UNFORGETTABLE

Nalini Shivkumar

Rema Mahalingam

Nalini Shivkumar and **Rema Mahalingam** teach at a women's college in Hyderabad. They have presented papers in national and international forums on gender issues and are interested in documenting women's concerns. The duo have edited a book titled *Women in Nation Building: A Multi-dimensional Perspective*, and have authored a coffee table book on women achievers, titled *Divas of Deccan: An Ode to the Women of Hyderabad*.

UNFORGETTABLE

THE ICONIC WOMEN OF SOUTH INDIAN CINEMA

NALINI SHIVKUMAR
REMA MAHALINGAM

RUPA

Published by
Rupa Publications India Pvt. Ltd 2015
7/16, Ansari Road, Daryaganj
New Delhi 110002

Sales centres:
Allahabad Bengaluru Chennai
Hyderabad Jaipur Kathmandu
Kolkata Mumbai

Photographs courtesy: E. Gnanaprakasam ('Photo Gnanam')

ISBN: 978-81-291-3531-5

First impression 2015

10 9 8 7 6 5 4 3 2 1

Printed by Parksons Graphics Pvt.Ltd, Mumbai

Contents

Preface

It was during our visits to other countries for international seminars that we realized the impact of Indian cinema, particularly Bollywood, and felt that South Indian cinema has not got due recognition, despite its huge contribution. There has been no documentation about the female icons of South Indian cinema and we felt enthused enough to write this book.

When films were shot under sunlight and the processing of the reels was done in complete darkness in wooden troughs, when the concept of cinema was an anathema to a conservative society, when effeminate-looking boys played the role of women, a few ladies broke the barriers of seclusion and defiantly strode into the world of cinema. Braving the threat of being ostracized by the society, these courageous women worked under difficult circumstances in order to provide for their families. They came out of the conventional mould of domesticity to carve a path for themselves. These are the forerunners who paved the way for young women of today to waltz into this industry.

Interestingly, some of the earliest heroines were singing sensations and passionate about stage performances. From 1931, these actors became an integral part of South Indian film lore; and being polyglots, they acted in films in all the four languages—Kannada, Telugu, Malayalam and Tamil. They are the true representatives of the culture and tradition of this period. The common denominator of these heroines is their talent and their dignified demeanour.

This book documents the memorable roles that made these actors legendary. These leading ladies have left a lasting impact for almost four decades despite the presence of very famous and charismatic heroes. The stars whose contribution has been discussed in this book are the gems in the treasure trove of cinema history.

While no single book can realistically hope to include the exhaustive list of women actors of this beautiful medium, we have written about thirty-four female actors who acted in women-centric films. There are many other prominent actors like Devika, Rajasree, Sukumari, Pandaribai, Nirmala, Kumari Sachu, Lata, Manjula, Ambika, Radha, Jayachitra, Sri Priya and Khushboo, who have not been featured because of several constraints, though they are also very popular and hugely celebrated stars of their times.

We dedicate this book to the wondrous women of South Indian cinema, who have given us unforgettable classics, which still linger in the collective consciousness of the people of India.

1

T.P. Rajalakshmi

Breaking the patriarchal establishment of defined roles for women, surged an extraordinary young Brahmin girl who dared to become a stage artiste, defying and breaching the confines of the conservative community in which she was born.

T.P. Rajalakshmi was born in November 1911 to Panchapakesa Sastri, the *karnam* of Saliyamangalam village in Thiruvaiyaru, Tamil Nadu. As a child, she had an amazing ability to sing any song she heard. Observing this talent in the young girl, a well-wisher introduced her to a drama company. Rajalakshmi studied only up to the fifth standard. Her family was in dire poverty and to add to her misery, she was married off at the age of eight. The marriage ended on a dowry dispute, and she remained with her parents. She was forced to join a drama troupe for their livelihood at a remuneration of thirty rupees a month. 'The family was ostracized,' recalls Kamala Mony, Rajalakshmi's daughter. 'But nothing stopped her.'

Initially, Rajalakshmi joined Aryagana K.S. Chellappa's Drama Company; later moved on to K.P. Moideen Sahib's troupe where she remained for three years. She played the lead role in all their productions and even travelled to Rangoon to perform. People used to watch her act and throw gold rings and chains to cheer her. 'She would collect it all and give it to the family,' recalls her daughter.

On her return from Rangoon, she joined the famous Cunniah Company, becoming the first female artiste in their group. Here, she played Sita to S.G. Kittappa's Rama, enjoying the status of a 'Special Drama' star. She even acted alongside M.K. Thyagaraja Bhagavathar, the popular film star of *Pavalakkodi* fame, when the play was staged in Madras (now Chennai). Nothing could stop her steely resolve and her tenacity in storming into the citadel of cinema, in an era when most women would not even dream of it.

As a precocious young lady looking for opportunities to grow, she joined the General Pictures Corporation, founded by A. Narayanan, to act in the silent film *Kovalan* in 1929. She moved to the Associated Film Company where she starred in *Usha Sundari* (1930) and *Rajeswari* (1931), playing the lead in the latter, opposite Raja Sandow.

When the Imperial Film Company was planning a talkie, *Kalidas*, they chose her for the role of heroine on K. Subramaniam's recommendation. Having learnt music and dance, she sang two *keertanas* (devotional songs), two patriotic songs and performed a *kurathi* folk dance in the film.

The film was shot in just eight days. Produced at a cost of 8,000 rupees, the film raked over 75,000 rupees in earnings. *Kalidas* (1931) was the first Indian multi-lingual film with dialogues in Tamil, Telugu, Hindi and Bengali.

It was a film based on folk mythology, on the life of the legendary third-century Sanskrit poet, Kalidasa, the creator of many classics like *Shakuntalam* and *Megha Sandhesham*. The story revolves around the beautiful princess, Vidyadhari (played by Rajalakshmi) who attracts the attention of a powerful and crafty minister in the court of her father, King Vijayavarman of Thejavathi. The minister wanted her to marry his son to reinforce his own power in the kingdom but she rejects his offer. To avenge his insult, he tricks her into marrying an illiterate simpleton, a goatherd (played by P.G. Venkatesan). Realizing her mistake, the princess prays for help to Goddess Kali, who bestows exemplary knowledge and literary abilities on Vidyadhari's husband. Thus, the humble goatherd is transformed into Kalidasa, the legendary poet. The film was a crude attempt at narrating a powerful story; there was no lipsync.

The first Tamil film, *Kalidas*, opened in Madras at Kinema Central. The release was a public event and people gathered in huge numbers to see the novelty of 'talking' pictures. When the film reels were brought to Madras, thousands gathered at Madras Central railway station and followed the reel box to Kinema Central. The fascinated crowd showered rose petals, broke coconuts and burnt incense sticks in the procession with the reels of the film, all along Wall Tax Road from the railway station!

Kalidas had about fifty songs in Tamil and Telugu. It included compositions of Saint Thyagaraja, the Carnatic classical music icon. When T.P. Rajalakshmi as the heroine appeared on the screen and sang the song *'Gandhiyin kai rattiname'*, few realized at that time that they were witnessing the birth of a cultural colossus—the world of Tamil film music. Tamil cinema popularized classical music by simplifying it for the masses.

'Manmada baanamadaa'...a song rendered by Rajalakshmi became very popular among young women. *'Indhiyargal nammavarkkul eno veensandai'*...was another song based on the

theme of the freedom movement. Some of the songs even featured the national slogan '*Vande Mataram*'.

In 1933, S. Vincent made *Valli Thirumanam*, a film that catapulted Rajalakshmi to stardom and earned her the sobriquet of 'Cinema Rani'. When *Valli* was released, a reel was lost. Nevertheless, the film ran to house full shows. Later, the missing reel was found and advertised in the newspapers. Those who had already seen the film went a second time, to watch the scenes they had missed!

It was around this time that she met T.V. Sundaram, a co-star whom she later married. She stayed in Calcutta (now Kolkata) to make several films such as *Kovalan* (1933), *Draupadi Vastrapaharanam* (1936), *Harishchandra* (1935), *Gulebakavali* (1935) and *Lalithangi* (1935).

On her return, she set up Sri Rajam Talkies. She was the first woman director in South Indian cinema, and the second in Indian cinema after Fathima Begum. A pioneer of different genres of filmmaking, she produced, directed, wrote, edited and played the lead role in her films *Miss Kamala* and *Madurai Veeran* in the 1930s. She was the first woman to achieve such distinction in the history of South Indian movies, perhaps even Indian cinema. She engaged well-known stunt actors of the day—'Battling' C.S.D. Singh and 'Stunt' Rajoo.

Rajalakshmi's *Miss Kamala* revolves around a well-to-do young woman who faces several problems because of her cruel guardians. The story is about how she escapes from their clutches and succeeds in achieving her goals in life.

Over time, the industry trends changed, but Rajalakshmi refused to change. She would not do anything that would sully the virtues of dignity and grace she espoused. During the filming of *Nandakumar* (1935), made by A.V. Meyyapan,

Stage actress, silent film heroine, movie star, vocalist, writer, director and producer ...first ever

Nostalgia of the old-world charm

with T.R. Mahalingam playing young Krishna, Rajalakshmi, in her role as Yashoda, refused to wear the costume designed for her because it was not in keeping with her sense of sobriety; she stood her ground and wore what she was comfortable in.

As she grew older, she switched to essaying the roles of a mother in films, but remained very choosy. One such film was *Jeeva Jyothi* (1947), where she plays a dignified Brahmin mother. Another was Joseph Thaliath's hit costume movie *Idaya Geetham* (1950), where she played the queen mother.

Although she was not considered conventionally good-looking, Rajalakshmi exuded a magnetic screen presence. In her personal life, she was a huge inspiration to the people of her times. Strongly protesting against social ills like child marriage and female infanticide, Rajalakshmi even adopted a girlchild in a bid to provide her with a secure future.

She was a true patriot, associated with the freedom movement and the Indian National Congress. She was close to the Congress leader, S. Satyamurthy. Deeply inspired by Mahatma Gandhi, she produced a film, *India Thai*. The film failed at the box office, leaving Rajalakshmi in a financial mess. She had to sell all the huge property she had amassed. Yet, she did not regret having produced the movie, and she declared that to be her small contribution to the cause. She braved the British Indian censors but gave in to a change in the title—*Tamizh Thai* (1940). Rajalakshmi was a proud nationalist. She would often sing patriotic songs onstage and the British officers would arrest her. Then the drama company would get her out of jail.

The street where Rajalakshmi lived was renamed as Rajarathinam Street. Rajalakshmi owned about ten to twelve houses there. Her residence #1, Rajarathinam Street was named as 'Rajmahal'.

When she was awarded the Kalaimamani in 1961, the charismatic actor M.G. Ramachandran (famously known as MGR) who did not want her to come in a taxi, personally sent his car to pick her up and dropped her back, reminisces her daughter.

T.P. Rajalakshmi was the first woman to earn the honorific title of 'Cinema Rani'. Her achievement is commendable considering that she had no family support and had to face the ire of the society for choosing the profession she did. Through it all she remained like a lotus in murky waters. Rajalakshmi will be remembered for her indomitable courage in the face of trials and tribulations, going through the crests and troughs of life, traversing from penury to riches and scaling the pinnacle of glory in South Indian filmdom with her respectability intact, given the challenges of the film industry, particularly for a hapless woman.

She passed away on 20 August 1964, leaving behind a brilliant repertoire of achievements in the archives of Indian cinema. She was the first woman to wear so many hats. Kudos to this great star for making women a force to reckon with in the film industry.

2

T.R. Rajakumari

When ace director K. Subramaniam, on a visit to leading actress Dhanalakshmi's house, noticed an apparently nondescript girl serving coffee, little did he know he was about to create history in the world of cinema.

When the girl was invited for a screen test, the make-up man—one of the best in India, Hari Babu from Bengal—dismissed the face, and refused to even apply powder, because of her dark skin! But his master insisted and lo, a star was born. Her name was T.R. Rajakumari. She was later conferred the sobriquet—'Dream Girl' of Tamil cinema.

Thanjavur Ranganayaki Rajayee was born in 1922 into a fairly well-known family who practised fine arts like dance and music for generations. Her grandmother and mother were grooming Rajayee to be a classical singer, since she had the required talent and a mellifluous voice, but destiny had charted out a different path for her.

Her aunt Dhanalakshmi, who was then playing lead roles in films, inspired her. On her aunt's advice she made herself visible and waited patiently for a chance in films. When

Ellis R. Dungan began work on *Kalamegam* in which Dhanalakshmi played the heroine, the niece was offered a comedy role, but both aunt and niece, Rajayee aka Rajalakshmi, refused the role.

Her first film was *Kumara Kulothungan* (1939), which passed away with a whimper. She did a few unsuccessful movies, like *Dana Sura Karna* and *Mantharavathi* (1941).

After the initial fiasco, came *Katcha Devayani* in 1941, which conferred stardom on her for her role as Devayani, daughter of the sage Sukracharya, in the mythological tale. Initially, the film failed to draw the attention of people, but when word spread of the spectacular beauty of the teenage heroine and the breathtaking picturization of the idyllic scenes, where the heroine cavorts in a pond, rides an elephant, exuding oomph and sensuality, people flocked to the theatres. *Katcha Devayani* was a stupendous success and Rajakumari became a rage, walking her way to fame. In several places, including Madras, the film ran for twenty-five weeks, marking a never-before milestone in the industry. Kothamangalam Seenu, her hero, who played Katcha in the film, was a popular actor of the 1930s and 1940s. The credit for making her look attractive and sensational goes to director K. Subramanian. The film was crafted artistically, and brilliantly choreographed, skyrocketing her to dizzying heights of success.

Then came *Manonmani* (1942), where she was paired with the then leading star of Tamil cinema, P.U. Chinnappa. The pair became very popular, and Rajakumari was made to look gorgeous, as the princess he sees in his dreams. The same pair was cast in *Kubera Kuchela* (1943). In her next film, *Sivakavi* (1943), which was very well received, she played a court-dancer, Vanji, who falls in love with the hero, M.K. Thyagaraja Bhagavathar, also known as MKT.

The year 1944 saw the release of *Haridas*, a folk myth about a sinner-turned-saint, again featuring MKT and Rajakumari. This iconic film had a 114-week run in one theatre in Madras—a record that remained unbeaten for half a century! Rajakumari plays the role of a vamp who lures the hero, only to destroy him later. All the songs were rendered by MKT himself and went on to become huge hits. A famous song-and-dance sequence from this film, *'Manmatha leelai kandaar undo'* is still remembered.

The MKT–Rajakumari duo with filmmaker Sundar Rao Nadkarni was considered the formula for box-office success, with the brief exception of *Valmiki*, when MKT was arrested in the sensational Lakshmikanthan murder case and C. Honnappa Bhagavathar replaced him as the hero.

Rajakumari then teamed up with P.U. Chinnappa, her erstwhile hero, and acted in a comedy, *Vikatayogi* (1946).

Her next significant movie was *Pankajavalli* (1947), which was again an adaptation of a folktale, where she plays the man-hating ruler of a kingdom where the women are treated as superior to men. And then comes a handsome man who wins her heart. Rajakumari gave a memorable performance in the title role. The film also included noteworthy music by the famous composer, Papanasam Sivan.

In 1953, Leo Tolstoy's classic *Anna Karenina* was essayed in Tamil as *Panakkari* by K.S. Gopalakrishnan, with Rajakumari playing the role of Anna and Chittoor V. Nagaiah, the suspecting husband who ill-treats his wife for being close to an army officer, played by M.G. Ramachandran (MGR). The film bombed at the box office, primarily owing to the anti-sentimental storyline, but her brilliant acting was appreciated.

Around the same time, another film, *Pitchaikkari*, a remake of a Malayalam film, became a major hit, and there was a joke

The first South Indian 'Dream Girl'

A scene from the famous drum dance of India's first magnum opus Chandralekha

In the box-office hit Gulebakavali *with M.G. Ramachandran*

that made the rounds then that those distributors who bought *Panakkari* became *pitchaikkaarans* (beggars), while those who bought *Pitchaikkari* became *panakkarans* (rich men)!

In her Tamil film career, Rajakumari acted as the female lead to many major film stars, including M.K. Thyagaraja Bhagavathar, T.R. Mahalingam, K.R. Ramaswamy, P.U. Chinnappa, MGR and Sivaji Ganesan.

Chandralekha starring Rajakumari was an epic period film, the first of its kind ever attempted in Indian cinema, boasting of fantastic sets like palaces, a moat and draw-bridge strong enough to withstand the weight of horses, riders and thronging crowds. Her brilliant rendering of the role, the drum dance, her resplendent costumes and her circus trapeze act were all major highlights at the time. The film was in the making for five years, and cost around three million rupees.

The king, seduced by Vasantasena (Rajakumari), abandons his wife (Kannamba) and his son. Vasantasena wants his son arrested and her own son made heir. She has the king and queen imprisoned while she attempts to seize power. The king's son escapes from prison and leads a revolt against Vasantasena and her general, Ugrasena. This film was scripted by Karunanidhi and showcased a huge star cast. Following massive publicity, *Chandralekha* released in 1948, created a sensation and smashed box-office records all over the country, making it the first 'all-India hit'. Its Hindi version opened the doors for South Indian producers to sell their films in the north. Rajakumari as Vasantasena the heroine, rose to great heights with this film and virtually carried the movie on her shoulders. Indeed this was her career-best role.

In 1948, she did another memorable film, *Krishna Bhakthi*, a folktale fantasy inspired by a French novel titled *The Monk*.

She plays a devotee of Lord Krishna, shrewdly thwarting the advances of the king's spiritual advisor who turns out to be a fraud. He repents and turns into a saint.

After a few unsuccessful films based on mythology and folklore, she turned producer with her brother Ramanna and produced films like *Vaazhapirandhavan* (1953), *Koondukkili* (1954), *Gulebakavali* (1955), *Paasam* (1962), *Periya Idathu Penn* (1963), *Panam Padaithavan* (1965) and *Parakkum Paavai* (1966). *Koondukkili* saw the rare coming together of the two superstars MGR and Sivaji Ganesan.

Gulebakavali (The Flower of Bakavali) was produced and directed by her brother T.R. Ramanna. MGR, Rajakumari and Rajasulochana were cast in the lead roles. The film is about a young man who sets out to find a mysterious flower, which is believed to have the power to restore eyesight. Rajakumari plays the role of a glamorous and captivating young lady. In his quest for the flower, the hero meets three women who turn out to be princesses and siblings!

Rajakumari distinguished herself by her sheer courtesy and grace, and was the first female superstar of the 1940s. She chose to remain single, was very disciplined and benevolent and helped all her family members settle down in life.

Vaanambadi, in 1963, marked the final drawing of the curtains, as Rajakumari withdrew completely from the spotlight. The 'Dream Girl'of the celluloid world retreated into complete seclusion, ensconcing herself in a world of prayer and quietitude, and died after a prolonged illness.

3

K.B. Sundarambal

Full many a gem of purest ray serene
The dark unfathomed caves of ocean bear

These lines of Thomas Gray would aptly describe this wondrous gem of South India who was fortuitously discovered, and as preordained, exploded into the world of cinema with her vibrant presence and her resonant voice pouring forth soulful music in profusion...her refrains are still reverberating in the precincts of all the temples of Lord Murugan, invoking the divine and enchanting millions even to this day.

K.B. Sundarambal, the 'Avvaiyar' of Tamil cinema was born in 1906, in Kodumudi village in Periyar district, Tamil Nadu. As a child prodigy with an innate genius for music, she resorted to singing ditties in trains in and around Trichy, to earn a few copper coins and alms. One story goes that the local deputy superintendent of police who was travelling in the train, chanced to hear her singing in full-throated ease and got her enrolled in Velu Nair's theatre. Another version is that it was Natesa Iyer, a railway official who took kindly to her after hearing her sing, helped her get a foothold in a drama troupe and also introduced her to director K. Subramaniam.

She acted for the first time in *Nalla Thangal* as one of the seven children thrown into a well by their mother, unable to feed them all. The film, based on a popular folktale, was a tear-jerker, a favourite of the Tamil theatre troupes. It offered a chance to showcase her potential in music. Around the same time, she started learning music from a harmonium player in the company. She excelled in her ability to traverse the entire diapason of notes in music at the top of the octave and in fast tempos. People observed and admired the timbre of her voice and the dignity of her performances. She became widely known as they toured all over the Tamil-speaking world—Myanmar, Sri Lanka and Malaysia. In Sri Lanka, K.B. Sundarambal met another touring star and theatre icon, S.G. Kittappa, who matched her in range, pitch and speed. As destiny would have it, they became a celebrated twosome, surpassing everyone else in the field and commanding a huge following. Their most talked-about pairing was in *Valli Tirumanam*, which blossomed into a real-life marriage off the stage.

When she was offered lead roles in films, she accepted only a few offers, which have proved to be landmarks. Her performance as Avvaiyar, the Tamil poet-saint (in the film by the same name), was so persuasive and compelling that till today, the actor remains almost synonymous with the legendary personality. Since there is no other accessible portrait of the historical poetess, Avvaiyar is depicted by using Sundarambal's image!

Avvaiyar (1953) narrates the folktale of an abandoned girlchild found by a devout, childless couple. This intelligent and beautiful girl Avvai, composes devotional songs and becomes an ardent devotee of Lord Ganesha. Her parents find a husband for her, but just before the wedding Avvai, dressed up as a bride, feels that it is her youth that is responsible for her new status. And in a moment of intense devotion, she prays for old age.

In promoting *Avvaiyar*, producer S.S. Vasan adopted a brilliant publicity strategy. As Avvaiyar was a familiar figure in conservative Tamil-speaking homes, he organized and requested groups of young women to visit such homes in Madras city and hand over invitations with vermillion and turmeric, requesting the people to see the movie. Vasan's plan worked and the masses were delighted at being personally invited to watch the film.

Nandanar (1935) is another movie starring KBS, produced by Assandas, that created history at many levels. She was paid a princely sum of one lakh rupees to play the lead male role. Now this was a big fortune indeed in 1935, when a sovereign of gold was sold at about thirteen rupees and petrol flowed, as if from a tap, at less than half a rupee per gallon!

It was the first time in the history of world cinema that a woman played the central male hero. A legend from the world of Carnatic music, Maharajapuram Viswanatha Iyer made his only appearance in cinema for a fee of merely 3,000 rupees, playing the rich Brahmin landowner, Vedhiyar, under whom Nandanar worked, and the film carried a scene where he had to prostrate himself before Nandanar. KBS was reluctant and apprehensive, for she was not a Brahmin, while Maharajapuram was a revered one! Such class and caste distinctions prevailed in those days. But the great musician was above such narrow-mindedness. To him, Sundarambal was Goddess Saraswati incarnate. He didn't mind incurring the displeasure of his community. The combination of such stalwarts starring in the film became big

The woman who played a hero, and received a whopping amount of 1,00,000 rupees in 1935 for her role in Nandanar

Personifying Avvaiyar, the legendary saint poet of Tamil Nadu

Cult figure and performer nonpareil

Musical genius, a great patriot and a political activist

news and moviegoers eagerly awaited its release. Director M.L. Tandon tackled the situation by making the two fall at each other's feet!

But the film was in for a lot of flak. Not everyone those days could accept a woman playing the role of Nandanar. So the critics came down heavily on the film as they felt it lacked realism, despite some appealing scenes and scintillating devotional music in the inimitable voice of KBS. *Nandanar* was shot in Calcutta and M.L. Tandon tried to make it a memorable movie, by bringing in farmers from the interiors of Tamil Nadu. But he was shocked when the senior technicians in the studio refused to permit the farmers inside, claiming that they were untouchables and the studio was as sacred as a Hindu temple.

The film negatives were destroyed in a fire that broke out under mysterious circumstances—the insurance company refused to pay the claim and won the case in the Madras High Court. Today, there remains no trace of this historic film, except for a handful of stills and some 78-rpm gramophone records.

Sundarambal's later movies included *Manimekalai* (1940), the epic story of the daughter of Madhavi and Kovalan of Silapathikaram, with KBS playing the lead role of Manimekalai who renounces worldly life to become a follower of Buddha.

She played Avvaiyar in *Thiruvilayadal* (1965), based on the theme of the divine sport of Lord Shiva. She virtually lived the role, often being identified with the saint poet, Avvaiyar. Her song in the film, *Pazham Nee Appa*, quickly grew to be the favourite of all Tamilians. During the screening of the film, several women went into a religious frenzy and the projector had to be stopped until the situation was brought under control.

Yet another memorable movie she acted in is *Karaikkal Ammaiyar* (1973), which literally means 'the revered mother from

Karaikkal'. It is the story of one of the three women amongst the sixty-three Nayanmars (devotees of Lord Shiva), one of the greatest figures in early Tamil literature from Karaikkal.

Sundarambal and her husband S.G. Kittappa were political activists during the Indian independence movement and they became ardent supporters of the Indian National Congress (INC). She continued to champion the movement, recording several gramophone discs extolling the struggle and sacrifices it entailed. Sundarambal always wore khadi sarees. Seeing her patriotic zeal and keen interest in serving the nation, she was chosen to be the first woman member of the Madras Legislative Assembly and was the first film personality to become a state legislative member in India. The couple became cult figures among theatre enthusiasts.

Her significant renditions in her vast repertoire of music include songs on the themes of the shocking incident of the Jallianwala Bagh massacre, the ideals of nationalist leaders like Mahatma Gandhi and Jawaharlal Nehru, and a clarion call on the freedom movement. When Pandit Motilal Nehru passed away, she famously sang '*Pandita Motilal Neruvai izhanduvittom*' in Raga Hindustan Kapi. This record became a bestseller and is today a collector's item. In fact, many of her gramophone discs became bestsellers and were bought and cherished over years in many Indian homes. Most of these discs were on sale for a mere two annas or twelve paise (one-eighth of a rupee). Her song '*Siraichaalai enna seyyum*' was often played at many INC party meetings held in the Tamil-speaking districts of the Madras Presidency. She was an ardent follower of Mahatma Gandhi and Rajaji (C. Rajagopalachari).

When her husband Kittappa died at a very young age, she chose to withdraw from cinema and refused to act with any other man for the rest of her life. She learnt to cope with his sudden demise and manage her finances, investing her money wisely. She restricted her outdoor activities, but continued to give classical music concerts, and made enough money for a comfortable lifestyle.

Getting over the despair of her bereavement, she tried to live a life of purpose, given her innate enthusiasm and confidence to forge ahead. She supported several deserving causes. Her attire of white clothes with sacred ash on her forehead and her rendering of devotional music conferred on her a quasi-saintly status.

In 1964, the Tamil Isai Sangam bestowed upon her the title of 'Tamil Isai Perarignar (Tamil Music Champion)'. In 1970, the government of India awarded her the Padma Shri for her contributions to the arts. K.B. Sundarambal, artiste extraordinaire, recepient of two national awards for singing, passed away on 15 October 1980. She remains permanently etched in public memory, as Avvaiyar, for her lead role in the eponymous 1953 film.

Success never eluded this amazing person. Nothing was insurmountable to this iron lady of indomitable will, every obstacle was a challenge and she pursued her goals with a singular force of concentration. Here was a woman who had the courage to stand up and don the roles she chose to, a patriot of rare calibre and an ardent devotee of Lord Murugan.

If success is measured not in achievements alone but in the impediments one has braved and overcome in the journey of life, K.B. Sunderambal certainly deserves the modern-day sobriquet of 'a woman of substance'.

4

M.S. Subbulakshmi

For a lay person to write about M.S. Subbulakshmi can be intimidating to say the least, and in the process to make sure that one does not plagiarize some of the aptly chosen epithets that have already been used to describe her, is another huge ordeal that one would face, adding to the apprehension of venturing to do justice to a celebrity larger than life, of almost an epical magnitude, a demi-goddess!

Talking about her foray into films would be unseemly without a prelude to her milieu in music that gave her a unique status unchallenged and unparalleled by anyone in the fraternity.

Madurai Shanmukhavadivu Subbulakshmi (popularly known as M.S.) was born on 16 September 1916 to Shanmukhavadivu, a veena player, and Subramania Iyer, a leading lawyer. Subbulakshmi grew up in what was virtually a temple of music. Not many know that Kunjamma, as she was fondly called, learnt to play the mridangam. She was constantly exposed to music because the family stayed close to the famous Meenakshi temple and she would hear the nadaswaram played there every day. This perhaps ignited the spark of her musical genius, a marvellous and extraordinary power that was being primed in her. She stopped her schooling when she reached the fifth standard and from then, it was music all the time. She had an unusual concentration on the tanpura *sruthi*. She received training in classical Carnatic music under the famous Semmangudi Srinivasa Iyer, and subsequently, in Hindustani classical music under Pandit Narayan Rao Vyas.

It was around this time, during one of her concerts, that Thiagarajan Sadasivam Iyer entered her life. He was closely following her concerts and felt that he could plan her path and career in music, observing that there was more to her. Sri Sadasivam Iyer, a great connoisseur of music, approached Subbulakshmi's mother and sought her daughter's hand. The mother consented and so did the daughter. He married her in 1940.

When producers approached M.S. Subbulakshmi to act in films, it was her husband who persuaded her to act in a few movies with specific financial objectives in mind, making sure that they were idealistic and chaste themes, with the accent on music. In 1939, Sadasivam and Subbulakshmi together formed their own film company and wanted to produce a mythological film, *Sakuntalai*.

M.S. Subbulakshmi starred in four of Ellis Dungan's films—*Sevasadanam*, *Sakuntalai*, *Savithri* (1941) and *Meera* (1945)—and the two that Dungan directed turned out to be Indian film classics.

Her first film was *Sevasadanam* in 1938, directed by K. Subramaniam, based on a novel by Premchand, *Bazaar-e-Husn*. The film championed the cause of women's equality and was a scathing attack on the dowry system, which often compels poor young girls to marry men much older than them.

The demi-goddess M.S. Subbulakshmi in Meera

The demure beauty epitomizing Meera

'She carries a veena in her throat!'— Eminent veena scholar Sambasivam Iyer

Sevasadanam, literally meaning 'the house of service', tells the story of an abused wife Sumathi (M.S. Subbulakshmi) who is driven out of her house by her husband and into prostitution. Later, she devotes her life to running an institution for the children of prostitutes. The film strongly depicts compatibility issues between such couples and sympathizes with the victims. Tamil film critic and historian, Aranthai Narayanan, observes in his book, *Thamizh Cinemavin Kathai* (The Story of Tamil Cinema), that '*Sevasadanam* proved a turning point in the history of Tamil cinema.'

Her second film, their home production, was *Sakuntalai* (1940), the story of the mythological queen Shakuntala, immortalized by Kalidasa in his play *Abhijñānaśākuntalam*.

Director Dungan, who shot *Sakuntalai*, later recalled how he could not get the desired reaction from her for a particular scene, so he sought permission from her husband to be rude to her, so as to enrage Shakuntala enough to unleash her pent- up ire on Dushyant. He succeeded in getting the desired shot. The film was a box-office success.

M.S. Subbulakshmi played the male role of Narada in *Savithri* (1941), to raise money to launch *Kalki*, the nationalist Tamil weekly, co-founded by her husband. Reviews reveal that when Narada descended from the sky, singing, the theatre reverberated with applause.

Her next film, *Meera* (1945), was 'visually opulent' despite being a black-and-white film because of the technical brilliance of Dungan (an excellent cameraman) and his cinematographer, Jiten Banerjee. They used a mould of her face, experimenting with different angles to make her look 'ethereal and angelic', and it worked. Her virtuoso rendering in Hindi of Meerabai (in the late 1940s), the austere Rajput queen who dedicated her life to Lord Krishna, had producers subsequently pleading with her to act in their films. But after *Meera*, M.S. Subbulakshmi withdrew from cinema.

She was truly a blessed star, extolled for her music, films and personal virtues. Princes and rulers have bowed to her music, as when the (then) Maharana of Udaipur said to her, 'I would have exchanged my whole kingdom for this Kalyani raga. Now I shall give you whatever help you need by way of horses and elephants in location shooting.' And he certainly did help them during the filming of *Meera*.

An excerpt from Ellis Dungan's reminiscences of directing M.S. Subbulakshmi states, 'As an actress, she worked hard to perfect her art. When time permitted, I also taught her a few words of English. By the time we completed *Meera*, she had mastered enough English to carry on a conversation. Since musicians always surrounded her in her home, rehearsing songs for a recital somewhere, I had to literally wait my turn to conduct film rehearsals. She was quite a busy lady and a lovable one...'

In Bombay Studio where the musical score for *Meera* was being recorded, artists who came in for other recordings would stop by and become rapt listeners. A thin newcomer, two long plaits dangling behind, refused to record her song after the M.S. session. 'Not now, not after that!' Lata Mangeshkar went on to become a legend of course, but she continued to remain a devoted M.S. fan.

In both appearance and lifestyle, M.S. Subbulakshmi remained conservative, with her flower-decked *kondai* (hair tied up in a bun) and her diamond nose and earrings. Possessing no jewels beyond what she wore and quick to give away the silk sarees gifted to her by admirers, she never tried to appear younger than she was. Thousands of people saw her as the embodiment of grace.

M.S. Subbulakshmi has always herself maintained that 'she is what she is', solely because of her husband. He was her friend, philosopher and guide. Her commitment to the chosen field was total, be it films or music, and her progress was meteoric. Hers was a rare combination of a pleasing stage personality coupled with humility, which served to embellish her image all the more. Her contributions to early cinema and music are truly timeless, alive and vibrant. Though she scaled new heights at every stage in her career, success did not make inroads into her equanimity or her impeccable demeanour; the native flavour was never lost in her rendering of songs in any language.

M.S. Subbulakshmi passed away at the age of eighty-eight, on 11 December 2004, in Chennai. But the rich legacy of music that she left behind will live on forever. The initials M.S. are two letters that spell magic and nostalgia for Tamilians, and transports them to the world of music. The last word in grace in South India is undoubtedly M.S.; the ultimate compliment for a woman in her twilight years is to be remotely resembling her, the colour of the Kanchipuram silk saree that she wore, a deep blue, is imprinted in the minds of thousands of women, and even today there is one more colour in shades of blue which silk stores stock, referring to it as 'MS blue'.

It is a daunting task to separate the great M.S. from the annals of Carnatic music and present her other facets, the lady has not only left behind an immortal legacy in music but has also created a cult following for her singing star image in *Meera* and *Sakuntalai*.

5

Pasupuleti Kannamba

Walking six feet tall bearing a statuesque figure, a dusky lady created a niche for herself in filmdom. Kannamba inched her way on the path she had chosen and proved that she was a female star to contend with.

Kannamba was born on 5 October 1911 in Cuddapah to Lokamba and M. Venkanarasaiah, a government contractor. She was their only child and grew up with her maternal grandparents in Eluru. Her grandfather, Nathamuni Naidu, a village doctor, encouraged her to study and learn music.

Once when she was watching the play *Harischandra*, staged by the Navala Nataka Samajam in Eluru, she was so enraged when she saw that the actor who played Chandramati did not do justice to the role, she got up and shouted that she could perform better! She was barely sixteen then. When the actor who played Chandramati challenged her to come and act, Kannamba instantly jumped on to the stage, delivered the same dialogue, sang the song and acted so effectively without any rehearsal, that she caught the attention of the drama troupe. She was immediately chosen by the company for the roles of Anusuya, Savithri and Yasodha.

One of the organizers of this drama group, K.P. Nagabhushanam fell in love with Kannamba and married her in 1934. Later that year, they launched their own drama company called Sri Rajarajeswari Natya Mandali and performed all over the Madras Presidency and the Nizam's Territories.

When C. Pullaiah of Star Combines approached her for the role of Chandramati in their production *Harishchandra* (1935), she told him that there were twenty-two members in their drama troupe, and she was willing to act in his film only if everyone in her troupe was given a role. He agreed and she played Chandramati in the film. The film was shot at Shalini Cinetone, Kolhapur and that was the beginning of Kannamba's film career.

Thereafter, Saraswathi Talkie Company from Bezwada (Vijayawada) offered her the title role in *Draupadi Vastrapaharanam* in 1936. The film *Kanakadhara* shot her to fame, since it had scope for histrionics. Her next venture was *Gruhalakshmi* (1938), with H.M. Reddi and B.N. Reddi. A film with a social message about the consequences of drinking, it depicted a profligate dancer who seduces a respectable doctor into abandoning his virtuous wife Radha (played by Kannamba). The doctor becomes an alcoholic and is framed for a murder. Meanwhile, Radha is given shelter by her brother-in-law. In a dramatic turn of events, Radha falls down the stairs after a showdown with the dancer and becomes mentally imbalanced. There is a scene where Kannamba goes running all over the streets, screaming, 'There's no God, and no justice.' When this scene was filmed, it was so real that the policemen who were on the beat chased the lady thinking that she was really insane and was running helter–skelter.

A dynamic and proactive actress, Kannamba took the initiative to co-produce some great movies, like *Chandika* (1940) with Saraswathi Talkies, where she played the title role. It is a pseudo-historical film with court intrigues, and warring factions for power, and the film had Kannamba in the role of Chandika as a valiant woman, also planning to capture the throne. She donned a male costume in the film, gallantly rode the horse and indulged in some sword fighting for the first time. For a particular scene where she was supposed to be playing with tiger cubs for a scene, to prepare for the act, she got herself two tiger cubs and personally fed them, making an effort to be comfortable in close proximity with them. That was the kind of commitment and dedication she brought to every role she took up. It was no wonder then that Kannamba's performances were always charged with energy and drew huge crowds.

She faced a few debacles in Tamil films; her pronunciation of Tamil words carried a conspicuous Telugu accent. But she worked hard to change this and was soon the choice for the 1941 film *Kannagi*. She gave a stunning performance and immortalized the role. She has rendered the longest ever dialogue impeccably, which remains unparalleled in the history of Tamil cinema, winning her a huge fan following.

Her role as queen mother in *Manohara* (1954) was another milestone in her career. Even a veteran like Sivaji Ganesan was in awe of Kannamba's dialogue delivery, particularly in this film. He considered her his mentor. She played the role of mother to NTR in the Telugu version of the film titled *Raja Makutam* (1959). Tamil film distributors would insist and request that Kannamba be given more dialogues, as she was really a favourite with the Tamil audience, who enjoyed her immaculate and powerful dialogue delivery.

Her imperial presence made her the apt choice for many mythological roles. She was also accomplished in action scenes, having learnt sword fighting and horse riding since she wanted to play her role to perfection. Interesting snippets that made the rounds about her, were that she owned a lot of heavy jewellery and had the habit of storing them in big jars in her kitchen. It was even rumoured that she wore all her jewellery to sleep every night!

Noteworthy actresses, like Anjali Devi, recall how Kannamba gave them tips on dialogue delivery and even taught them the art of interacting with people. She was the one who paved the way for Telugu-speaking actors to make inroads into the Tamil film industry. She was known to be very gracious with her colleagues, often helping them out with her suggestions and guidance.

In Gudavalli Ramabrahmam's historical film, *Palnati Yuddham* (1947) her performance as Nayakuralu Nagamma was much appreciated. Kannamba didn't hesitate to play negative roles as well, acting in a wide range of roles right from being the queen mother, mother, sister-in-law, to being the wicked stepmother and mother-in-law, bringing life to all the roles.

Ashok Kumar was a 1941 Tamil film directed by Raja Chandrasekhar with Thyagaraja Bhagavathar, and Kannamba. The film was based on an age-old Buddhist folktale surrounding Mauryan Emperor Ashoka's son, Kunal. The Mauryan prince, Kunal, was courted by Ashoka's younger queen Tishyarakshita (played by Kannamba), and when he rejected her advances, he was falsely accused by the queen of trying to seduce her and was thrown into prison and blinded. The story, however, comes to a happy end with his eyesight being restored.

While all the popular actresses hesitated to take up the

Pasupuleti Kannamba in Thaayai Katha Thanayan

The majestic queen mother in Manohara

Kannamba with S.V. Ranga Rao

role of Tishyarakshita given the negative amorous shades of the character, Kannamba accepted the role without any inhibitions. For the song *'Unaikandu Mayangada'* rendered in the inimitable voice and style of M.K. Thyagaraja Bhagavathar, she had to learn how to dance, since she was not a trained dancer. Just for this sequence she learnt dance from the famous *nattuvanar*, Vaideeswaran Koil Meenakshi Sundaram Pillai, who commended her and said that she was a quick and an intelligent learner.

Another classic Telugu film she acted in was *Thalli Prema* in 1941, where she plays a rich advocate's wife, pining for a child. Her real life yearning for a child was perhaps distilled into her role and touched the hearts of people. It created a stir and is remembered as one of her finest films.

Yet another incident during the making of the film *Saudamini* (1951) that stands testimony to her dedication, as narrated by M.L. Narasimhan, is the scene in which she was left alone in the forest, caught in a heavy cyclone. On the sets, (rain) water was poured from above and a gusty wind was created using a giant fan, which in those days, was called 'aeroplane'. Kannamba was so fanatical about her acting that she always used to wait for the director to say 'Okay' before getting out of the mood and the scene. Though fully drenched, she did not get up even after the shot was over. When the worried unit hands rushed towards her, she said, 'How can I get up unless the director says "okay"?'

In *Raja Makutam* (1959), an adaptation of *Hamlet*, she acquitted herself brilliantly in the role of the queen, while in *Lava Kusha*, she played Kausalya so impressively that the film became a blockbuster and won the National Film Award for the Best Feature Film in Telugu. She produced several hits with the help of her husband, director Kadaru Nagabhushanam, under their production banner, Sri Rajarajeswari Pictures. She had the privilege of earning the highest remuneration in those days—85,000 rupees. In her immensely productive career, she acted in about 170 films in all, winning wide acclaim for all her roles.

Some of her other memorable films include

Sumati (1942), *Tulasi Jalandhaar* (1947), *Sudarshan* (1951), *Mugguru Maratheelu* (1946), *Mangayarkarasi* (1949), *Anarkali* (1955), *Uma Sundari* (1956), *Todi Kodallu* (1957), *Abhimanam* (1960) and *Athma Bandhuvu* (1962). Chittoor V. Nagayya's *Bhakta Ramadasu* (1964) was her last film. Among her peers, P. Kannamba enjoys the distinction of having acted with all the superstars of the time, including M.K. Thyagaraja Bhagavathar, P.U. Chinnappa, Chittoor V. Nagayya, S.V. Ranga Rao, M.K. Radha, M.G. Ramachandran and Gemini Ganesan. Kannamba was also a popular singer, rendering many songs in her films. Her gramophone record, '*Krishnam bhaje Radha*', became a big hit and broke sale records.

Never having children of her own, Kannamba adopted a boy and a girl. Her daughter, Rajarajeshwari, married director C. Pullaiah's son, C.S. Rao, who was also a film director.

Towards the end of her prolific career though, Kannamba's production ventures upset the applecart and she ran into serious financial problems, which affected her health and that was the beginning of her end. P. Kannamba died at the age of fifty-one. After her death, her husband wandered around lonely, poverty-stricken, and died in obscurity.

But Kannamba will be remembered as the first female superstar of South Indian films.

6

Dr Bhanumathi Ramakrishna

She never stooped, but conquered, embodying in real life the majesty of the princesses and queens she portrayed in several movies, as if tailor-made for her.

Dr Bhanumathi walked tall in the film world, where women feared to tread, thanks to her commanding personality. Her reputation of being intimidating and daunting preceded her, and there was always an aura of reverence that stood her in good stead as she traversed in the challenging world of films. Bhanumathi proved the respectability of cinema, believing that if a woman relies on her quotient of merit she need not compromise!

Gawky in all the romantic scenes in her early films, Bhanumathi would later recall how no hero had the courage to walk up to her and even hold her hand! For when any hero attempted to touch her, her instantaneous reaction was always anger. In a lighter vein, she remarked that perhaps that was why her romantic movies failed.

Bhanumathi was the third child of Saraswatamma and Venkatasubbiah of Ongole, Andhra Pradesh. She was barely thirteen and still in school, when her father's friend, producer-director C. Pullaiah, was looking out for a young teenage girl to act in his film for the East India Film Company on the subject of dowry, *Varavikrayam* (Bridegroom for Sale). He wanted a girl who could also sing, so at the behest of her father's friends, she was persuaded to take up the role. Pullaiah convinced her father that acting was a perfectly safe choice of profession, so long as one chose to remain professional and maintain a discreet distance from other people.

In the film, Bhanumathi played the eldest daughter, Kalindi. Her father borrows money to get her married against her wishes to the thrice-married Lingaraju and she commits suicide before the marriage. When the film released in 1939, she was noted for her distinctive voice modulation and her promise as a professional singer. Years later, talking about the film and her role, she rued,'See the irony? Even after six decades, girls commit suicide and the menace called dowry is still there!'

Subsequently, she acted in *Malathi Madhavam* (1940), *Dharma Patni* (1941) and *Bhaktimala* (1941). Her first popular film was *Krishna Prema* (1943). There was a brief hiatus where she withdrew from the public eye, because her films were not very successful. She married Ramakrishna (an assistant director) who insisted that she should not continue to act or sing in films. The idea of staying at home and cooking for her husband and going for a movie by bus in the evening was romantic for her. She had no qualms about the life she had chosen and settled down to domestic bliss.

It was at this juncture that B.N. Reddy was looking out for a young girl for his film *Swargaseema* (1945), so he decided to persuade Ramakrishna to let Bhanumathi act in the film. The story was about a publisher who has an extramarital affair with a village girl Subbalakshmi (played by Bhanumathi). The publisher spots great talent in her and transforms her into an urban girl. The travails of the hero's helpless wife and how he reunites with his family is the drama that unfolds. The classic hit song sung by Bhanumathi, *'Ooh pavurama'*, turned out to be a big hit. This negative role catapulted her to stardom. Later, she excitedly recounted, 'All the senior artists, like Sivaji Ganesan, Thangavelu and Balaiah told me that they had seen *Swargaseema* forty-fifty times and that they were my fans!'

When their son was born, Bhanumathi and Ramakrishna started their own studio and named it after him—Bharani. Her debut production was a fairytale-like melodrama, *Ratnamala* (1947), with her playing the title role in which the protaganist is conned into marrying the infant princeling, Chandrakanta. The novel plot with its interesting twists and turns, and visual effects appealed to family audiences.

Her maiden Tamil film was *Rajamukthi* (1948) where she found the confidence to star and sing alongside the classical music veteran, M.K. Thyagaraja Bhagavathar.

B.N. Reddy then cast her in *Malliswari* (1951), a period film on the Vijayanagar Empire. She played the role of Malliswari who was forced, by her mother's greed, to be a part of the king's harem. How she outwits the king and redeems herself forms the denouement of the story. She excelled in the title role, interpreting the character in her own inimitable style and has also rendered several hit songs in the film.

This film is listed among CNN-IBN's 100 landmark Indian films of all time and has been declared a classic. It was the first Telugu film to be screened at international film festivals like the Asia Pacific Film Festival. It saw a public re-release with thirteen prints and Chinese subtitles in Beijing.

In Malaikallan with MGR... the crowning glory

The uber-cool Bhanumathi

A powerhouse of talent with Sivaji Ganesan

Playing a mother in Annai

The first picture that Bhanumathi produced and directed herself, undertaking the musical score as well, was *Chandirani* (1953). She even played a double role in it. She made this film simultaneously in Telugu, Tamil and Hindi and released it in all the three languages at the same time from Kashmir to Kanyakumari. This is a Guinness record for a woman and perhaps no other actor or actress has ever achieved such a feat. She went on to perform along with top artistes of her era, prominent among whom were Sivaji Ganesan and M.G. Ramachandran. *Malaikallan* (1954) was a classic MGR film where he plays Robin Hood and rescues the damsel Bhanumathi. The film's success made Bhanumathi a much sought after heroine. *Alibabavum Narpatha Thirudargalum* (1956) was very entertaining and is remembered for Bhanumathi's popular songs and dances like *'Unnai vidamatten'* and *'Azhagana ponnuthan'*.

Madhurai Veeran (1956) was based on the legend of the same name written by the poet, Kannadasan. In this film, Bhanumathi plays the princess, Bommi, who is rescued by the hero, whom she falls in love with. It was a resounding success, celebrating a silver jubilee run in many theatres.

'*Rangoon Radha* and *Ambikapathi* (with Sivaji Ganesan) taught me the nuances of emotional acting,' claimed the star. *Rangoon Radha* was released in 1956 and *Ambikapathi* in 1956. She gave a scintillating performance as a mother in *Annai* (1962), where she would not give up her hold on her adopted son to his real mother even after he had grown up. She picked up languages easily and did not need dubbing for her Hindi films like *Nishan* and *Shamsher* with the seasoned Ashok Kumar.

Then following a long gap, Bhanumathi played the role of a grandmother (Mangamma) in *Mangammagari Manavadu* (1984). She resumed her acting career and portrayed different character roles in movies like *Atthagaru Swaagatham* (1988), *Muddula Manavaraalu* (1986), *Samrat Ashok* (1992), *Moratodu Naa Mogudu*, *Baamma Maata Bangaarubaata* (1990) and *Pelli Kanuka* (1998). Every film she did bore the stamp of her unique and original style of acting and won her a huge fan following. One of her last major films was *Peddarikam* (1992), the story of two feuding families. In it, Bhanumathi scores as the head of the family! The film was remade in Hindi as *Hulchul*.

The top heroes of the day such as Nandamuri Taraka Rama Rao (NTR) and Akkineni Nageshwara Rao (ANR) acted in the films produced by Bhanumathi's Bharani Studio. ANR was almost a permanent hero of their pictures. With ANR as hero, Bhanumathi produced *Rathnamaala* (191947), *Laila–Majnu* (1949), *Chakrapani* (1954), *Vipranarayana* (1955) and *Baatasaari* (1961). And with NTR as hero, she produced *Chandirani* (1953), *Vivaahabandham* (1964) and *Ammaayipelli* (1974). She also acted as the heroine alongside them in films made by other producers. Her film, *Vipranarayana*, went on to win a national award.

She enjoys a unique status of having acted in more than a hundred films in different languages, directed sixteen films, written screenplay and dialogues, composed lyrics and music, and directed and produced films, in addition to singing—probably the only lady to have worked on so many areas in the world of films. She earned the sobriquet 'Ashtavadhani' in the industry for the multiple (eight) facets to her personality.

Every film that Bhanumathi took up was a story from the feminist perspective, given her understanding of the problems faced by her fraternity. Her Telugu film, *Antha Mana Manchike*, was adjudged best film in the year 1972. The Tamil version, *Ippadiyum Oru Penn* (1975), was applauded as the best social satire. She produced a children's feature film titled *Bhaktha*

Dhuruva Markandeya in Telugu, Tamil, Hindi and Malayalam with child artistes under sixteen years of age, which was well appreciated by both critics and the general public.

Before signing any film, she would lay down a condition that allowed for no indecency or physical closeness with the hero in any scene whatsoever. Such was her command over the filmmakers!

Dr Bhanumathi was the first female recipient of State Honours in 1956, when the state of Andhra Pradesh was formed. She received the National Awards for Best Actress for *Annai* (Tamil), *Anthastulu* (Telugu) and *Palnati Yuddham* (Telugu). Later, Mr Annadurai, the then chief minister, honoured her with the title 'Nadippukku Ilakkanam' (Grammar of Acting) for her remarkable performance in *Rangoon Radha*. In 1966, she was conferred the national honour of Padma Shri by the Government of India. In 1984, yet another feather was added in her cap, namely the title 'Kalaimamani', conferred by the Tamil Nadu Iyal Isai Nataka Manram. Furthermore, honorary doctorate degrees were conferred on her by Sri Venkateswara University and Andhra University.

Dr Bhanumathi Ramakrishnan will be remembered as a versatile genius who stormed into the male bastion and worked on her own terms, acquiring a magnificence and dignity by dint of her competence and demeanour.

7

Anjali Devi

She enjoyed the rare status of her name featuring in the top slots of the credits with the hero's name following hers...

She famously earned equal wages, on par with the hero—1016 rupees per month...

She knew only regard and respect, never any discrimination...

While marriage spelled the end of a film career for heroines in her time, she enjoyed the privilege of being married with two children and making her entry to films...

Her devotion to Puttaparthi Sai Baba, and his blessings sustained her throughout her life... she recalled how a fan once came up to her in Puttaparthi and thrust a mangalasutra in her hands...

Even today, she is Sita personified to her fans after her memorable performance as Sita in *Lava Kusha* (1963)...

Anjali Devi, when interviewed a few years ago, came across as a spirited lady full of joy and mirth as she walked down memory lane.

Anjana, who was rechristened Anjali Devi for her career in films, began as a child artiste on stage at the age of eight, in the role of Lohitasya in *Raja Harishchandra*. She joined the amateur troupe, Young Men's Happy Club, in Kakinada. It was a mixed group of professionals from different walks of life. And that was where she met her husband, Adhi Narayana Rao, a writer, lyricist and musician. She had been married at the age of fourteen and was a mother of two sons, when the film industry set up the ramp for her!

Little did she think about a career for herself, until the well-known director C. Pullaiah, gave her the invite for a heroine's role. Unlike other couples, she was persuaded by her husband to take it up and she gave in with a lot of reluctance because she had a baby to attend to. Then there was no looking back. A number of films came her way, and she was swept in the wave. He was to her the anchor of her life, '*matha, pitha, guru, deivam*'.

Anjali Devi made her debut as a heavenly seductress in *Gollabhama* (1947) and set the screen on fire. This film became her instant springboard to stardom. She followed this up with *Aadhithan Kanavu* (1948) and *Mangaiyarkarasi* (1949) in Tamil. She learnt to speak Tamil and Hindi at the club and remembered MGR helping her with her Tamil diction.

Soon, Anjali and her husband set up their own film production company—Anjali Film Productions. Their first production, *Poongodhai* (1953), a bilingual film in Telugu and Tamil, was meant to be Sivaji Ganesan's debut film.

Contrary to the popular public impression that she has only acted in serious roles, Anjali Devi actually has to her credit a wide range of roles, starting from *Adutha Veettu Penn* (1960) with T.R. Ramachandran and Thangavelu, its Telugu version titled *Pakkinta Ammayi* and Hindi version titled *Padosan*. Pullaiah gave her a negative role (Mohini) in *Gollabhama* and cast her as Sita in *Lava Kusha*, adding to her repertoire of roles.

The evergreen romantic song 'Thesulavuthe' *in* Manalane Mangayin Bhagyam *with Gemini Ganesan*

The celluloid queen immortalized as Sita

The two legends—Anjali Devi with Vyjayanthimala in the film Penn *in 1954*

In Tamil cinema, Anjali Devi is a legend. She was always a part of the big league of actors with films like *Adutha Veettu Penn*, *Kanavane Kankanda Theivam* (1955), *Manalane Mangayin Bhagyam* (1957), which were all mega blockbusters of the times. Her films with MGR, *Marmayogi* (1951) and *Sarvadhikari* (1951) are appreciated even today.

Marmayogi was based on Marie Corelle's novel, *Vendetta*, based on folklore about kings and princes, aimed at projecting the image of MGR as a person who fought against injustice. Anjali Devi, as the power-crazy mistress, gave a truly memorable performance. Though the character had shades of grey, she won over the audience.

Anjali Pictures was the first to use the slow motion technique, hitherto not available in the South. Their productions were known for their mellifluous music. With *Anarkali* (1955) and *Swapna Sundari* (1950), their production house zoomed to great heights. The banner went on to produce twenty-eight films in Telugu, Tamil and Hindi. One cannot forget musicals like *Runanu Bandham* (1960), *Sati Sumathi* (1967), *Sati Sakku Bai* (1965), *Swarna Manjari* (1962), *Mahakavi Kshetrayya* (1976) and *Bhakta Tukaram* (1973). Anjali Pictures became a household name for musicals and period films. The government of Andhra Pradesh awarded it the Golden Nandi Mahakavi Kshetrayya.

A series of blockbusters in various languages followed—*Bala Raju* (1948), *Mahatma Udangar* (1947, Tamil), *Swapna Sundari*, *Panduranga Mahatyam* (1957), *Jayabheri* (1959), *Raksha Rekha* (1949), *Ek Tha Raja* (1951, Tamil)—and many more, with Anjali playing the lead in all of them. She never looked back and went on to complete around 400 films as the heroine in Telugu, Tamil and Hindi.

Swapna Sundari was an imaginary love story about a celestial being and a common man, starring ANR and Anjali Devi, and they became a hit pair. Anjali as the Gandharva kanya looked ethereal and played her part to perfection. *Jayabheri* was a big musical hit, which again had ANR and Anjali Devi in the lead. It was a film based on caste discrimination. *Bala Raju* was a folklore love story. This box-office success had a hundred-day run and Anjali Devi, as Mohini, enthralled the audience with her dance numbers, especially in the song '*Theeyani vennela reyi*'. *Lava Kusha*, her landmark movie, was a classic that took about six years in the making. It immortalized the lead cast—NTR as Lord Rama and Anjali Devi as Sita. There were several versions that have been made since then, but only this film remains etched in the memory of Telugu audiences. Her portrayal in this film was so realistic that she is verily looked upon as Sita in the collective consciousness of Telugu film buffs even today. Her performance won her the President's Gold Medal for Best Actress.

Another film from the early years of her career that saw great commercial success was *Keelu Gurram* (1949), in which she plays the vamp who is cruel to the royal family. But breaking this image, she went on to do a pious role in *Lakshmamma Katha* (1950).

She also did several character roles, such as playing sister-in-law and mother, and was the epitome of the Indian woman on screen, depicting powerfully the myriad problems that engulf a woman in the Indian context.

Like every other film star, she too had her crests and troughs, facing severe financial losses in the making of a Hindi film. When all was lost and she was face-to-face with the harsh reality that one is alone in distress, she sought spiritual refuge in Sri Sathya Sai Baba. With faith, hope and his blessings, she bounced back with the devotional film, *Sati Sakkubhai* (1965), followed by *Bhakta Tukaram*. Both these films turned out to be multi-lingual superhits.

She shared her space on celluloid with legends such as M.G. Ramachandran, N.T. Rama Rao, Akkineni Nageshwara Rao, Sivaji Ganesan and Jayalalithaa. Three of them became chief ministers of their respective states. Anjali Devi's first recognition came in 1943 from Sir Arthur Hope, the governor, in the form of a gold medal and a citation, in appreciation of the play *Street Singers*, written by Adinarayana Rao.

Anjali wanted to educate her sons and make them professionals, making an effort to keep them away from the film field. True to her wishes, her elder son, Chinna Rao, became a software engineer, and the younger one, Niranjan Kumar, a general surgeon. Both of them live in the US.

Anjali Devi has been honoured by the states of Tamil Nadu and Andhra Pradesh but was disappointed about not receiving any award from the central government. Anjali Devi has served as the vice president of the Film Chamber of Commerce, as a senate member in Sri Venkateswara University, Tirupati, and as the first woman president of the South Indian Artists Association. She was known for her keen sense of social responsibility and contributed generously towards the cause of education.

Anjali Devi is a legend saga in the history of Indian cinema, linking pre- and post-independence India. She is no more yet her memory is fragrant—she had an incomparably prolific innings, spanning 400 films over sixty-five successful years.

8

Vyjayanthimala

True to the significance of her name in the spiritual idiom, evoking celestial images of a garland of forest flowers woven by Andal to adorn her Lord Krishna, Vyjayanthimala in its entire connotation is the name her orthodox Brahmin parents Vasundhara Devi and Ramaswamy had chosen for their beloved daughter. Her mother was a leading actress in Tamil cinema in the 1940s and acted in *Mangamma Sapatham* (1943), the first ever Tamil film to be declared a colossal hit at the box office. Vyjayanthimala is a Vaishnavite by birth and initiated to the Aandal cult, which, till this day, she never fails to invoke for blessings before giving any public dance performance.

Vyjayanthimala's childhood was spent in her humble home in Tiruvallikeni, Madras, where she grew up under the watchful eye of her grandmother, Yaduguri Devi. At the age of five, she was chosen to perform a classical Indian dance for Pope Pius XII at Vatican City, with her mother in the audience.

A performing classical dancer would have certainly been very visible at a time when life was not so fast paced, and with the cherubic face of a sixteen-year-old on stage, would a clarion call from the medium of cinema have been far behind? Her face did catch the attention of filmmakers, and that's how her first film in Tamil happened.

When cinema beckoned her she drifted into it as Mohana, an aspiring dancer in *Vazhkai* (Tamil) in 1949, and then as Mohini in *Jeevitham* (1950, Telugu) and Latha in *Bahar* (Hindi) in 1951. She was just meant to be a pretty young girl and perform classical dances, which she did with absolute ease. She learnt Hindi at the Hindi Prachar Sabha in order to dub her own voice for her character in the film. There was not an iota of doubt that it was her dances that breathed life into the films, which were hugely successful.

Vyjayanthimala's *Nagin* with Pradeep Kumar was her tour de force. The film was the biggest hit of 1954 and enjoyed the tag of being a 'blockbuster'. The story was about two Adivasi tribes in conflict over their local economic rights. She plays the role of Mala, daughter of the Nagi tribe's chief, who vows to kill the son of the Ragi tribe's chieftain. Film reviewer Vijay Lokapally of *The Hindu* said, 'The ethereal Vyjayanthimala, barely eighteen, illuminates the screen with her stunning beauty, moving around daintily from one song to the other.' Close-up shots in the film highlight her ability to convey so much with so little effort.

Nagin was a precursor to her rise in Hindi cinema as an iconic actor, who combined her talents of acting and dancing to rule the silver screen on her terms. The lilting cadence of '*Man dole, mera tan dole*' rendered in the enchanting voice of Lata Mangeshkar, to the bewitching dance of Vyjayanthimala was a treat to watch and had the audience returning to the theatre for more. She has always had the mandatory dance sequence in practically every film she did, superbly showcasing her inimitable classical style.

The first female superstar of Bollywood

Dancing her way to stardom

In Irumbu Thirai *with Sivaji Ganesan*

Not content with her image as a dancer extraordinaire, Vyjayanthimala was keen to take on more significant roles, and around this time, she heard about the story of Devdas, based on Saratchandra Chatterji's novel. While all the leading ladies of the day wanted to play Paro, it was Vyjayanthimala who offered to play Chandramukhi. In fact, the auditioners she would be inappropriate for the role as she was very young, but she eventually bagged it. Bimal Roy cast her as Chandramukhi opposite Dilip Kumar in the critically acclaimed *Devdas* in 1955. Her determination and zeal to play the part did not go unrecognized; she was appreciated for her histrionics and her scintillating dances. Subsequently, she won the Filmfare Award for Best Supporting Actress but refused to accept it, stating that her role was a leading, not supporting, one with equal importance in the film.

Following the acknowledgement of her acting skills with *Devdas*, Vyjayanthimala acted in *Devta* (1956), which was a remake of a hugely successful Tamil film, *Kanavaney Kankanda Deivam*. Surprisingly though, she accepted the supporting role of a vamp in the film. No role was insignificant to this great performer. In 1957, she did *Aasha*, a romantic comedy based on the English film *Wonder Woman*, with Kishore Kumar playing a good Samaritan who is framed in a murder case. Ultimately, virtue triumphs and he escapes and marries his lady love, played by Vyjayanthimala. This film was also a box-office hit. It was remade in Tamil in as *Athisaya Penn* (1959) in which she co-starred with Telugu actor Akkineni Nageshwara Rao for the first time.

Sadhna, which released in 1958, is a black-and-white social guidance Hindi film, produced and directed by B.R. Chopra. The film revolves around Rajini (played by Vyjayanthimala), depicting a prostitute's love affair with a professor. Chopra had taken up the theme of rehabilitation of prostitutes, a highly controversial topic in those times. Film buffs credited her with the rare courage to accept negative roles like the one she played in this film, that of Champabai, acting alongside Sunil Dutt.

Another very successful movie that won her critical acclaim and awards was *Madhumati* in 1958, where she plays the lead role. *Madhumati* came to be known as the first film of its kind in the gothic genre, based on the theme of reincarnation and revenge. Devendra is in love with Madhumati, played by Vyjayanthimala, who commits suicide to save herself from the advances of the villain. Her performance as Madhavi, Radha and the ghost Madhumati zoomed her to the zenith of stardom.

In the same year, she acted in a mega production in Tamil, *Vanjikottai Valiban*, along with Gemini Ganesan and Padmini. She played the role of Mandakini, a stubborn and ambitious princess. The film had a great theatrical run and was labelled as a blockbuster at the box office. Even today, this film is remembered for the dance performance of Vyjayanthimala and Padmini in the '*Kannum kannum kalanthu*' song, so much so that the song became more popular than the film itself and is still regarded as one of the best dance sequences in Indian cinema.

In 1960, Vyjayanthimala concentrated largely on Tamil films in order to keep in touch with the industry. Her first release was S.S. Vasan's *Irumbu Thirai*, the Tamil version of *Paigham*. Her subsequent release was the magnum opus *Parthiban Kanavu*. Apart from Tamil, the film was produced in the Telugu and Sinhala languages. She also acted opposite the legendary M.G. Ramachandran for the first time in *Baghdad Thirudan*, another truly memorable film.

Following her successful re-entry in Tamil cinema,

Vyjayanthimala signed on Dilip Kumar's home production film,*Gunga Jumna* (1961). In this dacoit drama, she enacted the role of Dhanno, a washerwoman who falls for her childhood friend Gunga (played by Kumar) and eventually killed during a gun fight. In order to prepare herself for this role, Vyjayanthimala had to learn Bhojpuri. Her performance as a simple and graceful villager talking in the Bhojpuri dialect earned her rave reviews. In 1964, she co-starred with Dilip Kumar for the sixth time in Ram Mukherjee's *Leader*.

Later that year, she starred in C.V. Sridhar's *Nazrana* with Raj Kapoor. The film was a remake of the highly successful Tamil film, *Kalyana Parisu*, released in 1959. Then followed *Then Nilavu* (1961) with Gemini Ganesan. After a two-year break, Vyjayanthimala regained her place in Bollywood through Raj Kapoor's first technicolour film, *Sangam* (1964), the first Indian film shot outside Asia, in Europe. The film's story was considered Bollywood's greatest love triangle. For her role as Radha, caught between her husband and her former lover, Vyjayanthimala's display of emotional maturity won her the Filmfare Best Actress Award.

Jewel Thief, in 1967, made Vyjayanthimala and Dev Anand a hit pair. Her splendid dance number, *'Hothon pe aisi baat main'*, became a huge hit. Her last release in the year was *Hatey Bazarey* with Ashok Kumar. She played the role of a widowed young woman, Chhipli, who falls in love with a civil surgeon.

Saathi (1968) is a tear-jerker with an engaging storyline. In this tale of sacrifices, Vyjayanthimala steals the show with a lively performance. She left the industry after shooting for the historical Hindi film *Amrapali*, (1966) which was based on the life of Nagarvadhu (a royal courtesan) of Vaishali.

Vyjayanathimala married Raj Kapoor's personal physician,

Dr Bali, and has a son, Suchindra Bali. She was the first actress to have earned sobriquets like 'Numero Uno', 'Female Superstar' and 'Twinkle Toes', the first to pave the way for other South Indian actresses in the film fraternity. She introduced semi-classical dance to Bollywood, and was also a role model for all the aspirants to be trained in dance before they ventured into filmdom. The myriad choicest adjectives that have been lavished in describing her beauty, her repertoire of exquisite dance nuances, her captivating performances, all bear testimony to the finest heritage that she has bequeathed to the film industry in the South, as well as in the North, where many have attempted to tread and lagged behind.

Vyjayanthimala, now in her seventies, performs on stage to a packed auditorium even today, a feat in itself that speaks volumes for the charisma of this glamorous lady who could defy age and still appear resplendent.

9

Savitri

For a movie buff Savitri spells sheer nostalgia, capturing and evoking a montage of powerful scenes from her classics enshrined in the annals of South Indian cinema. There has been no challenge to the highest encomium 'Nadigayar Thilakam' (actress par excellence) conferred on her. The only other actor who shares this honour is Chevalier Sivaji Ganesan. She is also one of the very few film artistes to have a statue raised in her honour, one other being M.S. Subbulakshmi. Among the many lofty tributes paid to her, there is one that must be recorded for posterity, coming from her fraternity, 'There never was nor will ever be another Savitri'!

Savitri was born in 1935 to Nissankara Guruviah and Subhadhramma in Chirravuru (near Tenali) in Guntur, Andhra Pradesh. Her father died when she was six months old. She began learning music and classical dance at the age of eight and performed stage shows while still in school. She showed an interest in an acting career from the age of thirteen so her uncle took their family to Madras to help her get an entry into films.

She was introduced by producer S. Krishnamoorthy to

L.V. Prasad who was looking for a heroine for his Telugu film, *Samsaram* (1950). Savitri was first given a lead role as a heroine but she was very nervous, and was relegated to a small role in the film. Later, she was given a cameo in *Roopavathi* (1951). The movie was a flop, but it did help her overcome her nervousness and instilled in her a newfound confidence that she could act. The third time, when director K.V. Reddy was looking for a dancer for their film *Pathala Bhairavi*, he asked Savitri if she would give one small dance performance in the film and she readily agreed. The male dancer, Pasumarthi, was the dance director of the film. The movie was released in 1951 and became a huge hit. For the first time people took notice of this newcomer who could showcase a whole range of emotions in just a song-and-dance sequence.

A few minor roles followed till she became a star with *Pelli Chesi Choodu* in Telugu, titled *Kalyanam Panni Paar* in Tamil (1952). She bagged the dream role of Parvathi in the Telugu and Tamil versions of *Devdas* in 1953, an all-time classic and perennial favourite, with a soulful performance by Savitri.

Savitri established her great acting credentials with *Ardhangi* in Telugu, titled *Pennin Perumai* in Tamil (1955). She gave a very moving performance as a woman who is compelled to marry a mentally retarded man (played by A. Nageshwara Rao in Telugu and Gemini Ganesan in Tamil). She nurses the man back to health while teaching a lesson to her scheming mother-in-law. The film was re-made in Hindi, as *Bahurani* (1963).

The year 1955 saw yet another big hit of Savitri—the bilingual *Missamma* in Telugu, titled *Missiamma* in Tamil. The film, directed by L.V. Prasad, was a comedy about a couple pretending to be married in order to get a job, as the condition is that it is for a married couple only. The Tamil version in particular launched the Gemini Ganesan–Savitri pair (N.T. Rama Rao played the lead in the Telugu version opposite Savitri.) She broke her image as a tragedy queen and proved her credentials in comedy as well.

Savitri never used glycerine, and she proved her lachrymose spontaneity in a tragic scene in *Maya Bazaar* (1958) giving a perfect shot as desired by the director. Her drag act, sans make-up, as Ghatotkacha in the film *Maya Bazaar*, at the young age of twenty, was considered world-class.

The mid 1950s to late 1960s were her halcyon days and the period marked Savitri's ascension to great heights as an actress, with masterpieces in Tamil and Telugu. She was cast in the big league with stalwarts like Sivaji Ganesan, Gemini Ganesan and Nageshwara Rao where she proved her might and match time and again. She did only three films with MGR. Some of her important films in this period were *Kalathur Kannamma* (1959), *Kappalotiya Thamizhan (*1961), *Pasamalar* (1961), *Karnan* (1963), *Pavamannipu* (1961), *Raktha Tilakam* (1963), *Kaikodutha Deivam Navarathri* (1964), *Thiruvilaiyadal* (1965) and *Kandan Karunai (1967)* in Tamil and *Aradhana* (1962), *Moogamanasalu* (1963), *Varakatnam* (1968) and *Maro Prapancham* (1970) in Telugu. She even acted in a few Kannada films towards the end of her career; she played the role of a mother in films like *Thaayige Thakka Maga* (1979) and also acted in *Chandanada Gombe* (1980).

In *Pasamalar*, a tear-jerker and a sentimental drama of the bonding between a brother and sister, Savitri and Sivaji blazed through their roles, making it a watershed in the history of Tamil cinema, so much so that in Tamil parlance, '*pasa malar*' has become an idiomatic expression for affection between siblings. Savitri even went on a diet to reduce her weight for

Claim to fame in the epic film Maya Bazaar

Dynamics of emotion in Navarathri

In the title role in Kallathur Kannamma *with the child prodigy Kamal Haasan*

the second half of the film. The sentimental scenes in this film left a lasting impact on the audience.

Pavamannippu is a tale of communal harmony where she starred alongside Sivaji and Gemini Ganesan. The story about three children adopted and raised by foster parents in Muslim, Christian and Hindu households is a complex melodrama with a dishonest man, his villainy and its consequences. These were films where she had amply demonstrated her outstanding histrionics. *Pandava Vanavasam* (1962), where she played Draupadi, is perhaps her most acclaimed mythological film.

Another memorable film was *Gundamma Katha* (Telugu) that was released in 1962, partially inspired by Shakespeare's *The Taming of the Shrew*. The plot revolves around the story of a proud mother, Gundamma, and the way she was brought on track by her two young sons-in-law. She plays Lakshmi, the stepdaughter, in the film. It was later remade in Tamil as *Manithan Maravillai*. K. Viswanath, the doyen of Telugu cinema, exclaimed that Savitri 'emotes through her eyes.'

The screenplay of *Kalathur Kannamma* is based on the story *The Forgotten Factor*. It is a love story of a rich feudal landowner's educated son (Gemini Ganesan) and a poor but educated girl (Savitri), the daughter of the feudal bigwig's lowly servant (S.V. Subbaiah) both unaware of the identity and background of each other. Savitri gives a classic finish to the role by her fine depiction, which is etched in her audience's memory.

Yet another movie, *Kanyasulkam* (1955), which was adapted from the famous play of the same name, was made with a message to eradicate the social evils of the time like child marriage and prostitution, and to encourage widow remarriage. In this movie, Savitri played the prostitute, Madhuravani, with artistic ease.

Soon offers started pouring in, and producers wanted to cast her in their movies. Savitri could switch between roles very convincingly; while her romantic comedies were highly enjoyable, she could just as easily take on homely character roles, playing a good wife or daughter-in-law taking care of the whole family. She has also done triangle love stories, and has acted in mythological movies, bringing those characters alive.

It would be an understatement to say that Savitri was a very popular actress in Tamil. She married Gemini Ganesan, while acting in *Manam Pola Mangalyam* (1954). In her hundredth film, *Konjum Salangai* (1962), in which she was paired with Gemini Ganesan; she immortalized the song '*Singaara velane deva*' with her flawless lipsync. Her amazing performance as Santha, the humble flowerseller, was matchless. Both the protagonists competed with each other on screen, casting a spell on filmgoers. The melodious song enhanced the magic of the scene.

There were a few producers who wanted to make a film based on the famous Telugu novel written by Bucchibabu titled *Chivaraku Migiledi* (What Will Remain in the End). They wanted to cast Savitri in the role but she did not evince any interest. They approached Akinneni Nageshwara Rao and requested him to convince her. The ploy worked and she did the film. Though not commercially viable, the film won great appreciation from the critics and Savitri herself considered it her best performance. In 1960, she received the Rashtrapati Award for this film.

One of the reasons for the downslide in her career graph after 1965 was perhaps the ungainly weight she put on, particularly unacceptable in the industry when glamour was fast becoming the order of the day. Of course, this also spelt a general decline in moviemaking standards. She only had a few odd releases to her credit at this time, including *Thattungal Thirakkapadum* (1966), *Kandhan Karunai* (1967) and *Saraswathi Sabatham* (1966). They were all delayed releases. She did continue to act with NTR and ANR till 1970. She had no films with Sivaji for six years after the release of *Thiruvilaiyadal*; *Praptham* (1971) was their last film together.

Notable among the awards and recognition she received are state awards, such as Kalaimamani from the government of Tamil Nadu, Nata Siromani by the government of Andhra Pradesh and a stamp issued in her name. The Sanskrit title 'Mahanati' which means 'Supreme Actress' was another honour bestowed on her. She was a role model for all the heroines of her time. She acted in a total of 318 films in the Telugu, Tamil, Kannada and Hindi languages, recording an average of eight films released per year. She was aptly called the 'Ingrid Bergman of India'.

Her downfall was when she could not retire from movies gracefully like her contemporaries, Padmini and Sarojadevi, but tried to linger on, attempting direction. She directed five movies and most of them were remakes—*Praptham–Mooga Manasulu*, *Kuzhanthai Ullam–Chinnari Pappalu* (1963), *Chiranjeevi–Neerkumizhi*, *Vintha Samsaram–Vietnam Veedu* (1971). She produced her own movies and lost all the money she had earned. She began sinking into a financial abyss, felt personally let down, went into depression and finally died after prolonged suffering.

Many artistes fade away into oblivion since public memory is short. But Savitri is a striking exception. She will be remembered as long as celluloid lives on, because her films mirror life itself with their veritable kaleidoscope of human emotions and passions, rendered in all their diversity. She is one of those rare actors who imparted a Shakespearian magnitude to the roles she enacted, making the audience experience a cathartic impact. It would not be a hyperbole to say that she has not been surpassed!

10

Padmini

Regal in her presence, with a chiselled and captivating face that complemented her stately figure and the poise and elegance that training in classical dance endowed her, Padmini was a visual treat and a connoisseur's delight on the silver screen, a damsel who was admired and acclaimed not only for her classic beauty but also for her memorable histrionics. She was hailed as the queen of South Indian cinema in the 1950s and 1960s.

Born in Travancore, Kerala, on 12 June 1932, to Thankappan Pillai and Saraswathi Amma, Padmini was their second daughter. The three sisters—Lalitha, Padmini and Ragini—became popular dancers in different genres like Kathakali, Bharatanatyam and folk dances, and came to be called the Travancore Sisters.

Padmini was around ten when she gave her *arangetram* (first formal dance performance). Her mother was grooming the girls for a career in dance and films. She was spotted during her dance performance by the famous dancer Uday Shankar, who was, at the time, looking out for dancers for his Hindi film, *Kalpana* (1948). It starred Uday Shankar and his wife Amala Shankar and

Padmini made her screen debut as a seventeen-year-old. Film offers soon started coming her way.

S.S. Vasan of Gemini Studios cast Padmini in the lead role in *Mr Sampat* (1952), an adaptation of R.K. Narayan's novel of the same name. Her first character role, though, was in *Ezhai Padum Paadu* (1950), an adaptation of Victor Hugo's *Les Misérables*, and the film was also made in Telugu as *Beedala Patlu*.

Padmini soon emerged as a multifaceted, multi-lingual actor, comfortably switching among all four South Indian languages as well as Hindi, without any need for dubbing.

Her first milestone was *Panam* in 1952, where she was paired with Sivaji Ganesan. This film truly marked the start of her successful career.

She soon became a powerhouse of talent to reckon with; her films *Madurai Veeran* and *Amaradeepam* (1956) and *Vanjikottai Valiban* with Gemini Ganesan (1958) and *Mannadhi Mannan* (1960) became classics and box-office hits. People began to rave about her beauty, dance and emoting prowess.

Vanjikottai Valiban (1958) made history with the fascinating dance duel between Padmini and Vyjayanthimala, one of its kind in the annals of Indian cinema, pairing as it did the two most beautiful faces and most celebrated dancers of the time on one platform, their twinkle toes weaving an ensemble of exquisite movements set to lively classical music and lyrics, all part of the narrative. Their zestful rivalry both on and off screen made it a visual treat for connoisseurs of dance. This scene is imprinted in the minds of all those who have seen the film and till today has remained unparalleled and much-talked-about vintage performances.

No doubt, the credit for integrating graceful classical movements and nuanced facial expressions into cinematic song picturization goes to both these actresss; their dances became big hits and raised the bar for film dances. It became almost mandatory for film aspirants to be well trained in classical dance.

One of Padmini's highly appreciated movies was *Thangapadhumai* (1959), a brilliant adaptation of the Kannagi epic. In addition to her other talents, Padmini proved her extraordinary skill in dialogue delivery. She was known to be very disciplined on the sets, often seen to methodically rehearse her lines and try out different variations.

Her contribution to Malayalam cinema has also been significant. She acted in a number of Malayalam productions, the most famous being *Snehaseema* (1954), an adaptation of Alfred Tennyson's famous story-poem *Enoch Arden*.

She forayed into Hindi films with *Jis Desh Mein Ganga Behti Hai* (1960) opposite Raj Kapoor. The film captured her exquisite beauty, finesse and elegance. The film bagged many prestigious National and Filmfare Awards. Padmini was nominated for the Best Actress Award.

She also acted in an Indian–Soviet film, *Journey Beyond Three Seas* (1957), based on the travelogues of Russian traveller Afanasy Nikitin. In it she plays the role of Lakshmi, a royal dancer. In the Hindi version *Pardesi* (1957), she acted with Prithviraj Kapoor. She learnt the Russian language to do justice to her role in the film. The Russians were great admirers of Indian movies and even named their children after Raj Kapoor (Raj) and her (Lakshmi, her screen name). In fact, the film had such a strong impact on Russian audiences that following the film, a stamp was officially released in honour of the actress.

She did another film, *Aashiq* (1962), with Raj Kapoor. Her other Bollywood films were *Payal* (1957), *Afsana* (1966), *Vaasna* (1968), *Chanda aur Bijli* (1969) and Babubhai Mistry's *Mahabharat*

(1965), all in the 1960s. Sanjeev Kumar, the hero of *Chanda aur Bijli*, greatly appreciated her performance in the film.

One of the most successful films of the 1950s starring the Travancore Sisters was based on a folktale, *Thookku Thookki* (1954), starring Sivaji Ganesan, and the song, '*Sundari soundariye*', sung by the three sisters became a huge hit.

Uthama Puthiran, released in 1958, starring Sivaji and Padmini, is adapted from Alexander Dumas'*The Man in the Iron Mask*. The story is about a queen who gives birth to twins, one child is forcefully abandoned; and the two grow up, one becoming virtuous, the other avaricious. The two meet and are daggers drawn until the mother intervenes in the denouement. Padmini gave a memorable performance as the heroine. The songs from this film like '*Mullai malar mele*', '*Anbe amuthe*', '*Kathiruppan kamala kannan*', '*Unnazhakai kanniyargalkandathinale*' have an evergreen quality.

At the peak of her career, in 1961, her mother got her married to Dr K.T. Ramachandran, and Padmini relocated to the US. After seven years of blissful married life, she was once again offered good roles in films. She now had the consent and encouragement of her husband to start her second innings in the film industry, and after that, there was no looking back.

She played the role of a mother in very significant landmark movies like *Vietnam Veedu* (1970) and *Penn Deivam* (1970), which brought her immense fame and recognition. In *Vietnam Veedu*, she plays a Brahmin wife wearing a nine-yard saree and speaking the typical Brahminical dialect, torn between her children and her retired husband who is emotionally distraught while trying to come to terms with his retired status. *Chitthi* in Tamil (1966) (and its Hindi version *Aurat*) was another hit movie in which she portrayed a young woman compelled to

Mohanambal and Shanmughasundaram—the clash of titans in Thillana Mohanambal

Vintage wine in the film Vietnam Veedu

A heady cocktail of class and style

The charismatic pair in Mannadhi Mannan

marry an elderly widower with a family and the difficulties she encounters. The film *Thillana Mohanambal* came her way in 1968. She used to shuttle back and forth from the US to act in films. In this film, Padmini played Mohanambal to Sivaji's Sikkil Shanmugasundaram, two brilliant and impulsive artistes vying with each other to excel professionally in two different genres of classical dance and music, when they realize they are in love. It was truly the role of a lifetime for both of them, and together, they set the screen on fire. They made the characters come alive, giving the story a magnificent and larger-than-life lustre. It became a cult film.

Her other unforgettable Tamil films, which enhanced her status and made her a classic actress, were films like *Ethirparadhathu, Meenda Sorkam, Theiva Peravi, Mannadi Mannan, Madhurai Veeran, Raani Samyukta, Rickshawkaran, Arasilankumari, Punarjanmam, Amara Deepam, Kuzhandaikaga, Pesum Deivam* and *Irumalargal*. Some of these films with Gemini Ganesan, Sivaji Ganesan and M.G. Ramachandran gave Padmini an iconic image all her own.

Among her notable Malayalam films was *Adhyapika* (1968) in which she gave a sensitive performance as a teacher who sacrifices for her family and ultimately dies under unfortunate circumstances.

The tremendously popular pairs of the 1950s and 1960s included Gemini Ganesan–Savitri and MGR–Saroja Devi, but the awe-inspiring combination of Sivaji–Padmini set a new record—they acted in sixty films together.

She was the only multi-lingual star to have had the unique opportunity of starring with the several megastars like Sivaji Ganesan, M.G. Ramachandran, Akkineni Nageshwara Rao, Sanjeev Kumar, Shammi Kapoor, Ashok Kumar and the first

'Showman' of the Hindi film industry, Raj Kapoor. She was not merely cast for the glamour quotient but had an equally major role, which got her as much recognition as the hero.

Fazil's *Nokkethadhoorathu Kannum Nattu* in Malayalam (and its Tamil remake *Poovey Poochudava*) marked Padmini's re-entry in films much later; her role as a grandmother won her a Filmfare Award in Tamil in 1985 and accredited the movie with box-office success. She had always longed to do an art film, at least a small role in a Satyajit Ray film, and she got her chance with *Vasthuhara* directed by G. Aravindan in 1991.

She won the Best Actress Award of the Film Fans Association in 1954, 1959, 1961 and 1966, besides winning the prestigious Kalaimamani Award from the Tamil Nadu government in 1958. She was conferred the title 'Natya Peroli' for her legendary Tamil film *Thillana Mohanambal* in 1968. She also won another Filmfare Award in 1985 for her role in *Kaajal*. She was known to be socially responsible and never hesitated to do her bit for the country. During the Indo-Pakistan war in 1965, she went out to the war front and performed for the wounded Indian soldiers. She was a member of the Congress party and gave speeches in many political meetings during the 1967 and 1971 Lok Sabha and assembly elections for the party.

Padmini ruled the South Indian film industry during her day, not just because she had an enchanting face but by dint of her perseverance and intrinsic discipline. She was a thorough professional who spent hours together rehearsing her lines, her dancing skills and her multi-linguistic ability; above all, her easy camaraderie with the fraternity and her instantaneous affinity with the media and her fans will always be remembered.

She died of a heart attack in 2006 in Chennai—stars may come and go but Padmini is beyond compare!

11

B. Saroja Devi

This 'Abhinaya Saraswathi' would never have become a star if her grandfather had succeeded in having his way. Born in 1938, as the fourth daughter to her parents, Saroja Devi's grandfather tried hard to persuade his son to abandon the baby! But her father refused and the rest, as they say, is history. Her father was the man behind her success. His encouragement propelled her to reach Amazonian heights, winning the highest national civilian awards—the Padma Bhushan and the Padma Shri. She holds the world record for acting in the most number of films in the lead role as the heroine.

Saroja Devi's legendary beauty caught the attention of some of the most prominent figures of the time in India, including the then prime minister, Jawaharlal Nehru, who complimented her charming looks. She was a reluctant star to begin with; her single-minded goal was to be a teacher.

B.R. Krishnamurthy spotted her talent at the age of thirteen, at a school function, but she refused his film offer. A few years later, she debuted with her first film in Kannada, *Mahakavi Kalidasa* (1955). In the words of veteran stage director and film actor C.R. Simha,'Sarojamma, as a teenaged heroine, created such an impact through her very first film, *Kalidasa,* that she became the reigning female superstar of three South Indian languages and held that position for nearly two decades.' Her debut film won her a national award. She later recalled, 'In most of my films, I wore only traditional sarees, only occasionally I wore a salwar kameez. I had made it very clear to my directors that I would never ever wear a swimsuit or a sleeveless blouse!'

Simultaneously, she made her entry in Tamil films. B.R. Panthulu signed on the fledgling actor for a dance sequence in his movie, *Thangamalai Ragasiyam* (1957). Even in that minor role, the young star cast a magical spell on her audiences.

Saroja's victory run in Kannada continued. Her performance as the dancer in *Amarashilpi Jakanachari* (1964) who inspires the sculptor Jakana, well surpassed the screen presence of her hero, Kalyan Kumar. This film brought her dancing talent into the limelight. It also happened to be the very first full-length colour film in Kannada, which was later remade in Telugu with Saroja playing the female lead. The film in which she bagged the most sensational role was *Kittur Chennamma* (1961). She was hardly twenty years old then. Her acting potential was tapped to the fullest in her role as the patriotic Rani. The actor brought to life the extraordinary freedom fighter's story. Saroja became iconic as Chennamma, playing the younger, widowed and aged character. She captured the emotion of a childless widow imprisoned by the British poignantly on celluloid. She was forced to transform her melodious voice into a thundering tone for delivering intense and fiery dialogues; *'Nimage naavu needa beke?'* (Why should we pay the taxes as your subordinates?) is a dialogue that any old-timer can recollect even today. Her melodramatic essaying of the role revealed the mature actor in her.

Saroja Devi's career graph skyrocketed when she was paired with all the leading heroes of Kannada, Tamil, Telugu and Hindi filmdom. She set records in her time, rubbing shoulders with cine greats like Rajkumar in Kannada, N.T. Rama Rao and Akkineni Nageshwara Rao in Telugu, M.G. Ramachandran, Sivaji Ganesan, Gemini Ganesan and S.S. Rajendran in Tamil, and Sunil Dutt and Shammi Kapoor in Hindi. Bengali superstar Uttam Kumar also wanted to work with her. She earned the title, 'Chaturbhaashe Taare' (Star of Four Languages). Her unique style of dialogue delivery earned her the title 'Kannadathu Paingili'. Veteran actor V. Shantaram complimented her as a 'real actress, expressing real emotion'.

Saroja's entry in Tamil cinema was equally dramatic as her debut film in Kannada. MGR chanced to see her when she was shooting in the Vauhini studio in Chennai; he decided to cast her in his film *Thirudathe* (1961). Owing to a delay, he cast her in *Nadodi Mannan* (1958) instead. She could hardly speak in Tamil at the time, but he motivated her to learn the language. Her pairing with MGR in her very first Tamil movie paved the way for her mercurial rise in Tamil stardom. She was bracketed in the same category as MGR and accorded the same reverence. Her fans lapped up her beauty and her childlike innocence. Her eyes spoke volumes, rendering dialogues unnecessary. What is surprising is that she simultaneously acted in four languages, working four shifts a day. Fortunately, she could easily switch from one shoot to the other as make-up, hairstyle and costume were kept very simple those days. She insisted on dubbing for all her movies on her own. Saroja Devi's success story is exceptional indeed, for we must remember that she had no film lineage or godfather to back her in the industry.

Her next successful film was *Kalyana Parisu*, paired opposite

Kannadathu Paingili—the charming Saroja Devi

Emotion-charged role in Paalum Pazhamum

Enchanting the audience in the chart buster…'Love birds love birds' in Anbe Vaa

Casting a spell with MGR… the all-time hit pair

the romantic hero, Gemini Ganesan. This family drama was a super-duper hit in 1959. After this film, Gemini and Saroja became a winning romantic pair, acting in several films together. *Kalyana Parisu* is a love triangle where two sisters fall in love with the hero but the younger sister (played by Saroja) sacrifices her love. It was a commercial success due to the exceptional performance of the lead pair. Director Shridhar remade the movie in Telugu, this time, casting her opposite ANR. Later, it was remade four times, twice in Telugu and twice in Hindi!

Yet another memorable Kannada movie of hers with Rajkumar was *Bhagyavantharu* (1977). The lead pair play disillusioned parents who die of cancer and cardiac arrest respectively. Their performance was so realistic that Rajkumar's wife could not bring herself to watch them both die on screen!

MGR and Saroja Devi seared the silver screen together in nearly twenty-seven films. Almost all of these films were hits. Some of the more popular ones include *Thirudathey* (1961), *Thai Sollai Thattathey* (1961), *Paasam* (1962), *Thaayaikaatha Thanayan* (1962), *Asai Mugam* (1964), *Periya Idathu Penn* (1962), *Dharmam Thalaikkakkum* (1963), *Neethikku Pin Pasam* (1963), *Pannakkara Kudumbam* (1963), *Padakotti* (1964), *Nadodi, Thalibahakiyam, Naan Anayittaal* (1965), *Petralthaan Pillaiya* (1966) and *Parrakkum Pavai* (1966). Her most memorable performance opposite MGR was in *Anbe Vaa* (1966), where she plays a rich little spoilt girl. This film was such a resounding success that she was cast in the same mould in movies like *Enga Veettu Pillai* (1965), *En Kadamai* (1964), *Panathottam* (1963) and *Thayin Madiyil* (1964). But she was refreshingly distinct in every one of them. Her movies are also remembered for the beautiful costumes worn by her. In fact, following these films, she became a fashion connoisseur. Scores of women followed her fashion style and the outfits and jewellery worn by her in these films became a rage. *Arasa Kattalai* (1967) was her last film with MGR, as he did not want to cast her as the lead heroine after her marriage.

The charming superstar reached the pinnacle of fame in 1967. She consented to an arranged marriage with Sri Harsha, an engineer. The marriage reception was a grand affair attended by the who's who of South Indian cinema. 'M.S. Subbulakshmi sang at my wedding!' she fondly recalls. When she was toying with the idea of calling it a day—'My mother told me to stop acting but my husband said that talent should not be wasted'—she received a green signal from her husband and embarked on her second innings in films. Her famous Midas touch resumed and all the films she acted post-marriage were box-office hits.

Saroja Devi took the Tamil film industry by storm, starring opposite Sivaji Ganesan in wonderful films like *En Thambi* (1968), *Anjal Petti 520* (1969), *Thenum Paalum* (1971), and *Arunodayam* (1971). The magical pair of Gemini Ganesan and Saroja Devi made their mark again in *Panama Pasama* (1968), *Thamarai Nenjam* (1968), *Malathy* (1970), *Kann Malar* (1970), among others. Directors unhesitatingly cast her opposite younger heroes like Ravichandran in *Odum Nadhi* (1969) and R. Muthuraman in *Paththu Matha Bandham* (1974, her last film in Tamil), and they turned out to be very successful films too!

Saroja Devi bid adieu to Tamil films in 1970. After that, she only accepted offers for Kannada films and soon became the highest paid star, giving superhit films opposite Rajkumar and Vishnuvardhan in mythological as well as social drama genres. Her 150th film was *Sri Renuka Devi Mahatme* (1977). One film after the other, the iconic star had played the lead role in over 200 films without ever having to play the supporting role!

She refused to sign any films after the untimely demise of

her husband. The broken-hearted actress remained in mourning for almost a year. She resumed shooting only in 1987 to honour her prior commitments. The eight films that she took on were cameo roles, but as always, she was the cynosure of all eyes. Unwillingly, she gave in to popular demand and churned out one more successful film, *Parambariyam* (1993), opposite Sivaji. And she went on to play a few noteworthy character roles in the year 2000.

Saroja Devi's success story is exceptional indeed, for we must remember that she had no absolutely film lineage or godfather to back her in the industry. Diligently, she made her way purely on her own merit and was decorated with several awards during the five decades she graced the film industry. She is the only leading star today to have received the Lifetime Achievement Award thrice! Even today, she is a charismatic figure in tinsel town, one who will always be fondly recalled by veteran cine lovers and who continues to inspire and motivate the aspiring stars of tomorrow...

12

Vijaya Nirmala

'Start, long shot, close up, profile, block shots, cut!' Words that have come easy to a star who, after enjoying the limelight on celluloid crashed into the male-dominated profession of wielding the megaphone. There were other predecessors (woman directors) like Bhanumati, Savitri and G. Varalaxmi, but she raced ahead of them all, creating a watershed in film history. Vijaya Nirmala, a prolific director, had all the leading stars, including Sivaji and Akkineni Nageshwara Rao, dance to her tunes. 'My everlasting regret is not having directed the legendary N.T. Rama Rao,' she muses.

Vijaya Nirmala created history when the *Limca Book of Records* for directing the maximum number of films in Indian cinema recognized her. She became a trendsetter, featuring in the *Guinness Book of World Records* (2000) as well, directing forty-two films—the most for any woman director in the world! And her journey continues...

The director–actor's association with filmdom began at a very early age, as a child artiste. Vijaya's aunt, Rao Bala Saraswathi, a singer of repute at the time, took her under her wing and introduced her to the right people. Her training in acting began with a Tamil movie directed by R. Panthulu, who taught her to emote with a bribe of 'puri potato'!

Her second innings commenced when she was seventeen. The child had blossomed into a vivacious beauty. Ace photographer A. Vincent cast her in his first directorial venture in Malayalam, *Bhargavi Nilayam* (1964), a horror film with her in the lead role as Bhargavi. She dubbed for the film in her own voice. Her very first movie was a success, enjoying a hundred-day run. This film was her launch pad to stardom.

Her first Telugu film was *Rungula Ratnam* (1966), where she was introduced as Niraja. This was followed by another landmark debut film in Tamil, *Enga Veetu Penn* under the 'Vijaya banner'. She was rechristened as Vijaya Nirmala. The prefix 'Vijaya' became her lucky mascot and true to its meaning, it spelt victory for the star.

A Telugu film, *Saakshi*, directed by Bapu, marked a turning point in the actor's life. This film won rave reviews in the Tashkent film festival. The lead pair, Krishna and Vijaya Nirmala, went on to become a hit pair, acting in forty-seven films together. Their on-screen chemistry was further cemented in real life by marriage. Post-marriage too, every film of theirs did well at the box office. They became a rage in Telugu filmdom—the two stars were a perfect foil to each other. Multifaceted Vijaya was a good wife who managed to strengthen the family by bonding with her stepchildren as well.

During the shooting of *Saakshi*, Nirmala was so inspired by director Bapu that she wanted to follow suit. But she was advised against it, as she would lose her status as an actor; moreover, she was told that if she failed as a director, she would be neither here nor there. This made her procrastinate. She had been receiving wide acclaim for her performance in several Tamil, Malayalam and Telugu films. One film in particular, *Panama Pasama*, brought her laurels for her role as Alek Nirmala. Though this was a supporting role it was impressive. Nirmala presented another facet of her talent as a comedian. She plays the character of a supposedly rich daughter dazzling her mother-in-law with her so-called riches. The dialogue,'I going Malaysia,' became extremely famous. The song '*Elandapazham*' was a racy number that won many hearts. Her role served to bring much relief in an otherwise heavy tear-jerker. She stood out despite the multistar cast of Saroja Devi, Gemini Ganesan and G. Varalaxmi. Her pairing with Nagesh in the movie was received very well.

She earned a name for herself in Malayalam movies too. In *Anweshichu Kandethiyilla*, her acting received as much attention as did the heroine, K.R. Vijaya. She was as good as Sharada in *Karutha Pournami*. These Malayalam movies sharpened the actor in her.

Vijaya Nirmala was at ease acting in any capacity, whether heroine, comedian or support lead. She was never scared to be pitted against versatile actors, both male and female, carving a niche for herself. After several runaway hits like *Bangaru Gaajulu* (which won the Nandi award) and *Soppu Seepu Kannadi* (comedy), Nirmala realized her dream of becoming a director. She debuted as a director with a Malayalam movie, *Kavitha*.

'It was cheaper to produce a movie in Malayalam than in any other language,' she said. Heeding her husband's advice she established her own production house. As a director, Vijaya Nirmala quickly established full control over the cast, unit, budget and the shoot plan. Since she was not good at sketches, she planned her shots using Kondapalli toys! Unlike other directors, she would concentrate on long block shots and close-up at one go. 'This was to avoid wastage of film footage,' she explains. Economy was her watchword while making films.

Her first directorial venture registered victory and signalled her arrival as a director. She bought the film rights of a famous feminist novel; there was to be no song or dance in the film and she dared to cast her husband in the lead role! This was a brave move, as Krishna was a hero of the masses in those days. She remembers, 'My husband agreed and I was thrilled!' She faced problems with the great character actor Gummadi who was not satisfied with her style of shooting. 'Since he was sceptical, I called off the shooting for the day and asked him to watch the rushes of the film the next day'. If he was satisfied, he could continue, she recounts. True to his word, Gummadi turned up the next day, watched the rushes and donned the pancake, pronto. He gave a new title to the director, 'Pani Rakshasi', meaning 'a devil workaholic'!

Vijaya Nirmala, as a director, went on to invent new ways and techniques to make a film unique, proving she was as capable, if not more, than the men in the profession. Nageshwar Rao was stumped by her style of filming. When she was shooting for the film, *Hema Hemulu*, the hero had to change costumes in quick succession and Vijaya Nirmala kept taking the shots back to back. At one point, the actor was so confused that he asked her whether there was any film left in the camera! The film had two great stars in it, ANR and Krishna. Vijaya Nirmala showed her genius as director, employing highly technical shots in the fight sequences and the climax scenes. There was a sequence that was shot at one go, using nearly 2000 shots at the same time. Both heroes were amazed at her speed and her skill. Sivaji, too, praised her for her judicious use of his call

Captivating looks

With Jaishankar in her characteristic elan

sheets and for wrapping up the shoot within twenty-days with another twenty days given over to the film *Gnana Oli* (1972). So surprised was he that he tried to convince the director to shoot another movie in the remaining days. To this day, Vijaya Nirmala treasures this compliment coming from the stalwart.

Though she remade *Devadas* (1974), her dream project, the movie did not do well at the box office but was appreciated for its superior technical excellence. One of the shots in the movie showing Devadas drinking and an engine driver stoking coal into the burning cauldron of the engine was adapted in the Hindi version starring Shah Rukh Khan. This was indeed proof of the director's creativity to showcase a novel way of shooting a scene. Vijaya Nirmala reached the zenith as a director with *Alluri Sita Rama Raju* (1974), which was also the hundredth film starring her husband. The dedication and involvement of the seasoned director resulted in the film becoming a legend. What is noteworthy is the fact that she acted in and directed her films! Her cameo role in this movie along with the song '*Osthadu na raju*', a highly popular number, added to the success of the film. She always wore both hats most comfortably. She could still be a director's actor, as seen in several movies like *Akka Chellelu* (1970), *Devuda Chesina Manushulu* (1973) and *Pandanti Kapuram* (1972). These were mega movies which upped her star status.

Her dedication as an actor, too, was praiseworthy. She learnt to ride horses, play the veena, and drive scooters and cars. Today, at the ripe age of seventy, she is learning to swim! The actor–director's record of 350 films in all, across Telugu, Tamil and Malayalam, leaves one awestruck and serves as an inspiration for aspiring youngsters to follow in her footsteps. The partnership of Vijay Nirmala and Krishna stands testimony to their marital and professional compatibility as the first family of Tollywood. She has also produced serials for the small screen. Indeed, Vijaya Nirmala's name spells stupendous victory. She has received the Raghupathy Venkaiah Award for her contribution to the Telugu film industry. The doyen hopes to complete half a century in filmmaking—her grit and confidence that have made her the most distinguished film director in filmdom will make this possible. May her tribe grow forever more!

13

Jamuna

'A woman, in public life, should always hold her head high, displaying a little bit of arrogance and pride.' Silver jubilee star Jamuna lived by this philosophy throughout her film career. Undeterred by the sobriquet, 'the arrogant actor', she dictated her terms and lived by her own rules. This Satyabhama of the Telugu film industry exuded her trademark boldness and beauty both on and off screen. She ruled the Telugu film industry for two and a half decades, acting in nearly 189 films in Telugu, twenty in Tamil, sixteen in Hindi and five in Kannada. Her roles acquired a legendary quality, just like her beauty. Fortunately for her, the characters she essayed were a reflection of her own personality—bold and beautiful. Both on and off screen, her actions unhesitantly expressed her thoughts, irrespective of the consequences. Her role model was none other than Bhanumati, the actor nonpareil.

Early in her career, the valiant actor was mired in a controversy involving two leading male stars of her time. They boycotted her and she was almost ostracized by the elite of the film industry. 'She was branded as a headstrong and arrogant person. Such rumours began doing the rounds in the industry, confounding her life. It did hurt her a lot during those agonizing three years. She never once let fear overcome her. As luck would have it, other producers began to cast her in women-centric roles. 'These producers felt I could carry the entire film on my shoulders. I acted with lesser-known heroes like Jaggaiah, Kantha Rao, Balayya, Ramana Murthy and Satyanarayana between 1959 and 1961. All those films were successful,' she recalls.

The courage displayed by this actress is praiseworthy. She never cowed down even when a famous producer asked her to apologize for the benefit of the film industry 'I have done no wrong, why should I apologize? If I don't get films, I am ready to quit.' The word 'compromise' was alien to her nature. Luckily for her, she had tremendous support from her parents and other industry members. The issue was solved and the matter amicably settled with the intervention of two senior producers. Soon the floodgates of opportunity opened once again. Jamuna became a force to reckon with after the release of the two movies, *Gundamma Katha* (1962) and *Gule Baga Vali*, where she was paired opposite the two reigning movie moguls. She is the only female star in South Indian cinema to have taken on male domination and emerged triumphant.

Jamuna was born in a Brahmin family in Hampi, a small hamlet in Karnataka. Her father moved to Duggirala in Guntur to trade in tobacco and turmeric. The Kannada girl became a naturalized Telugu *bidda*. Right since childhood, little Jamuna was a powerhouse of talent, opting to sing and dance in different dramas. As expected, she was picked up by a producer to act in a film. Her first few films received lukewarm responses yet the feisty girl was noticed. She broke this spell of failed films with *Illarikam* (1959) opposite ANR, a social drama, which became a silver jubilee film. Jamuna overshadowed the hero's performance with her own, essaying the role of a rich girl with gay abandon, especially in the superhit song '*Niluvave vaalukanula daanaa*!' People who saw her in this song began comparing her beauty with the full moon. Opportunity knocked at her door with *Missiama*, another very successful film. Savitri played the lead role in this film, but Jamuna was highly appreciated for her dapper appearance. Savitri and Jamuna went on to act in several films and came to be known as Akka Chellilu—reel-life sisters. Savitri was always protective of the younger star and played her elder sister in real life too.

Jamuna's parents accompanied her to all the studios, keeping a strict watch on her; in fact, her mother was responsible for her make-up and costume. She was very firm about Jamuna wearing the right clothes. The actress remembers, 'God forbid, if those tailors' hands touched me while taking measurements, she would watch them with eagle eyes and hit them!' Jamuna fondly recollects another incident where she had to wear a long gown for a waltz based on an English tune. She was paired opposite NTR and ANR. The song was a dream sequence where ANR is a cook who dreams about a modern girl. Naturally, Jamuna had to wear a gown for this scene. 'My mother was very much against this. She insisted on frills covering the upper portion of the gown, so much so the producer came running home to convince my mother!'

As a heroine, her portrayals were highly individualistic with a trace of audacity. She was not known to play the demure, comely or coy maiden. In all her movies, she had a haughty swagger and a seductive appeal, which never crossed the limits of decency. Her roles in *Gundamma Katha*, *Mangama Sapatham* (1965), *Gule Baga Vali Katha* and *Letha Manasulu* (1966), are ample

Jamuna, the quintessential beauty

Carving a niche in Telugu cinema

Courting stardom with the thespian

Anbulla Maanvizhiye with Jaiashankar in Kuzhandaiyum Deivamum

testimony to her skillsets. She expressed a characteristic vanity and playful naughtiness, which made most of the songs from her films memorable. In songs like '*Shri variki memante enta paraka*,' Jamuna plays a wife wooing her husband. The chemistry between ANR and Jamuna is so evident for all to see in the song '*Andala o chilaka*'; this song enhanced her glamour quotient and widened her fan base. Similarly, in the movie *Letha Manasulu*, the music ably supported the refreshing romance of the young couple. The famous song '*Mauname gani manusupatina*' is an all-time favourite from *Gundamma Katha*, starring the lead pair Jamuna and ANR. This was a comeback movie for Jamuna, after the earlier unpleasant controversy. And she proved to the industry what a jewel in the crown she was. Some other notable movies she acted in were *Mooga Nomu* (1969), where she pulled off an emotional enactment very successfully—she was as good as Savitri was in the Tamil original, *Kaluthur Kannamma*. *Muddu Bidda* (1956) and *Eedu Jodu* (1967) were films that won her appreciation in every frame. She was just as successful when paired with superstars like Sivaji and Gemini in *Thangamalai Rahasiyam* (1957), *Nichya Thambulam* (1961) and *Nalla Theerpu* (1959). Jamuna earned credit for performing a wide variety of roles such as a vamp in *Mohini Rukmaangada* (1962) as well as character roles and ornamental cameos. Jamuna accepted her offers based on the story, her role and the credibility of the producer. She was adamant about acting in *Bangaru Thalli* (1971) despite severe discouragement. The film's success proved her detractors wrong and she received a flood of offers following this film.

Jamuna is one actress who led an impeccable life off screen, without being embroiled in any gossip or rumour linking her with her male leads. She married a zoology professor chosen by her parents, who claimed that he was the right person to handle their temperamental daughter. Her wedding was celebrated on a grand scale. 'Savitri Akka dressed me as the bride, even lending her diamonds,' she recounts. All the industry bigwigs, including NTR, graced the occasion. Jamuna offered to quit her acting career (she was at the peak of her success at the time), but her husband encouraged her to continue, claiming, 'it was God's gift to her'. Like Saroja Devi, she too, delivered several hits after marriage, squashing the belief that fans would not accept a married heroine. Jamuna's stupendous success in her career after her marriage was seen in *Shri Krishna Tulabharam* (1966), in her performance as the memorable Satyabhama. So effective was she in this role that critics felt that there cannot possibly be another Satyabhama to equal her in film history. Jamuna and Satyabhama became synonymous figures in people's minds! 'I worked hard to essay this role. While shooting for *Milan*, I used to rehearse the role of Satyabhama in between shots. I would stand before a mirror and practise how to hold my hand on the hip and draw with my toes on the floor.' This pose, in fact, became legendary, adding sheen to her superb performance in the movie. Another role that brought her much acclaim was *Muga Manasulu*. As Gauri, she captivated the audience with her big mesmerizing eyes. She bagged the same role in the Hindi version. This won her the Filmfare Best Supporting Actress Award. Time and again, Jamuna claimed her place amongst successful female stars like Savitri and Sharada. The lady had her signature uniqueness as an actor, which kept her in good stead.

Movies like *Letha Manasulu* were remade in Tamil. She acted with relatively lesser-known male leads like Harinath (Telugu) and Jaishankar (Tamil). In the Tamil version of the film (*Kuzhandaiyum Deivaimum* 1965), Jaishankar accidently fell on her during the shooting of the song (*'Anbulla maanvizhiye'*). Her head bore the brunt of his entire weight and though this did not affect the shooting then, it impacted her health in her later years. But the song became very popular.

Jamuna delivered several hits, always giving her best shot, playing noteworthy roles in movies like *Ramu* (1968), remade in Tamil, *Tahsildar Gari Ammayi* (1971) and *Collector Janaki* (1972), among others; these were evergreen roles that stood the test of time in cinema history. She gave another stellar performance in *Pandanti Kapuram* (1972), as the unforgettable Rani Malini Devi. This role was earlier offered to Bhanumati, who rejected it as it had shades of grey. Jamuna immediately accepted and immortalized the role of a vindictive woman. It seemed tailor-made for her! Her fans began to call her Rani Malini. For a while, these women-centric characters even rendered their male leads redundant! Brand Jamuna was the order of the day throughout the 1960s and 1970s. She had absolutely no competition despite being surrounded by many heavyweights at the time.

Jamuna is widely appreciated for her wonderful balancing act, on both her professional and domestic fronts. Her son is a professor of media studies in the US and her daughter is a budding painter. She herself basks in the companionship of her husband.

Jamuna decided it was time to pay back to society and made her entry into politics. She was chosen by Indira Gandhi to contest the parliamentary elections from Rajahmundary. 'It is ironic that I was opposing NTR, my hero of several films. I used to only criticize his ideology and never the man,' she says. She has done yeoman service as the state president of the Old Artists Association. While heading this organization, she enrolled approximately 10,000 elderly artists as members, extending several benefits to them.

The soon-to-be octogenarian actor now wants to lead a quiet life, spending her time in communion with God and playing with her grandchildren. The Andhra Nargis' timeless beauty will be appreciated unto eternity; as the Bard put it, *age cannot wither her nor custom stale, her infinite variety...*

14

Manorama

'I had never done comedy before and was scared, but Kannadasan convinced me into doing the role. I think he was right because if I had begun as a heroine, I would not have been able to last this long.' The star was never to regret this chance. She became a legend, doing 1500 films and entering the *Guinness Book of World Records* for acting in the maximum number of films at the time. She also has to her credit over 1,000 stage performances, a veritable feat in itself! She enjoys the distinction of having acted with Annadurai and Karunanidhi, who later became chief ministers of Tamil Nadu.

Palathur Papa alias Gopishantha had a steep climb to the top. The journey took half a century and five years to be precise, traversing to reach the summit. Manorama the legend was created. Cloning this actor par excellence would be next to impossible. Her life story begins in Rajamannargudi in Tanjore district. The saga of the actor rechristened as Manorama commenced here.

To supplement her income young Manorama began to sing for Terukuthu or street plays and doubling up as a playback singer for the stage artistes. It was during one such show that she was baptized as 'Manorama', by the drama director and harmonist. She was forced to act when the heroine refused to play her role. And that is how 'acting happened by accident', claims the star.

Lady Luck smiled on her after she joined S.S. Rajendran's Nataka Mandram. During one of their shows, thespian Kannadasan signed her on for his movie. The actor was initially hesitant to play the comedienne in *Malayitta Mangai* (1958), but the gamble paid off and a historic comedienne was born. Her compelling performance in the movie brought the house down and Manorama was on her way to stardom. She became a numero uno comedienne, acting with stalwarts like Thangavelu, Cho Ramaswamy, Nagesh and Tengai Srinivasan. Manorama had the required craft while acting with the veteran Thangavelu. She has entertained the audience as the daughter of Thangavelu in the full-length comedy film, *Galatta Kalyanam* (1968). She plays the spinster who is averse to marriage. Attempts to change her mind by Nagesh as the suitor and Thangavelu as the father make for a rib-tickling comedy. She did very well for herself when paired with Thangavelu in *Ponnuku Thanga Manasu* (1973) and *Vallavanukku Vallavan* (1965). The comedy act did not come easy. It required precision, timing and a down-to-earth approach. The consummate actor did this with effortless ease albeit a little loud and dramatic. She deserves a bugle blast for her repertoire. Her most cherished dream came true when she played the lead heroine in *Konjum Kumari* (1963). Here too, the smidgeon of comedy was visible. The actor evolved her own style, using different slang and dialects, which added to her versatility.

Ace director A.P. Nagarajan utilized the actor's prowess in mythologicals like *Thiruvilayadal* (1965). Despite doing a cameo role in this film, she attracted plenty of attention. He cast her again in *Saraswathi Sabatham* (1966), where she perfected her craft. *Thillana Mohanambal* (1968) was a game changer that showcased Manorama at her best. Jil Jil Ramamani (the character she played) elevated her star status to a whole new plane. The character's vivacity, innocence and openness was simply superb. Undaunted by the presence of two theatrical geniuses like Sivaji and Padmini, she delivered a performance of a lifetime. 'Even today, when I see it, I become my own fan,' she reflects with pride. A.P. Nagarajan, the director, exacted a finely chiselled masterpiece from Manorama. Her act was a rare combination of dramaturgy and comedy, which earned critical acclaim. Her character became a cult figure, adding a whole new dimension, which held the audience spellbound. Her favourite mentor and director cast her again in *Raja Raja Chola* (1973), where she provides comic relief as Poonkodi. 'He was truly a man of many talents, a "*sakalakala vallavan* (master of all arts),"' she said. This film was also the beginning of a mutual admiration between Manorama and the doyen, Sivaji. She would lovingly address him as 'Anna'. The star nostalgically recalls her last meeting with Sivaji to seek his blessings on her birthday. During the course of their conversation, she was elated to hear him praising her to his wife. Other great comedians like Cho and Nagesh also were a perfect foil to her acting. She has acted in more than hundred films with them. Her most unforgettable act with Cho was in *Bommalattam* (1968). The song *'Vaa vaathiyaare uttaande'* broke new ground in the realm of comedy. Manorama's rendition of the song in true Madras slang and her comic capers with Cho wrote a new chapter in comedy. Both were perfectly in sync and their collaborative effort made the act evergreen. Even today this song evokes much laughter, reigning high on the actor's

The unforgettable Aatchi of Tamil cinema

Jil Jil Ramamani in Thillana Mohanambal

'Muthu kulika varigala' *upped her star quotient*

The riot act with Mouli, another seasoned comedian

list of best performances. Its humour defies the passage of time and remains immortal.

Manorama was happy to continue her first love (singing), especially after the raging number in *Bommalattam*. She was rightly called 'Suraiya of South Indian cinema', being compared with the singing star of yesteryears in Bollywood. Her tryst with singing began under the music director, M.A. Kumar. Manorama sang along with L.R. Ishwari in the famous '*Thatha Thatha pidi kudu*' in the film, *Magale Un Samathu* (1964). This phenomenal singer–actor belted out such wonderful numbers as '*Muthu kulika varigala*' in *Anubhavi Raja Anubhavi*. This song skyrocketed her to the hall of fame shared by singers like P. Susheela. Manorama's disarmingly funny antics in the song became a rage. The song became so popular that it was included in the Hindi version too! Her singing talent was exploited in about sixty films. Another song based on a folk tune, '*Pogathe pogathe en kanava*' similarly climbed the popularity charts. HMV released an album of her songs titled '*Vaa vaathyare*' and it sold like hot cakes.

Manorama, the uncrowned queen of comedy, has often been compared to Lucille Balle, the great Hollywood comedienne. A volcano of talent, she gave her best when she was paired with Cho and Nagesh, especially in *Aayarathil Oruvan* (1965) and *Anbe Vaa* (1966), *Paar Magale Paar* (1963) and *Pattikada Pattanama* (1972). In these movies, she played a faithful servant, a village girl and a good friend. In *Kasethan Kadavulada* (1972), she excels in the role of a domineering second wife controlling the purse strings at home. Her caricature of the snooty rich woman sent the audience into peals of laughter.

Manorama progressed into doing character roles after an outstanding stint as a comedienne. She has given memorable performances in so many Kamal Haasan starrers that she almost became a permanent fixture in his films. The most noteworthy ones include *Singaravelan* (1992) and *Michael Madana Kama Rajan* (1990) and a dignified cameo in *Vazhve Mayam* (1970). She was equally comfortable acting in Rajinikanth films like *Billa* (1980), *Thanga Magan* (1983) and *Naan Adimai Illai*. The actor had a difficult role of an older woman falling in love with the hero (Satyaraj) who is in disguise in *Nadigan* (1986). 'This was a tightrope balancing act as I had to retain the dignity of the character' she recalls. Another challenging role was in *Savaal* (1981), as Burma Papa speaking the Burmese refugee language.

The actor claims her characterization in *Chinna Gounder* (1992) remains her most favourite role to this day. The song sung by her was an impromptu one written and shot on the same day. The poignancy with which she sang it earned her abundant praise and admiration. She was in her element in films like *Kadhalan* (1994), *Nattamai* (1994), *Gemini* (2002) and *Saamy* (2003), playing key roles in each. Her most notable role as the domestic help, Kannamma, who helps the family to resolve their problems, was in *Samsaram Athu Minsaram* (1986). The actor effectively showcased the dynamism and boldness of an enterprising domestic help. Later, *Chinna Thambi* (1991) reiterated her penchant for playing serious roles. As the mother of the protagonist (Prabhu), she is at once indulgent and understanding. The star always claimed that she unconsciously imitated her own mother on celluloid.

Manorama had the distinct honour of being paired opposite Mehmood, the Bollywood king of comedy, in *Kunwara Baap* (1974). She held her own in the film, flamboyant and flashy, dubbing the dialogues in her own voice. She treasures her role in *Unakkum Vazhvu Varum* (1978) as a talkative girl forced to act as a dumb person. The laugh riot that she created is unarguably one amongst her most stellar acts. The actor rates her character in *Unnal Mudiyum Thambi* (1988) as one of her most challenging and satisfying roles till date. It brought out another facet of her acting calibre. With this role Manorama became an accomplished star.

She paid attention to even the smallest jingles and advertisements where she lent her voice or her presence, be it in the electronic or print media. She rightly deserved the honour of the Padma Shri and Kalaimamani Tamil Nadu state award. Manorama the legend can never be surpassed in a long time!

Manorama has carried on undeterred in her long and passionate innings, giving her very best to Tamil, Telugu and Malayalam cinema. This charismatic comedienne has an immortal place all her own in the annals of South Indian cinema. Her formidable talent will be remembered long after she ceases to wear the grease paint.

As she herself aptly puts it… 'The only job I know is acting, which I will do till my last breath. My fervent wish is to die with my make-up on.'

15

Sowcar Janaki

A mother is one who will spare no efforts to protect her offspring and her unconditional love will make her do anything for her child. This is the story of a young mother who chose a profession which no woman from an orthodox background would opt for as her livelihood. At seventeen, she was left with only one alternative based on her previous stint as an AIR (All India Radio) artiste. So she chose to act.

Sankaramanchi Janaki (her name after marriage) was married off at the tender age of fifteen solely to nip her acting aspirations in the bud. It all began with eminent filmmaker B.N. Reddy's curiosity to see the girl behind the familiar voice in AIR. He offered her a chance to act. When an excited Janaki mentioned the offer at home, all hell broke loose. Her brothers and mother forced her to tie the knot to prevent such antics. Her famous voice was instrumental in getting her married. The family of Sankaramanchi Srinivas (radio supervisor at Kakinada) came asking for her hand. Before she could bat her eyelid, the youngster entered into the shackles of matrimony. Should we say the radio played a significant role in her marriage and stardom simultaneously?

Janaki was born in an educated but orthodox family in Rajahmundry. Her father, a paper technologist, was educated in England. He was an extremely progressive man and her mother was a devout woman. It is little difficult to believe that a girl from such a family would pursue an unconventional profession like acting. Janaki was truly destiny's child. Every decision of hers seemed predestined. How else can one explain the event of a teenaged married woman, a mother, becoming a renowned cine star!

The actor's better half was a good husband but not a breadwinner. Naturally, this responsibility was thrust upon her and left with no choice, she went looking for acting opportunities to keep the home and hearth going. The seventeen-year-old with a child in hand now approached the famous B.N. Reddy who had initially offered her a role. Seeing her plight, he arranged for a screen test. L.V. Prasad was to direct this film, a maiden venture of Vijaya Productions. Janaki was elated to play the lead role in their film *Shavukar* (1950), opposite NTR. 'Directly from being a mother confined to the kitchen, I had to face the camera' she says. The role of Subbulu fitted her like a glove. She was to be paid a princely sum of 2,500 rupees. 'With the signing amount, I bought clothes and baby food for my child.' She was very fortunate to have been under the baton of a genius like Prasad. 'He would show me how to act but encouraged me to have a style of my own,' she fondly recalls. The director would never hesitate to reprimand her in order to extract the right emotions.' The film was a runaway hit, receiving applause and critical acclaim. Janaki became the only star to have the title of a film as a prefix to her name.

She came to be known as Shahukar Janaki, which later became the legendary 'Sowcar'. To this day, she remains proud of this title that her ardent fans conferred on her. The star treasures the unprecedented glory showered on her.

Very strangely, she was asked to go back to being a housewife as she was no star material. She neither had the looks nor the charisma for the glamorous roles. Despite these discouragements she fought tooth and nail and continued undeterred. 'I did not give in to desolation as this was my only means of livelihood.'

Success did come to her by and by; she went on to bask in the limelight with all the leading male stars in the four languages. 'NTR had immense faith in me and allowed me to share space with him on the silver screen in movies like *Kanyasulkam*,' (released in 1955) says the star. She proved her detractors wrong in the role she played in this film, that of Buchiamma, the young widow. Known to persevere, she made use of every opportunity to make her mark in the industry. In the film *Venkateswara Mahatyam* (1960), she became popular as a fortune-teller. Her mastery over the particular accent and voice modulation required to play this character won her critical appreciation. Even Dr Radhakrishnan, the former President of India, praised her role in this film. The heroine had successfully demolished two abiding mindsets seen in the industry—that an actor cannot be married and that a high glamour quotient is a must.

By the time she acted in *Rojulu Marayi* (1955), she had three children. Yet she could slip into the shoes of the protagonist easily, playing an innocent shy and young girl romancing ANR. It was tough balancing both domestic and professional fronts but the 24/7 mother gave her best to her children at home and to her films simultaneously. The twenty-hour work schedule sometimes made her carry the image of a role to her home (there was no time to switch over), which would scare her children! 'Once after returning from the shoot of *Iru Kodugal*, I continued to behave like collector Janaki, even after reaching home. My children began to cry,' she reminisces. This particular movie (1969) was a trailblazer in the social genre, casting the female protagonist in a much more powerful light than the male lead. She did other epic films like *Uyarntha Manidan* (1968), *Pachai Vilakku* (1964), *Paarthal Pasi Theerum* (1962), *Paar Magale Paar* (1963) and *Motor Sundaram Pillai* (1966). In all these archetypal films, Sivaji and Sowcar were the lead pair. In *Motor Sundaram Pillai*, Sowcar plays the veena in one scene. The director took the assistance of the great veena maestro, Chitti Babu, to lend an authentic touch when shooting the scene. K. Balachander, who directed Janaki's most memorable movies, recalled how she was initially hesitant to enter a pool of water in his film, *Neerkumizhi* (1965), but later agreed to do it in the spirit of the role. 'Such was her dedication,' claims the thespian.

A turning point in her career came with the film *Pudiya Paravai* (1964). This was Sivaji's first home production and he was insistent on casting Janaki in a glamorous role, much against the wishes of the director, Dada Mirasi. The role had shades of grey and veered towards being vampish. Janaki gave a convincing portrayal as the alcoholic club dancer out to ensnare the hero. The sophistication and the sensuousness exhibited by the actor in the dance number '*Paartha nyabakam illaiyo*' became immortal. She overshadowed the other heroine in the film who was famous for her looks and glamour! 'Any role that is unusual, unconventional, has a special appeal for me. Maybe it has something to do with my psyche, as I love

The ebullience of Sowcar Janaki in her maiden appearance

Making her presence felt in Ethir Neechal

Pitting talent with the doyen

Sharing the limelight with Bhanumathi in Annai

complex characters. Very few actors would have accepted such a role at the peak of their career,' she mentions. It also helped the star to break away from the prevalent stereotype of emotionally high-strung characters. She did yet another role with shades of grey in *Doctor Chakravarthy* (1963, Telugu), where she plays the possessive wife of ANR. Her stamp of individuality in her expression in the scene where she keeps looking at the watch, as she is bored became quite famous. *Kaviya Thalaivi* (1970) was from her own production house, directed by her mentor, K. Balachander. It was a story where the protagonist sacrifices her life for her daughter's sake. Janaki played a double role. She essayed the mother and the daughter better than Suchitra Sen did in the Hindi version, *Mamta* (1966). 'It was a lifetime role which impacted me greatly,' says the actor.

Her favourite director identified her talent to act in comedies like *Ethir Neechal* (1966) and *Bama Vijayam* (1967). Her comic timing was so well appreciated that she was repeated in the Telugu (*Mugguru Kodalu*) and Hindi (*Teen Bahuraniyan,* 1968) versions. Later, at the height of her career, she made the unusual choice of acting on stage, joining K. Balachander's theatre group in 1965.

The multi-talented actor has executed several characters in her time, ranging right from a blind village girl to a sophisticated lawyer. She was not comfortable dancing but she has danced beautifully in the movie *Akka Chellelu* (1970), to the famous song '*Paandavalu paandavalu tummeda*'. Even here, Janaki made her own style statement.

These films gave her career a quantum leap. The star went on to do 400 films in various South Indian languages. The seventy-five or so Telugu films she acted in made her a celebrated icon in Tollywood, giving her a permanent place among the all-time greats. In Tamil, she made a name for herself, etching memorable roles with her subtle pitch in dialogue. She has to her credit thirty Kannada movies (ten with Raj Kumar). Her best appearances were in *Mahishasura Mardhini* (1959), *Sati Shakti* (1963), *Tayige Takka Maga* (1978) and *Shabdavedhi* (2000), which won her much acclaim and recognition. She also did two films in Malayalam and a few in Hindi. She dubbed for all the movies in her own voice with the perfect accent demanded by the language. She was sought after by Tamil directors who cast her in movies like *Thillu Mullu* (1981), *Thodarum* (1999) and *Vaanavaraayan Vallavaraayan* (2014). Her acting in *Thillu Mullu* as a widowed socialite remains popular with cinema lovers even today; the ease with which she alternated between the two characters never fails to evoke a smile.

The Tamil Nadu state government bestowed on her the Kalaimamani award, which was given away by then chief minister, Karunanidhi. She was also the recipient of the Lifetime Achievement award instituted in the name of the legend, ANR (Swarna Kankanam). She was conferred with the Sivaji award as well. The star was appointed as a jury member for the National Indian Films awards committee and has chaired the State Telugu Films awards committee.

A significant facet of Janaki is her impeccable English, her perfect diction and accent. She is a very private individual and hates to share her sorrows. Her adversities have taught her to face life head on. The octogenarian actress now enjoys the company of her two daughters and one son, four grandchildren and two great granddaughters. Janaki, the actor, is also a gourmet cook. She likes to believe in the maxim, 'Looks go and cooks stay'.

Sowcar Janaki has truly earned pride of place in the hundred-year history of Indian cinema, reigning on the silver screen for six decades and still going strong. She has enjoyed every moment she spent in this world of fantasy. Her only wish that remains unfulfilled is to share the same frame with the great Vyjayanthimala. An actor who once embarked on this path to merely earn a livelihood is still going strong with the same passion. She hopes to make her mark on celluloid as long as she breathes.

16

Urvashi Sharada

Kanyasulkam (1955), a revolutionary Telugu film, was the launch pad for a nine-year-old impish girl from Tenali, Andhra Pradesh. A girl who blossomed into a tall, beautiful woman with aquiline features. Thanks to her genes, she also inherited a deep sonorous voice. The voice belied her dainty looks. Saraswati Devi, rechristened Sharada, became one of the most accomplished actresses of early modern South Indian cinema. She was known for her finest performances, which left a lingering melancholy long after the movie was over.

It was her mother who made her entry into films possible. Such was the enthusiasm of the mother that she sent her daughter to Madras to learn Bharatanatyam. The grandmother accompanied the little girl when she shifted to Madras. She was a strict disciplinarian who laid down rules and would watch the young girl like a hawk to ensure the heroes did not touch her during the drama rehearsals, which were to be only on Sundays!

Sharada joined Annapurna Studios and was guided by the great star, ANR. She acted as his sister in their production titled

Iddaru Mitrulu (1961). It was ANR who moulded the budding actress. 'He showed me how to walk, talk and even hold the mirror.' This role fetched her public acclaim.

Malayalam cinema was quick to notice the talented actress and pitchforked her to the zenith of fame as the uncrowned tragedy queen, leaving the viewers misty-eyed with her acting prowess. 'My mother gave birth to me while Malayalam cinema gave me life.'

She looked and played the part of a Malayali so well that a famous director like S.S. Vasan asked her to learn Telugu to act in his film! This unassuming star claims she is a director's actress, giving them the complete credit for her iconic portrayals. 'My long dialogues lasting nearly five minutes, in the movie *Anthapuram* (1998), was completed in one shot. Thanks to my director.'

Sharada became a multi-lingual actress, simultaneously acting in Kannada, Telugu, Malayalam and Tamil. Some of her noteworthy films in the mythology genre are *Valmiki* (1963, Kannada and Telugu) and *Arunagiri Nathar* (1964, Tamil). *Kattu Thulasi* (1965), *Muraippennu* (1965) and *Iruttinte Athmavu* (1966) were powerful presentations that still stand the test of time. *Irutinte Athmavu* was a low budget film, culturally rich, highlighting family drama. She matured as an actress as Amukutty in the film. It was a fine enactment of a girl's deep love for a man whom the world declared as mad. Sharada was at her absolute best in this film and it gave her a firm foothold in the Malayalam film industry.

Sharada entered the annals of film history with a high-voltage performance in *Thulabharam* (1968), directed by A. Vincent. This is a story of two friends who part ways due to certain events in their lives. Vijaya (Sharada) ends her friendship with Vatsala (Sheela), after the former's father's death. Vatsala's lawyer father is responsible for this tragedy as he loses the case. Vijaya gets married to a trade union leader and leads a life of abject poverty. The protagonist shows her love for her husband and children during such trying circumstances. Sharada immortalized the role of Vijaya as a wife and a mother. In moments of grief, she spoke with her eyes. She handled the role with utmost dexterity, which it demanded. It is no wonder that she won her first Filmfare Award for Best Actress (then known as the Urvashi Award) for this film. She recalls, 'Even today when I see the film, I cannot sleep for three days, I doubt if I can ever be Vijaya once again.' Her sterling act as a struggling mother protecting her children was equivalent to that of Nargis in the classic *Mother India* (1957). The actor raised the bar and created a benchmark, which few actresses could follow. This film was remade in four languages with Sharada playing the lead in all four versions.

Triveni (1970) portrays Sharada as the central protagonist in a love triangle. Sharada and Prem Nazir is a young couple in love. The young hero goes in search of greener pastures promising to return and marry her later. Meanwhile she gets married to a wealthy old man for mere companionship. In the climax, her hero of old returns to find his lady love married, with a child. Her husband dies and the lovers are reunited. The actress was a scene-stealer in the film, displaying an ideal combination of passion and affection. It was as if the story gave her a readymade platform to tell the world about the effervescence of falling in love and the maturity of a married woman adjusting herself to a compromise. Sharada's characterization won her the Kerala State Best Actress Award.

In *Tara* (1970), she bagged a double role, playing both mother and daughter. The unusual characterization elevated the movie to another level altogether. As expected, Sharada did justice to both the roles and won the Kerala State Best Actress Award for the second time.

Malayalam films continued to give Sharada her dream run. Several opportunities came her way to showcase her talent. One such film was *Swayamvaram* (1972), directed by Adoor Gopalakrishnan. The director wanted fresh faces for the film and he approached several colleges to conduct auditions but found no fitting response. Eventually, he offered the role to Sharada. The film had a profound impact on the young audience. The story is a journey from illusion to reality. It's all about a couple, Vishwam (played by Madhu) and Sita (played by Sharada), who get married against their parent's wishes. The film outlines the struggle faced by the newly married couple since it is an inter-caste marriage. Sharada once again infused a touch of dignity into the character, projecting finely the valiant struggle, first as a wife, then as a widow. The film ends in typical Adoor Gopalkrishnan style—leaving the conclusion to the audience. Sharada registered an act that re-inforced her image as a classic tragedy queen. It received wide critical acclaim and was awarded four National Film Awards—including Best Film, Best Director and Best Actress.

Nimajjanam (1979) was a pathbreaking film where the story lives up to the title that means renunciation or immersion. The story revolves around a woman (played by Sharada) who forsakes her life as a form of punishment for having been raped by a bullock cart driver. As was wont of those times, the woman had to bear the cross all alone for a crime committed against her. Sharada gives an outstanding account as a beautiful wife accompanying her husband who falls prey to the lust of an illiterate man. She displays her remorse and shame unparalleled in the film industry. She rightly deserved the Filmfare Award a third time, a record that no other actress could boast of!

Urvashi Sharada—talent in abundance

Essaying myriad roles with absolute ease

A volcano of emotions

A touch of poignance with A.V.M. Rajan

Sharada played Draupadi opposite N.T. Rama Rao in his magnum opus *Daana Veera Soora Karna* (1977), departing from her tragedy queen image to be crowned the dialogue delivery queen. Initially, a nervous Sharada had to face several retakes for her shot. But NTR brought out the unabashed actress in her, making the great director–actor proud. Her enactment of the malevolence and angst of Draupadi was brilliant. In the key scenes, her voice came to the fore, aiding her torrential downpour of words mouthed by Draupadi.

She went on to do several successful films with the late thespian, the most noteworthy one being *Justice Chowdary* (1982). This multi-starrer had NTR in a double role. Sharada is cast as his beloved who sacrifices her love for that of another woman. Her son (played by NTR again) wants to take revenge on his father for this injustice done to his mother. Sharada dies ultimately, with her son being accepted by the father. She excelled even in this ordinary role and managed to carve a niche for herself amongst all the bigwigs who acted in the film. This later opened the floodgates of character roles, which she executed with assurance and style. One such memorable movie was *Major Chandrakanth* (1993), another multi-starrer.

Sharada's consecutive success in multi-lingual films is a record of sorts. She thrived equally in Hindi, Kannada, Telugu as well as Malayalam films. The actress has done fifteen films with her Telugu co-star Shoban Babu, all of them being box-office grossers. They shared a wonderful on-screen chemistry. Their last film together was *Evandi Aavida Vachindi* (1993), which was also a runaway hit. Another cameo role was in *Nyayam Kavali* (1981), where she played a lawyer. During the shooting of this movie, her mother was on her deathbed. And yet, the true professional that she was, she proved her belief in the maxim, *the show must go on*. Sharada received kudos for her role as a policewoman, in *Pratidhwani* (1986). Her character roles with Chiranjeevi and Junior NTR have received excellent reviews. She must be the only actress besides Anjali Devi to have been at such ease playing lead as well as supporting roles. Her failing health prevented her from acting in films later on and she stopped accepting offers gradually. After a hiatus though, she made a come-back in a Malayalam movie titled *Naayika* (2011), a story of a female film star. It was a kind of biopic and she played the lead role of Gracy, displaying the same verve and enthusiasm she had shown in her early years.

Politics and films are sometimes intertwined. Sharada had her limelight in politics as well, as a member of parliament of the Telugu Desam Party from the Tenali constituency. 'I entered politics without knowing anything about it. My main aim was to serve society through politics.'

'I only accepted films which I felt comfortable doing. And as it always happened, only good roles came to me. I think the highlight of my characters was that they were always moulded within the parameters of our culture. Nowadays, Western ideals are definitely having an impact on our lives, but I believe that we have to draw a line somewhere so that such ideals will not affect our cultural ethos,' says the actor. The intensity that she breathed into each of her characters made her a cut above the rest. It is impossible to do justice to this iconic star in a few words; her unforgettable roles are too many to number here. She was decorated with the NTR Lifetime Achievement Award in 2010. Her success story is something unimaginable and probably serves as an inspiration to the young stars of today. She remains as graceful and dignified today, as she was in her heyday.

17

Sheela

Malayalam films stand out in the firmament of Indian cinema for the bold and compelling themes they present with stark realism and fine sensibility. It has in its rich repertoire some brilliant themes and expositions, on par with Hollywood.

Mollywood has created a niche for Sheela Abraham, for the mammoth number of films and the sheer gamut of roles she has played.

She is the only heroine who has entered the *Guinness Book of World Records* for co-starring with Prem Nazir as the heroine consecutively in more than hundred films.

She strode the silver screen with a physical presence that is at once paradoxically resilient and vulnerable, with an expressive face that projects her myriad range of emotions and a body language that can gesticulate her quick reflexes, Sheela was the numero uno choice for powerful roles. Her big moment, she pointed out, was when the audience clapped when she makes her entry, in a long shot as a rich and elderly widow in her second innings in *Manassinakkare* (2003).

Clara Abraham aka Sheela was born on 24 March 1945 in a

Syrian Christian family. Ironically, she made her debut in Tamil with *Paasam* (1962), with MGR and Saroja Devi in the lead, and followed it up with *Bhagyajathakam* (1962, 'Good Fortune') in Malayalam, with Sathyan. After that there was no looking back, with numerous film offers coming her way.

Chemmeen (1965, 'Prawns') is her most iconic Malayalam film, based on the 1956 novel of the same name by Thakazhi Sivasankara Pillai. It is the story of the relationship between Karuthamma, the daughter of a Hindu fisherman, and Pareekutti, the son of a Muslim fish wholesaler. The story revolves around a myth about chastity that floats among fishermen communities in coastal Kerala. Myth has it that if a married fisherwoman is an infidel when her husband is out at sea, the sea goddess (Kadalamma) will consume him. The film was based on this novel and Sheela lived the role of the fisherwoman!

Picturized beautifully against the seascape backdrop with realistic performances by Sheela and Madhu, *Chemmeen* received great reviews and was instantly recognized as a technically and artistically brilliant film. It is cited as the first notably creative film to have come from South India. It was also the first South Indian film to win the Indian President's Gold Medal for Best Film in 1965. It was screened at various international film festivals and won prestigious awards at the Cannes and Chicago festivals. The film was included in the list of 100 greatest Indian films by IBN Live. *Chemmeen* was dubbed and released in Hindi as *Chemmeen Lahren* and in English as *The Anger of the Sea*. Sheela had arrived, enjoying an unprecedented and stupendous success, immortalizing her in the annals of Indian cinema. Recently, when filmmakers wanted to remake the movie, they wanted to recast Sheela and Madhu to bring back the magic of their romance, age notwithstanding.

Velutha Kathreena, a heroine-centric movie made in 1968, was based on the novel of the same name by Muttathu Varkey on the theme of untouchability and depicting the atrocities meted out to untouchables, and the protagonist is Katreena played effectively by Sheela who endures the ill treatment owing to her skin colour. The actor was quick to cash in on this emotive portrayal.

Then the film *Kallichellamma*, made in 1969, was a real challenge, where she plays a rustic girl who goes through many trials and tribulations. This film, too, was an adaptation of a novel. The commendations received were a ratification of her outstanding act. In *Vazhve Mayam* (1970), Sathyan and Sheela are a newly married couple who are happy enough until the bug of suspicion creeps in and shatters their marital harmony, leading to their estrangement. He later realizes her innocence, feels remorse and wants to go back to her. As fate would have it, it is too late and she is married to another by then. Heartbroken, he becomes an alcoholic and dies pathetically, and she too breathes her last, fighting to prove her fidelity. Sheela gave yet another mind-blowing performance in this film.

In *Kannapanunni*, a 1977 Malayalam film based on Kalaripayattu, a traditional martial art of India native to Kerala, she plays the role of a strong yet humane princess forced to marry a poor woodcutter. It was the hundredth film featuring Prem Nazir and Sheela as the lead pair.

In *Kadathanattu Makkam* (1978), she faces a death sentence on the allegation of being in love with a boatman, despite being a princess. Sheela has certainly proved her prowess in the wide range of themes and roles she has played impeccably. No role was insignificant to her—she would get to the skin of the character she was given.

The uncrowned queen of Malayalam cinema

The doctor duo, MGR and Sheela

Walking into history with Chemmeen

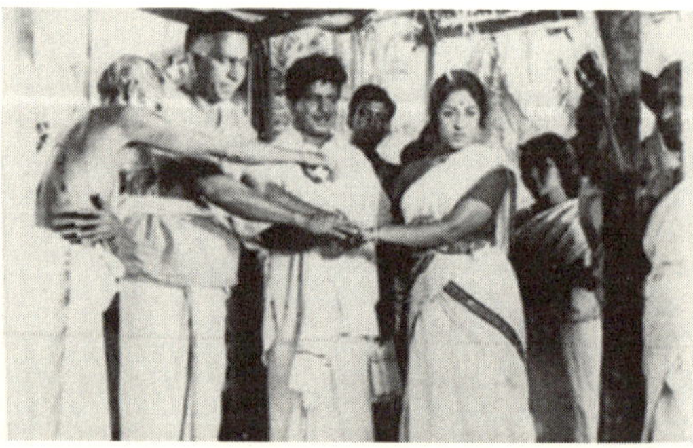

An earthy portrayal

Armed with the experience and knowledge she had gained in the field, she took to direction in the 1970s and 80s, directing two films, *Yakshaganam* (1976) and *Shikarangal* (1979). She wrote the story, script and screenplay for these films, and they were later remade in Tamil as well.

Besides films, she has directed a tele-film, *Ninaivukale Neengividu*, featuring actress Jayabharathi. She has authored a book titled *Kuilinte Koodu* and has written many short stories. She has also dabbled in painting.

Sheela has had the good fortune of getting wonderful, challenging and diverse roles in her first innings and she acted for almost two decades. Then she married actor Ravichandran and withdrew from the arclights for twenty years.

Her return was also very significant and she had plum roles coming her way. In *Manassinakkare* (2003) which means 'beyond the mind', Sheela as Kochu Thresia is a rich widow, who longs to live life to the lees, but is ignored by her children who are caught in the rat race for making money. This is when she meets the young man Reji (Jayaram) in whom she finds a companion, and looks up to him as her son. Reji also reciprocates and eagerly fulfils all her wishes. They have fun together, indulging in all simple joys and savouring good food, and even get arrested by the police for gambling.

This was her come-back film and she proved that age cannot stale her potential and artistic sensibility. The Malayalam filmdom was quick to induct her for elderly and substantial roles.

Sheela won great appreciation for her sensitive rendering of the hysterical mother in *Akale* (2004), an adaptation of the American classic by Tennessee Williams—*The Glass Menagerie*. She essayed the role of Margaret Evans, an Anglo-Indian lady, who lives in a seaside house with her two children, Rose (played by Geetu Mohandas) and Neil (played by Prithviraj Sukumaran). Margaret's husband who is in the navy sets sail one day and never returns. She earns her living by stitching and making small handicraft items to bring up her children. Her son, Neil, works in a factory but he is unable to decide whether he should help his mother and sister or live his own life. Later, Rose ends up in a mental hospital where she dies. Sheela's execution of this challenging role was indeed inimitable.

She took on the role of Elizabeth Mammen in the film *Pathaka* (2006). The film is about a young politician with a clean image who puts in genuine efforts to serve the state and the series of problems created by his opponents and the ensuing twists and the turns. Sheela, as the politician's mother, wants him to become a great leader just like his father. In *Thaskaraveeran* (2005), Kochu Baby played by Mammootty escapes to Mumbai to get away from the disrepute the family faces, only to become a don in Mumbai. Years later, he happens to come back home, persuaded by the affection of Meenakshiamma (played by Sheela) who is like a mother figure to him. Sheela won a lot of critical acclaim for her performance in this film.

This actress doesn't want to rest on her laurels; she wants to do her bit for the society, which lavished love on her, and made her so special. Sheela's dream is to play the role of an AIDS patient, or any role that could convey a message to society. Yet another newfound interest to her was politics, and so she joined the Congress, and maintains that she only wants to serve the people.

The veteran actress is a winner of several national and (Kerala) state awards. Her other accomplishments include winning the Lux Award five times, the South Indian Filmfare Award seven times, the Screen Videocon Lifetime Award, the

Sathyam Memorial Award and the Kerala State Award for Best Actress.

Cinema is a demanding field, and it is indeed phenomenal to have a record of around 500 films in all the southern languages. She enjoys an equanimity that is rare for a person in this field and she attributes it to her sense of satisfaction. Malayalam cinema has indeed conferred upon her the honour and glory due to her for her huge contribution to the film industry, and today in her twilight years, she sips from her cup of joy savouring her significant and euphoric moments. Another star whose fame will never fade…

18

K.R. Vijaya

A quintessential Dravidian beauty with lustrous hair, expressive eyes and emotive lips, Deivanayagi, rechristened as K.R. Vijaya, began her tryst with celluloid in the early 1960s. Punnagai Arasi (Queen of Smiles), was from a mixed parentage of Malayalam- and Telugu-speakers, which explains her comfort in all the four South Indian languages. She began her historic journey from Palani, a quaint little temple town in Tamil Nadu. Her father was a member of a drama troupe led by M.R. Radha, a famous villain in films at the time. Acting was in her genes and it manifested on the stage at a very young age. She began to act and dance in various stage shows. Gemini Ganesan spotted her in one such show and thus began a much-loved chapter in South Indian cinema history.

An agent introduced her to director K.S. Gopalakrishnan and she was given one of the lead roles in his film, *Karpagam* (1963). The young actor gave a credible performance despite being pitted against the seasoned actors of the time (Gemini and Savitri). Her clear diction and fluent dialogue delivery made the director's work easy. The protagonist, Karpagam, transforms from a bubbly girl to a loving wife yearning for a child. She showers all her love on her niece, finally sacrificing her life to save the child from a raging bull. This film brought her into the limelight and her successful sojourn lasted for the next forty years.

Server Sundaram (1964) reinforced her talent as an emotive actor. Vijaya gave a convincing account of the daughter of a hotel owner. Sunderam (a waiter) falls in love with the owner's daughter, Radha (played by Vijaya). This movie is written by K. Balachander and directed by Krishnan-Panju. Vijaya displays the optimum combination of her beauty and talent in the film. The success of the film added to her star status.

K.R. Vijaya's foray into Telugu films began with *Sri Krishna Pandaveeyam* (1966), a multi-starrer with NTR in the lead. She plays the young Rukmini with absolute grace, lending the role just the right amount of glamour. She matched the veteran NTR frame to frame. If NTR was majestic as Krishna, Vijaya was the shy and coy young Rukmini out to charm Krishna in the song '*Priyurala siggu eleni*? (Why do you feel shy?)'. Her portrayal of Rukmini was realistic. This character came brilliantly to life and catapulted her to the hall of fame of Telugu cinema. Popular heroes like NTR, ANR and Shoban Babu Harnath gave her their full support. Her portrayals were engaging and entertaining and gave her the opportunity to showcase her facile talent. In the same year, she acted in a film with a fairytale theme, *Paramanandayya Sishyula Katha*. It was a multi-starrer with NTR in the lead. Vijaya as Chitralekha (the celestial maiden) gives a dazzling performance, exhibiting her dancing repertoire in the dance competition with Vijayalaxmi. This dance sequence became the highlight of the film. She fit the character like a glove and amply proved her versatility as a dancer.

Punnagai Arasi K.R.Vijaya

Dignity and sobriety with Muthuraaman in Dheerga Sumangali

On the path to stardom with Gemini Ganesan

Matching excellence in histrionics in Thirusoolam

She distinguished herself in social genres like *Bale Thammudu* (1969), a remake of the Hindi film *China Town* in which NTR plays a double role. Vijaya plays the female lead role energetically, showing traces of humour. The train scene in this movie attracted a lot of praise. Father (Ralengi) and daughter (Vijaya) travel in a train; the hero (NTR) enters the compartment disguised as a sanyasi. Ralengi is taken in by the predictions of the soothsayer, who uses the opportunity to woo his beloved in the guise of a song. Vijaya is blissfully unaware and what follows is a rib-tickling comedy. The three enlivened the entire scene with their natural acting.

The first Tamil movie in which she played a mythological role was *Namma Veetu Deivam* (1972). Subsequently, she dazzled her fans as a goddess in several movies like *Thirumal Perumai*, *Kandan Karunaai* and *Annai Velankini*. Ace director A.P. Nagarajan cast Vijaya in an epic film, *Saraswathi Sabatham* (1966), along with several legendary artistes like Sivaji, Gemini, Harnath, Devika and Savitri. Vijaya, as the beggar girl who is transformed into a beautiful queen, gave a very effective portrayal of both characters. After this film, she played several mythological roles in Tamil, Telugu and Kannada and created a benchmark for all these roles. 'My fans would come to me and say that whenever they went to a temple or did some puja at home they would see me in the deity.' The producer and directors also insisted on casting only her in their mythological films. There is an instance of a producer who threatened to stage a hunger strike in front of her house until she accepted the role in his movie, *Shukravara Mahalaxmi* (Telugu). But the actor in all humility admits, 'I have no imagination and creativity; my director was my guru on the sets. I followed his instructions.'

K.R. Vijaya acted in some of the marvellous Tamil classics

like *Pattanittil Bootham* opposite Jaishankar. She became famous, appearing in a one-piece bikini (a shocker in those days) but she carried off the costume with great dignity. Glamour became her second name in films like *Ooty Varai Uravu*, where she was very sensuous in a saree in the dance number '*Thedinen vandhathu*'. She made a mark in films opposite Sivaji, including *Iru Malargal* and *Paladai*. Her compelling screen presence was on par with the veteran Padmini. *Tanga Padakam* and *Thirusoolam*, again opposite the thespian Sivaji zoomed her to a coveted status in Tamil cinema. This pair acted in about thirty-five films together (1964–1999).

She was also the favourite heroine of MGR, playing the lead with him in movies like *Nalla Neram*, *Vivasayee* and *Naan En Piranden*, cementing her superstar image.

In her six Kannada movies, K.R. Vijaya essayed a mélange of roles which were appreciated both by the industry and filmgoers for her sensitive performance.

Her debut film in Malayalam was *Odayil Ninnu* (1965), directed by K.S. Sethu Madavan. She was fortunate to have shared screen space in the film with geniuses like Prem Nazir, Sathyan and Kaviyoor Ponnamma. Her character is that of an orphan raised by the rickshaw-puller (Prem Nazir). She refuses to acknowledge him when she grows up and realizes her mistake only when her father is on his deathbed. Vijaya as an arrogant girl internalized the character, winning several accolades. *Sakunthala*, directed by Kunchakko, gave her recognition for her eloquent characterization and her stunning beauty. Prem Nazir in the lead and the melodious songs made it a box-office grosser. *Anarkali* was a historical film, again by Kunchakko, in which she played the beautiful court dancer, Anarkali, with Prem Nazir playing Prince Salim and Sathyan playing Emperor

Akbar. She donned an important role in the film *Ayodhya* with Prem Nazir once more as hero, notching up another success. *Anveshichu Kandethiyilla* was a film to remember, where she plays a nurse pining for love in an otherwise dull life. She is paired opposite Satyam. The 1979 starrer *Ezham Kadalinkkare*, directed by I.V. Sasi, was a runaway hit and K.R. Vijaya rode on the crest of its success. She holds the record of having acted in hundred Malayalam films out of the 400 films in her kitty. Probably she is the only actor to have acted in hundred films each in Telugu, Malayalam and Tamil. She has a monopoly on this record. The star has had the honour of acting opposite all the leading Malayalam heroes from Satyan to Mammootty and Mohanlal. She graduated to playing middle-aged roles, as she did not shy away from acting her age in Telugu, Tamil and Malayalam, acting opposite younger stars. In movies like *Appu*, she plays the mother of Murali, and later, in *Mr Brahmachari* she is the mother of four daughters and the grandmother of actor Balakrishna in *Simha*. She has even been the mother of Kamal Haasan and Rajinikanth. Her mother role (of Mammootty and Rahman) in *Ithiri Poove Chuvannapoove* won her the Best Actress Award.

The magic of her mythological portrayals was seen in Kannada films like *Ondagona Baa* (with actor Somayajulu) and *Om Shakthi Mahime*. In Telugu, she is the eternal Kausalya in *Sri Rama Rajyam* with Balakrishna in the cast. She did a recent cameo in the Tamil film, *Virudhunagar Sandhippu*. She has even starred opposite Raj Kumar and Feroz Khan in two Hindi films. Lack of time prevented her from accepting more Hindi films.

K.R. Vijaya married a leading industrialist, Velayudum, who added to her star value by making her the proud co-owner of a ship and an aircraft.

The Tamil Nadu government has felicitated the actor with the highest recognition, the Kalaimamani Award. She is also the recipient of the Chevalier Sivaji Ganesan Award and the Lifetime Achievement Award. The actor had a taste of the small screen, acting in successful tele-serials like *Kudumbam*, *Raja Rajeswari*, *Anandham* and *Madisaar Maami*.

The humble star confesses… 'I haven't planned my life or career; in my childhood, I did what my parents wanted me to. I have never been to school; the little I know is only from the movies.' God is her troubleshooter, she claims. 'From my childhood, if I had any problem I would close my eyes and place my problem before God and I would get the answer.' The iconic star has an enviable record of 400 successful films in all the South Indian languages and Hindi.

19

Dr J. Jayalalithaa

'In my stars I am above thee, but be not afraid of greatness; some are born great, some have achieved greatness and some have greatness thrust upon them...'

These lines from Shakespeare's *Twelfth Night* epitomize Jayalalithaa, the unforgettable star who carved her destiny out of the adversities she faced, and wrought her fortunes 'at the flaming forge of life'. For all her reluctance to be an actor, she created history as one of the leading luminaires of South Indian cinema. Her brave journey to the top is more dramatic than any film script.

She was born in the lap of luxury. Unfortunately, bad times fell upon the family when Jayalalithaa was very young and her happy childhood came to an abrupt halt. Her mother insisted on her following her footsteps to augment the family income. Her first association with the world of celluloid came about in 1961, with an English movie, *Epistle*, directed by Shankar Giri. She was introduced by ace director B.R. Panthulu in a Kannada film, *Chinnada Gombe*, opposite Kalyan Kumar. Thc alabaster-skinned girl attracted a lot of attention in her debut movie.

Another famous director, Sridhar, cast her in *Vennira Adai* in a convincing performance as a girl with a mental disorder falling in love with her psychiatrist.

Panthulu struck pay dirt by taking on board the new leading lady for the charismatic MGR in *Aayirathil Oruvan*. This pair went on to create history, weaving magic at the turnstiles as she played the sizzling Poongodi. Following this film, they did twenty-eight films together, beating Saroja Devi's record of twenty-seven films, becoming the most popular pair of Tamil cinema. Jayalalithaa replaced Saroja Devi in *Adimai Penn* as the latter was married by then. MGR reshot the movie with Jayalalithaa doing a double role opposite him. She also lent her voice for the song '*Amma endral*' in the film. The pair was repeated in movies like *Kavalkaran*, which became a box-office grosser. Jayalalithaa became a rage. Many of her movies with MGR are timeless and memorable till today.

In *Kudiyiruntha Koil*, she dons a glamorous role wearing sleeveless blouses and tight-fitting salwar kameezes. The crackling romance between MGR and Jayalalithaa in *Ragasiya Police 115* (1968) contributed greatly to the success of film. The dance numbers in the movie showed off her nimble-footedness. The actor did a completely different role in *Nam Naadu* (1969) as Alamelu/Ammu, the tender coconut vendor. Her simplicity, innocence and naïve appearance as a village belle was a stark contrast to her earlier roles. The two actors, despite their age difference, scorched the screen with their performances, backed by scenic locales and foot-tapping songs. The star was the first leading lady to wear Western clothes and shoes custom-made to match the costumes. Despite the ornamental nature of the role in her movies alongside MGR, Jayalalithaa had a bubbly screen presence all her own, enlivening the narrative. *Annamitta*

Kai (1972) was the last movie starring this legendary pair.

Then began the Jayalalithaa–Sivaji Ganesan saga with *Motor Sundaram Pillai* (1966). She played the daughter of Sivaji, falling in love with the boy next door, in which she stood out amongst the star-studded cast and the movie ran for a hundred days. Her next film with Sivaji was the full-length comedy *Galata Kalyanam*. In this film she was equal to the versatile veteran in her comic timing, playing the role of a girl who is a fashionista, spending outrageous amounts on her clothes. Her comic capers during the romantic interludes with the hero made for some rib-tickling humour.

Jayalalithaa's portrayal as a prostitute turned wife of the hero (Sivaji) in *Engirundho Vandhal* propelled her to the forefront of filmdom. The agony and anguish emoted by her is a perfect complement to Sivaji's performance as a deranged man. The Jayalalithaa–Sivaji duo went on to become a pair to reckon with after the release of *Enga Mama* (1970). Sivaji turns the waif into a refined urban girl ready to take on her cunning fiancé. She stepped firmly into the shoes of the character and did a splendid job. The movie also had several scenes showcasing the comic timing of both stars.

Director C.V. Rajendran showcases the star in *Sumathi En Sundari*. Sumathi, a popular star, yearns for a normal life. At the first available opportunity, the protagonist manages to give the slip and run away. She finds refuge in an estate, falling in love with the manager (Sivaji Ganesan). Jayalalithaa excels as a plain homemaker treasuring her marital bliss. She also successfully emotes the agony and anxiety in the scenes that show her being caught.

In *Pattikada Pattanama* (1972), Jayalalithaa returned to her tried and tested portrayals. The actor was back to her suave, snooty appearances and behaviour while Sivaji provided the perfect foil, as a rustic rural hero. He is instrumental in kindling the traditional sentiments of the heroine. She deftly handled both the modern girl and the woman loving her husband and pining for her child. The songs *'Ennadi rakkamma'* and *'Urmi melam'* were well-loved numbers, which added to the popularity of the movie. The film won the National Award and Filmfare Award for Best Film. Jayalalithaa walked away with the Filmfare Best Actress Award, being the first in that category to receive the award after it was introduced in 1972.

Her competent performance was then seen in movies like *Savaley Samali*, *Needi*, *Pattum Baratamum* and *Chitra Pournami* (which was their last movie together). She had proved equal to the legend in the eighteen movies that they had acted in. Seventeen of them were box-office grossers.

Jayalalithaa had the ability to break away from the mould and be very comfortable opposite Muthuraman, Jaishankar, Ravichandran and Nagesh. She delivered seven hits starring opposite Jaishankar in films like *Muthuchippi*, *Nee*, *Yaar Nee*, *Vairam*, *Gauri Kalyanam*, *Thanga Gopuram*, *Vandhale Maharasi*. The actor even showed her singing talent in the song *'Kangalil aayiram'*.

Ravichandran–Jayalalithaa was another profitable combination that registered six winners like *Naan*, *Bhagdad Perazhagi*, *Moondrezhuthu*, *Magarasi* and *Madi Veetu Mappillai*. Three of the five movies with Muthuraman enjoyed a run of over hundred days. *Suryakanthi* (1973), a black-and-white movie, fetched Jayalalithaa yet another Filmfare Award. She was at her best in her trademark Western outfits and her traditional sarees, acting first as a beloved, and later, as the wife of the protagonist. She also crooned two songs *'Oh meri dilruba'* and *'Naan endraal adhu'* with stalwarts like T.M. Soundarajan and

S.P. Balasubramaniyan. *Shanmugapriya* was also received well at the box office, further reinforcing the success of the pair. Jayalalithaa starred in *Thirumangalyam* (her hundredth film) with Muthuraman. This film had a huge star cast who were good performers yet Jayalalithaa came across as a seasoned actor proving her mettle. The actor's penchant for singing was fulfilled in the songs '*Thirumangalyam kollum murai*' and '*Ulagam oru naal pirandhadhu*' in the film.

Major Chandrakanth, a suspense thriller, had her acting as the beloved sister of Nagesh who kills her boyfriend for jilting her. She won critical acclaim for her role. There was an optimum blend of naivete and maturity portrayed by the star. She bid farewell to Tamil cinema after *Nadhiyai Thedi Vandha Kadal* with Sarath Babu.

Jayalalithaa thrived in mythological roles as well, in films like *Kandan Karunai, Saraswati Sabatham, Adhiparashakthi, Annai Velangani* and *Sri Krishna Leelai* in Tamil. She has also acted in Telugu mythological films like *Sri Krishna Vijayam, Sri Rama Katha* and *Sri Krishna Satya.* Her performance as Satyabhama, opposite the legendary NTR, fetched her her third Filmfare Award for Best Actress.

The polyglot star has acted in twenty-eight films in Telugu. She made her debut in *Manshulu Mamathalu* (1965) as a lighthearted girl. Unfazed by the presence of thespians like Savitri, ANR and Jaggaiah, she gave a good account of herself in the movie. *Aasthiparulu* was another multi-starrer with ANR, Jaggaiah, Krishna Kumari and Vanisri. Despite being a new entrant, she did justice to her role with her inimitable charm. She was cast opposite NTR in *Chikkadu Dorakaddu* along with a legion of stars like Kantha Rao and Krishna Kumari. The young Jayalalithaa unerringly essayed her role, paving her way

Jayalalithaa's phenomenal celluloid presence

Trail-blazer duo

Breakthrough film Major Chandrakanth

to unparalleled stardom. Such was her popularity amongst the Telugu directors that she was cast yet again in *Thikka Shankaraiya* along with NTR and Krishna Kumari. This film uncovered her talent of being at once coquettish and delightfully outrageous with the hero who is slightly crazy. She went beyond the confined clichés in *Baghadad Gajadonga* with NTR. This famous pair also did movies like *Kadaladu Vadaladu* and *Katha Nayakudu*. She acted in two more movies with ANR—*Adrushta Vanthalu* and *Aadarsa Kutumbam*. These movies gave her the right canvas to showcase her acting prowess as a mature and a refined performer. She did not hesitate to play a lead role with a vampish slant in the Krishna starrer, *Gudachari 116*, and the stars aligned to ensure her victory even in this new avatar. She has acted in two movies with Shoban Babu, the most mentionworthy being *Doctor Babu*. She was hailed as a prodigious star illuminating Tamil and Telugu celluloid.

Chinnada Gombe, her launchpad film, helped her carve a niche in Kannada movies. She was paired with Kalyan Kumar in movies like *Mavan Magalu*, *Mane Aliya*, *Namma Kartavya* and *Badukura Dari*, increasing her popularity.

The actor's foray into Malayalam films was restricted to just two movies, *Jesus* and *Uppu*. Both reaffirmed her status as a consummate actor.

Jayalalithaa confidently acted in the Hindi movie *Izzat*, holding her own as an adivasi girl; this was her only venture in Bollywood.

The 1960s and the mid-70s witnessed Jayalalithaa reigning supreme as the uncrowned queen of Tamil cinema who had completed hundred films in a decade, no mean achievement for an actress. The actor rewrote her destiny to be immortalized as one of the distinguished stars to illuminate the skyline of South

Indian cinema. Her tempestuous life filled with trials and triumphs propelled her into two high profile careers—politics and cinema.

The celluloid arena immortalized her acting and politics would record her as one of India's most illustrious statesmen.

20

Bharati Vishnuvardhan

She is like a river flowing quietly, sometimes gushing rapidly, soaking in the sun and drenching in the rain, yet absorbing everything to ensure a smooth flow and continuity. Bharati Vishnuvardhan, the doyen of Kannada cinema, has contributed to the Indian film industry for nearly four decades. Like other icons of her time, she has been an integral part of Tamil, Telugu, Malayalam and Hindi celluloid. As most stars of that era were, she too, was a good dancer with an expressive face. She has been the reigning queen in Kannada films for two decades (1960s–80s), her name etched indelibly in the history of South Indian cinema, and the star is still not ready to hang up her boots...

Bharati is a mix of Marathi and Kannada blood. Her Marathi-speaking parents had migrated to Karnataka. Her father, Raghavachar, was the man behind her success. He encouraged her. 'My father had seen a spark in me and on the insistence of Chinni Sampath Master, the famous choreographer, he brought me to Madras,' recalls the actor. Bharati found her niche in Kannada films. Her debut film was *Love in Bangalore* opposite

Kalyan Kumar. This film helped her step on the threshold of fame and become a phenomenal star of Kannada films. Dame luck smiled on her and she got an opportunity to make her mark in Bollywood. *Meherbaan* opposite Sunil Dutt upped her star quotient. She captured eyeballs in the song '*Aayega aayega ek chail chabila*', and fulfilled the director's vision of a sensitive performance. Post this film's box-office success; the actor joined the bandwagon of recognized stars of Bollywood. The busy actor riding on the wave of fame did a great balancing act both in Hindi and Kannada films simultaneously. Very few actors can boast of such a feat! She gave a good account of herself in Kannada movies like *Sandhya Raaga* (it won her the National Award). Nuances of her versatility raised her box-office stature and she had filmgoers awestruck with her prowess. In *Doddi Doddappa* under the banner of the famous B.R. Panthulu, she was rubbing shoulders with the icon Dr Rajkumar. *Gange Gowri* (1967) was the first of their films, which brought her critical acclaim. The pair did several successful films for nearly a decade and all were mega hits. After *Gange Gowri* Bharati became a household name.

She added another feather to her cap with her entry into Tamil filmdom in *Nadodi,* a multi-starrer with Saroja Devi and M.G. Ramachandran. *Uyarntha Manithan* earned her many laurels, competing with stalwarts like Sivaji, Sowcar Janaki and Vanisri, and was noticed for her refreshing performance under the guidance of Krishnan Panju. Bharati had the knack of making a facile switch from Kannada to Hindi and Tamil with the ease of a true professional. The schoolteacher role in *Sadhu aur Shaitan*, directed by Bhim Singh, won her high acclaim.

Her victory run in Kannada movies continued, with Rajkumar and her in the lead in many successful films like *Rajashekhara*, *Amma*, *Manasakshi*, *Balu Beligathe*, *Nammasamsara*,

Mayor Muthanna, Gandendu Hennaaru, Sri Krishna Deva Raya, Hasin Thorana, Kula Gaurava, Sri Krishna Rukmini and *Satyabhama.* Bharati earned critical acclaim for her performance in all these movies, acting alongside stars like Jayanti, Saroja Devi and Rajashree. The Raj Kumar–Bharati pair has been a part of over two dozen films becoming a renowned 'hit pair'. Their milestone movie was *Bangaarada Manushya,* which ran for two years.

Bharati managed to captivate the Telugu audience too. She was lucky to be paired with the heavyweights of Telugu cinema like NTR, ANR, Jaggaiah, Shoban Babu and Krishna. Some of her well-appreciated films were *Ninne Pelladutha* with NTR, *Bangaru Gajula* (Nandi Award for Best Film) with ANR and Vijaya Nirmala, Gaula Gopura with ANR and Rajashree, and *Arda Rathri* with Jaggaiah, *Sipahi Chinnaiah* with ANR and K.R. Vijaya, *Jai Jawan* with ANR, *Naa Thamudu* with Shoban Babu, *Neram Siksha* with Krishna and Chandra Kala. Telugu filmmakers and filmgoers acknowledged the actor known for her natural acting talent. She reached the pinnacle of fame with the K. Vishwanath movie, *Amma Manasu*, with Chalam and Jayanthi. She pulled off a big one with *Anaga Anaga Oka Thandri.* This was almost her last big hurrah in Telugu (1974).

Bharati also became a familiar face in Bollywood. She carried on her tryst with Hindi films like *Do Kaliyan* (cameo). In *Mastana*, she enacted the role of Sharda, opposite Vinod Khanna. She acquitted herself well despite the presence of Padmini. The Balraj Sahni starrer, *Ghar Ghar Ki Kahani,* had her playing Seema with a young Rakesh Roshan. Movies like *Seema* (Bharati–Rakesh Roshan) received a lukewarm response at the box office. Her most mentionworthy performance was in *Purab Aur Paschim* in which she gave a very good verdict of herself as Gopi, who falls in love with the hero, Manoj Kumar. She later marries Vinod

Khanna who is besotted with her. Her subdued acting as the second heroine won her huge appreciation. The superb success of this film opened up a plethora of opportunities for her in Hindi cinema till 1990. She exhibited an irreplicable synergy in the Mehmood movie, *Kunwara Baap*. She did poetic justice to her role as a mental patient in *Naya Din Nayi Raat*. Then there was a cameo in *Uttar Dakshin*, a film starring stalwarts like Sanjeev Kumar. Her poignant emotive performance reaffirmed her acting prowess. She bid adieu to Hindi cinema after the film *Aao Pyar Karen*, where she played the mother of Shilpa Shetty.

Bharati's debut film in Malayalam was *Padicha Kallan* (1969) where she played a second lead. After this, she touched base with Malayalam movies again only in 1986, with the film *Uppu*. Her role as Khadeeja was very well received. Another five-year gap later, she resurfaced in *Saanthawanam*, where she did a cameo. The actor was very much sought after in character appearances as Mohanlal's mother in *Devaasuram* and a supporting role in *Oru Yaathramozhi*. She was the director's favourite as the mother of Mohanlal, in *Varnapakittu* and *Narasimham*. She gave a dedicated performance as Alice John in *Mazhathullikkilukkam*, which had Sharada as Anna. In this Akbar Jose film, the two stars play spinster sisters who own a huge estate. Bharati then made a killing with her cameos in *Achan Kompathu Amma Varampathu* and *Nakshatra Thaaraattu*. She did not hesitate to play the role of a grandmother in *Karumaadikkutan*. Her last film was *Photographer* (2006).

Sridhar, the destiny maker of several stars, chose Bharati for his film *Avalu Kendra Oru Manam*, a multi-starrer with Gemini Ganesan and Kanchana. This love triangle was remade in Hindi. The young and pretty Bharati made a great romantic pair with Gemini Ganesan, especially in the song, '*Unnidathil ennai koduthen*'. She starred in about thirty movies in Tamil

Muddu nati, *Deccan beauty*

As successful in Tamil films

With Rajkumar—the winning combination of several hit films

with all the popular stars of the time, like MGR, Sivaji, Gemini, Jayshankar, Ravichandran and A.V.M. Rajan. With MGR, she acted in movies like *Nadodi* and *Anna Mittakai Chandrodayam*. She did several movies with Jayshankar, including *Nil Gavani Kadhali, Ponvandu, Ner Vazhi, Kadal Paravai* and *Poovum Pottu* (A.V.M. Rajan and Bharati).

Bharati had the opportunity to act under the baton of legendary directors of the likes of B.R. Panthulu, Prakash Rao, Sridhar, Krishnan Panju and K. Viswanath. She delivered performances in her own inimitable style, showcasing her plentiful talent, rendering all her roles immensely memorable.

The Bharati–Vishnuvardhan pair was a tremendous success at the box office. They were first paired in *Onde Roopa Eradu Guna*, which was a runaway hit. *Devara Gudi, Anna Athige, Makkala Bagya, Nagara Hole, Madhura Sangama, Rahasya Rathri* and *Bangarada Jinke* followed this film. They shared a wonderful chemistry as both were always on the same wavelength. This victorious duo registered several super-duper hits. Their onscreen chemistry spilled over into their personal life and they decided to tie the knot in 1975, the same year in which she completed her 100th film, *Bhagya Jyothi* in Kannada. After marriage, they almost became the first family of Kannada cinema. Both actors gave each other a lot of space, which only strengthened their bond, both personally and professionally.

But Vishnuvardhan's demise in 2009 left a great vaccum in Bharati's life. After that, she devoted all her energies in keeping alive the memories of her beloved spouse—be it building a memorial for him or organizing film festivals or charity events commemorating his death anniversary.

The versatile star felt she had a lot of acting still left in her. So she channelized it into doing some good character roles like

Preeti Prema Parinaya, directed by Kavita Lankesh. She earned laurels for her portrayal in this film, along with Ananth Nag, where they play two mature people falling in love. Another film that brought her accolades was *Kallarali Hoovagi* (2006). This was an exceptional film and it won the National Award. Bharati excelled in her performance as Ananth Nag's wife in this movie.

Bharati Vishnuvardhan has been active in films until 2012, her recent movies being *Tananam Tananam* and *Crazy Loka*. The star has been decorated with several awards and appreciation. She was honoured with a doctorate from Mysore University for her contribution to cinema exactly two years after Vishnuvardhan's doctorate was awarded by Bangalore University. They are the first film industry couple to receive such an honour. Bharati had been the president of the State Award Committee since 2011. She has also dabbled in TV serials and earned a name for herself in the serial *Janani*. Presently, she finds immense satisfaction in preserving and documenting the memory of her husband and loves playing with her grandchildren; her two daughters are her loving companions, filling the void left behind by her husband. As an individual, she is extremely philosophical and has always been known to take things in her stride. She admits she is very happy with the way life has treated her. 'From the first film, I became a heroine, and things went on for the better in my life. The State Award, National Award for *Sandhya Raaga* and scores of other awards kept me happy.'

Bharati joins the league of women who have made history with their felicity and aptitude to lend themselves to the celluloid world of all four South Indian languages as well as Hindi. These illustrious women have no parallel and have immortalized their names in the annals of Indian cinema history.

21

Kanchana

Kanchana (born Vasundara Devi), the bewitching star, endearingly known as 'the queen of the 70s', was a sublime blend of beauty and brains. Her real life story beats any reel life drama. Here was an actor who braved all storms right through her formative years with absolute grit and determination. The young girl had just finished her graduation when life dealt her a big blow—her father lost everything in business. Being the first born in the family, she became the anchor of the household and chose a career in the skies, becoming an airhostess, to help her family out. 'One day while I was about to sleep, I chanced to see an aircraft flying, and I decided to be a cabin crew member that night.' She was the ideal choice for an airhostess—tall, fair-complexioned, with a winning smile. Vasundara Devi became a very popular airhostess and was nicknamed Devi by the flight crew. This name stayed with her throughout her flying tenure.

Her flight into filmdom was another story of chance and coincidence. She had a brief affair with the silver screen soon after her matriculation, playing mythological characters like

Yogamaya (*Krishna Leela*) and Naga Kanya (*Suvarna Sundari*). Though she had enjoyed the short stint, it was forgotten during the intervening years. Once again, fate had a major hand in drawing her back to filmdom. During her flying days, she met several bigwigs from the cinema industry, and had even given a screen test during that time. It was director Sridhar who discovered this conventional Indian beauty on board a flight. The pretty hostess had captured his imagination and he instantaneously cast her in his mind's eye as a heroine. Kanchana had the poise and beauty to play the lead role in her debut Tamil movie, *Kaadhalikka Neramillai*, in 1964. With that, Vasundara Devi was rechristened Kanchana, and she illuminated the skyline of South Indian cinema for two and a half decades. In her very first film, she exuded confidence and style, immortalizing her role in the multi-starrer. The movie was a stupendous grosser running for 175 days, making Kanchana an overnight sensation.

Kanchana was the first educated star (graduate) in the South Indian film industry. This convent-educated quintessential actor went on to do more than 150 films in Tamil, Telugu, Kannada and Hindi. Her best performances were in films dealing with relationships, cheery romances and mythological genres. With every film Kanchana progressed from being an assured actor, bringing in the right measure of glamour with acting prowess. She had the fortune to act in roles of substance, especially her debut Telugu film, *Veer Abhimanyu* (1965), opposite Shoban Babu. Her role as Uttara fetched her admirers both young and old. To this day, it is one of her most memorable performances. The actor excelled in conveying the grief of a woman who loses her husband. Her monologue in the death scene announced her arrival as a powerful emotive actor.

Her pristine beauty was deftly showcased by most

directors of that era. She registered the same amount of success as Shubhadra in *Dana Veera Soora Karna*. 'I learnt a lot, acting opposite a great persona like NTR, who is a walking encyclopaedia of acting,' she recalls. She could very easily alternate between mythological and social genres. Her restrained acting in *Kalyana Mandapam* (Telugu) as a Devadasi wanting to lead a normal married life is one of the more noteworthy roles she has essayed. She delivered several hit films in Telugu, acting with major heroes like NTR, ANR and Shoban Babu. The actor was also paired with all the veteran male leads in Tamil cinema, including MGR, Sivaji Ganesan, Gemini Ganesan, Ravichandran and Jaishankar.

In *Adhey Kankal* (Tamil), she was paired with Ravichandran and gave a very good account of herself in this suspense thriller. She excelled in displaying the fear, love and anxiety of a young girl with just the right hint of maturity. The role was so well appreciated that she was also cast as the heroine in the Telugu version, *Adhey Kanlu*.

Kanchana was lucky to have been chosen by the ace director K. Viswanath to act in *Aatma Gowravam*, based on a novel by Yaddanapoodi Sulochana Rani. There were many firsts associated with this film. This was the debut directorial venture of K. Viswanath, which won him the Nandi Award for Best Film. Kanchana was paired with ANR for the first time; this pair went on to give several hits like *Manchirojulocchayi* and *Bhakta Tukaram*, among others. The director beautifully brought out her talent and turned her into a mature artiste. She did several glamorous roles with Krishna in films like *Nenante Nene* and *Dharma Daata*.

The lovely star took her own beauty, and the inevitable comments it attracted, in her stride, and comments gracefully, 'I got a lot of compliments; maybe I was destined to

Suave and sophisticated Kanchana

Kanchana in the popular film Kaadhalikka Neramillai

Exuding oomph in Adhe Kankal

Vibrant Kanchana with Balaji

receive them. But there were far more beautiful actors like Vyjayanthimala, Madhubala, Meena Kumari.' Director Sridhar cast his lucky mascot once again in *Sivantha Mann*. This was a big budget movie shot entirely in foreign locales like Switzerland and France. Unfortunately, the film did not fare well, but Kanchana's exposition as the princess of Vasantapuri garnered a lot of praise. She acted the part of the haughty royal personage in a very natural manner. Another most unforgettable performance by her was in the comedy film, *Uttaravindri Ulle Vaa*. She renders the role of an orphan woman seeking shelter in a house of three bachelors, while escaping the fate of being pushed into a brothel. The events that follow are a laugh riot in a chapter of accidents. This rib-tickling comedy gave her another chance to prove her multi-dimensional talent. She excelled in highlighting confusion, pretence and innocence. The lighthearted romance between her and Ravichandran accentuated the success of the film. In the same genre was the movie *Bhama Vijayam*, directed by K. Balachander. In this multi-starrer, Kanchana competed with veterans like Sowcar Janaki and Jayanthi. 'Serious acting is easy. But making people laugh is difficult. The dialogues written by Sadagopu ('Chitralaya' Gopu) were wonderful and helped me to essay the role,' she reflects. She was also cast in *Teen Bahuraniyan*, the Hindi version of the film.

Films like *Shanti Nilayam* (1969), based on *The Sound of Music*, brought her much acclaim and increased her fan base in Tamil cinema. She plays a governess in the film, and as the beloved of the protagonist Gemini Ganesan, she simply enchanted the audience, dazzling them with her striking looks. Luckily for the actor, she was not typecast into any one kind of role, but her exquisite persona made sure that she only played the lead heroine in her films, rather than a supporting role. Her histrionics were confined to effervescent roles, which never failed to leave a pleasant after-effect in a moviegoer's mind.

The appealing actor has also got a good verdict for her work in Kannada and Hindi films. These were cameo roles, nevertheless made memorable by the star. In her later years she accepted playing middle-aged characters in films like *Mauna Ragam* (Tamil) and *Gadasari Attaha Sogasara Kodalu* (Telugu), charming the audience. She donned the grease paint for a guest role in the Kamal Haasan starrer, *Sigappu Rojakal*, and the Kannada film, *Ananda Bhairavi*, with Girish Karnad. Her last appearance was in a Kannada film, *Devata Manushya*. This became her swan song and the actor decided to step away from the arclights after this.

Kanchana has been presented with the MGR Award for her invaluable contribution to Tamil cinema. She was specially handpicked by the chief minister, Selvi J. Jayalalithaa, an honour that deeply moved the actor. The Telugu film industry accorded her with the ANR Swarna Kankanam Award in 2007.

The reigning queen of the 70s had her unsavoury personal moments too, when the people she trusted let her down. Fortunately, her sister stepped in to give her the required moral courage and support. Kanchana channelized all her energies into worshipping the Almighty and later chose to live in complete anonymity. There were several rumours about her being in extreme penury, but the actor never bothered to set the facts straight. 'I didn't want to go back to the magazine that published it and ask for an explanation. Already, I had too many legal tangles to handle. I have renounced everything, but I still lead a materialistic life.'

Kudos to this admirable woman, for accepting her fate and living a quiet life, far away in Bangalore. Today, she is an epitome of equanimity and fortitude, one that many can learn from and emulate. She remains a true believer in the maxim, *Que sera sera*...Whatever will be, will be.

22

Vanisri

A small town girl without any great claims to good looks, knocks at the door of the motion picture arena. She enters, taking advantage of a small crack (read supporting roles), biding her time. When the opportune moment comes along, she triumphs as a star setting the silver screen on fire...

Ratna Kumari, hailing from Nellore, became an icon rechristened Vanisri by her mentor, S.V. Ranga Rao. She dominated the celluloid world for two and a half decades in challenging roles that made her a true legend. The young fat girl had a one single objective in her mind when she set out—to leave behind her footprints in filmdom. Her determination paved the way for a gritty growth story, rendering her a true successor of another legend, Savitri. Her looks and deportment in the early days was not the stuff heroines were made of, but the budding actress had a single-point agenda—to look beautiful on the big screen despite all her handicaps. She is rightly called 'the make-over queen', transmuting herself as she did into a refined beauty. The young star learnt the art of make-up on the job. And changed the look of the heroines of the time. 'I would read a lot of novels and the descriptions of the heroines influenced me. I started evolving my own style of dressing and make-up. I was the first one to try on different shades of lipsticks, bindis and nail colours that would match the sarees and I preferred bright colours,' she remembers. The star used her creativity to design new hairstyles, jewellery and even sarees. 'I brought in novelty by stitching two sarees with polka dots on them and wearing black colour outdoors. I would have constant arguments with the art and camera department because they thought it would look gaudy.' Little wonder then that within a very short period of time, she became a famous fashion icon, next only to Saroja Devi, who scripted the history of filmdom during the 1960s and 1970s.

Vanisri's first break was in *Marupurani Katha*, a remake of a Tamil film; when she was called by the producer she was surprised to find herself being cast in the lead role! But it was the Balachander-directed *Sukha Dukhalu* (1967) that brought her her first brush with fame. The competent director showcased her acting mettle in the memorable song, '*Ithi mallala velayani*'. Vanisri played a simple girl next door in the film and embraced resounding success. Though this was a supporting role, she never looked back after this film. Back to back, she did fourteen films a year in sixteen-hour shifts a day. So much so that her personal life was nearly non-existent. 'My reel life was my real life, with no time to wear the clothes and jewellery I bought for my personal use. I began to wear them in my films.'

Soon the actor became everyone's heart-throb, playing heroine to all the leading stars in Telugu and Tamil films. In Telugu, ANR and Vanisri became an all-time hit 'magical pair'. Filmmakers never tired of casting them together. Their claim was, 'ANR and Vanisri were born for each other.' Despite being frequently cast together, Vanisri would look different each time, adding a novelty in her own way to their pairing on screen. They scorched the screen together for nearly a decade. Movies like *Prem Nagar* and *Dushera Bullodu* became magnum opuses creating groundbreaking records. *Prem Nagar* was made in Tamil as *Vasantha Maligai* where Vanisri played the lead with Sivaji. This went on to become a huge blockbuster, proving that the modern Devadas continued to be a rage with moviegoers!

Her soaring success made her the highest paid actress of her time—she was paid two lakh rupees—much more than the earnings of any male superstar. Vanisri earned the encomium, 'Navrasa Natana', for her ability to artfully emote myriad feelings. She had the knack to mould herself into any character, be it a rustic village belle, an arrogant city girl or a mythological character. She had another title bestowed on her, 'Navala Nayika' (novel queen). She was a successful heroine of many movies based on popular novels; it seemed as though the characters in the novel were created just for her. As a testimony to the title, she came up trumps in roles such as Saroja in *Jeevana Tarangalu*, Latha in *Prem Nagar*, Sandhya in *Vichitra Bandham*, Jayanthi in *Secretary* (movies based on novels). In the period 1971–76, she acted in nearly eighty films with all of them becoming silver jubilee movies. It appeared as if cinema could not do without Vanisri! There were super-duper films like *Jeevana Jyothi*, *Jeevana Tharangalu*, *Krishnaveni* (Filmfare Best Actress Awards, 1973, 1974 and 1975). Her portrayal of the protagonist, Krishnaveni, added an entirely new dimension to her storehouse of talent. The emotions displayed by her as a victim of child abuse and how the ghastly incident surfaces during a visit to one of the tourist places is truly unforgettable. Vanisri successfully projected the indifference shown by the society towards the psychological trauma a woman goes through. She used all her craft to bring to the fore the agony suffered by such a woman in this film. Besides the recognition awarded to her, the film received critical acclaim. This was followed by *Bangaru Babu, Minor Babu, Bhakta Kannapa*, which proved her capacity to play social as well as mythological genres. With these roles, she inherited the mantle left behind by Savitri and did a great job of carrying it forward from where the late actor had left off. In the 70s, Vanisri alone was enough to script the success of the movie, proving that the male leads were only secondary (in this, she joins the ranks of stalwarts like Jamuna and Sharada). The producers were emboldened to cast her in double roles in *Ganga Manga* (Telugu) and *Vani Rani* (Tamil). The star essayed another indelible portrayal in *Jeevan Jyothi* where she plays both mother and daughter. She excelled as the mother, playing the part of an insane woman with poignancy and multifaceted talent. This execution notched her fame up one level. She was the launching pad for most young heroes to become popular stars (Chandra Mohan, Krishnam Raju in Telugu and Jaishankar in Tamil).

Vanisri left her mark in art movies as well, including *Anugraham* (Shyam Benegal) and *Gorinta Deepam* (Bapu). These roles were sans make-up and deglamourized, yet she proved her calibre; in fact, in *Anugraham*, she played a mute character. The trail-blazing star was also fortunate to be paired with Sivaji Ganesan in several Tamil box-office grossers. This helped her carve her niche in Tamil cinema. Sivaji became her great admirer and good friend. 'I was the first heroine to be invited to his home and served lunch by none other than his revered mother,' claims the star. This victorious lead pair acted in many hit films like *Uyarntha Manithan, Nirai Kudam, Vasantha*

Exuding a magnetic screen aura

In the same league as ANR

With Sivaji Ganesan in Vasantha Maligai

Great wavelength with Jaishankar

Maligai, *Sivagamyin Selvan* and *Kulama Gunama*. The last movie in particular was a multi-starrer, including the great Padmini. But this valiant actor competed with several superstars, proving equal to them. Vanisri had the opportunity to be associated with another great Tamil film icon, Gemini Ganesan. She gave the romantic star some uncomfortable moments with her skillsets in the film *Velli Vizha*. She was really lucky to bag the most challenging and coveted roles in Malayalam movies too, a prime example being *Baazigar* with Prem Nazir. This evergreen artist made her foray into Hindi films but met only with lukewarm success. The actor finally tied the knot with a doctor and settled down to being a full-time homemaker. She has a daughter and a son who have followed in their father's footsteps.

The seasoned actor could not stay away from the limelight for too long, though. She came back for her second innings. The Midas touch was evident when she landed plum assignments. She now played the arrogant wife and mother-in-law characters, giving them her unique touch and style. These roles provided her a wide platform to prove that there was much acting still left in her. She gave young heroes like Chiranjeevi, Nagarjuna and Venkatesh the jitters, acting, dancing and singing with them shoulder to shoulder. Being the firebrand that she is, acting with her proved to be a great challenge to these youngsters. Even at this stage, she maintained her reputation of yore, giving shots without any retakes.

Like some leading ladies of South Indian cinema, Vanisri also enjoyed a stint as a politician. She briefly canvassed for the Congress party, but quit the moment she realized that it was not her cup of tea. The benevolent actor turned her energies then to her sense of societal responsibility by establishing schools and starting an old age home. She has even founded a mobile theatre to spot talent! These avenues give her a lot of contentment and happiness. She thanks God for enabling her to give back to the society that gave her so much.

Having come full circle—iconic actor, dutiful wife and doting mother—Vanisri looks back on her life's journey and is happy about the way it has turned out. The pride and supreme confidence in her talent is sometimes manifest in statements like, 'If I was not in *Prem Nagar*...could ANR get that name and fame at all? It is because of our presence that those movies became super hits and ultimately ANR become very popular.'

Vanisri has been the recipient of many awards like the Kavignar Kannadasan Award, the Meena Kumari Award and the Madhavapeddi Prabhavati Award. She has no regrets about not being conferred the nation's highest civilian awards (the Padma Shri or Padma Bhushan). 'Nowadays, we can get them very easily if we are willing to spend some money,' she opines.

She decided to hang her boots when she was at the height of success as she felt she would not be able to change herself to keep up with the demands of ultramodern films, 'Where heroines had to play the vamps and the hero's dance movements made me very uncomfortable and I realized that Vanisri was not needed anymore in this field.'

Today, she hops between her three homes in Chennai, Hyderabad and Ooty, where her daughter is pursuing her Master's in medicine. This great actor may be away from the pancake make-up and the arclights but her name will be etched in the pages of cinema history for eternity...

23

Sujatha

Veni, Vedi, Veci, the actor came, saw and conquered the silver screen with her invigorating talent. She was a feminist to the core, always demonstrating a quiet strength in her reserve. Her brother introduced the reluctant star to the fantasy of acting. This true-blue Malayali had a transnational birth and upbringing as the daughter of Shankara Menon and Saraswati Ammal. Her father had migrated to Sri Lanka in search of greener pastures and became a teacher there. Sujatha was born in Galle and spent her early childhood there. The family moved to Kerala when she was ten. Convinced by her brother, she began acting on stage.

Sujatha had her first brush with cinema in *Do Kaliyan* as a child artiste. She progressed to doing adult roles in Malayalam films. Her glorious career began with the film *Tapaswini*. She went beyond the realm of talent, playing the character of a widowed sister of Prem Nazir. She left her imprint again in *Katha Nayika* and *Ernakulum Junction*.

But what really announced her arrival in South Indian cinema was *Aval Oru Thodar Kathai* (1974) directed by the virtuoso K. Balachander. He had noticed the dormant potential in this new artiste in *Ernakulum Junction*. He gave her a month's time to brush up her Tamil. By such time, she had already acted in forty Malayalam films. Though a late entrant to Tamil cinema, she created waves, earning the envy of many. *Aval Oru Thodar Kathai* broke every prevalent stereotype in the industry, its success hinged on the shoulders of its debutant heroine, Sujatha. With this film, both the actor and the director set a new trend in the portrayal of women, which was to become a cult later. The protagonist, Kavitha, is an urban woman who carries the responsibility of her family on her shoulders. She wears ultramodern blouses and even has a boyfriend in tow! To the outside world, she appears almost brazen and liberated, but in reality, she is just a young girl with her quota of chinks in the armour. The subtlety and sophistication displayed by the actor in the film were alien to the moviegoers of the time who were used to high melodrama. This was the beginning of parallel cinema history in South India. Sujatha's stylized work redefined the very portrayal of women in Tamil cinema.

She maintained the winning streak in yet another Balachander movie, *Avargal*. The actor played the role of Anu, a young mother who is a victim of her spouse's sadism. She brilliantly showcases the character's suffering and plight, especially when she is caught between the two men in her life, her husband (played by Rajinikanth) on the one hand and her admirer (played by Kamal Haasan) on the other hand, who is waiting to express his love to her. Sujatha consciously refrained from melodrama, scoring a winning point in this classic. She reminded the critics and her fans of Smita Patil, with a hint of Jaya Bhaduri (definitely a heady combination of quiet beauty and sophisticated acting).

The actor's dress sense spoke volumes of her inner dignity, sobriety and elegance. It also reflected a genteel culture without any pretence to glamour. Armed with her previous successes, she was all set to storm the bastion of Telugu cinema. *Gorintaku*, her debut Telugu movie, showed her playing a doctor falling in love with her classmate. This Shoban Babu–Sujatha starrer was a runaway hit with audiences rooting for her. She followed it with *Guppedu Manasu* and *Yedandasthula Meda*. Dasari Narayan Rao, the director, brought out the best in her like Balachander had done. Her emotionally powerpacked high-voltage performance in these movies struck the right chord in the hearts of scores of moviegoers. She transformed the run of the mill love story (rich girl falling for a poor boy) into a poignant story of sacrifice with her committed approach and almost out-shadowed the male lead in the film.

Sujatha went on to deliver several matchless roles, acting with such precision that it overawed her peers and seniors in the industry as well as film buffs. Her girl-next-door looks lent the perfect aura of realism to the characters she played—modern, self-reliant, independent, but with a touch of vulnerability. She inspired many women, particularly young girls, during the 70s as they could see themselves in the roles she played, be it Kavitha, Anu or Annam. Even when she did play the role of a rich girl, there was no plastic doll image associated with it. In *Gorintaku* and *Yedandasthula Meda*, she proved that a rich girl could be sensible and realistic. The actor never preferred verbose dialogues. She relied on her expressions to convey the story as she felt too much make-up and flashy clothes would take the attention away from acting. That explained her preference for cotton sarees, almost no jewellery and simple hairstyles in every movie she did. It is no wonder that each of her roles became an

As a lawyer in Vidhi

New wave star Sujatha

In another off-beat film, Mayangugiraal Oru Maathu

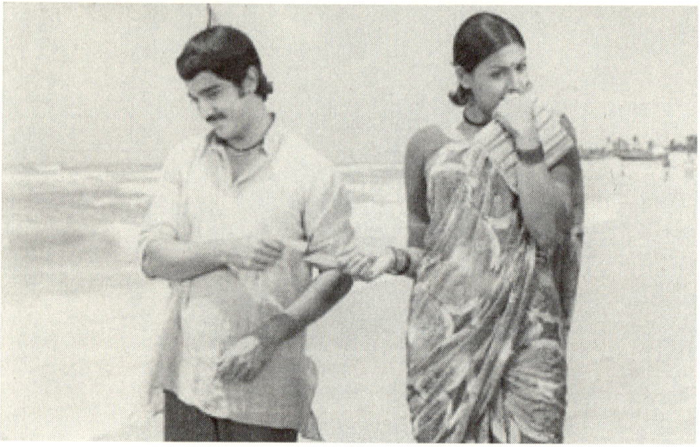

With Kamal Haasan in Kadal Meengal

inspired enactment. Yet she never became a poster girl for her fans because they accorded her an indefinable respect. Sujatha never aspired for the number one slot. She was focused with an eye for the minutest details, which helped her walk through every film successfully.

In *Noolveli*, a Balachander exclusive, Sujatha turned around a morbid theme into a thought-provoking narrative with her unique rendition. She delivered another winner in *Vidhi* as a lawyer fighting for justice for her client, a rape victim. Her fans can still vividly recall the court scene where she argues for the rape victim in her perfectly modulated voice. This was a hardhitting blockbuster, which bracketed her along with Sharada, the lead in the original version *Nyayam Kavali*. After *Vidhi*, the star played heroine-centric roles in several films like *Alaya Deepam*, *Unnai Naan Sandithen* and *Naan Padum Padal* among others. There was an invisible tenor of advocacy without aggression in most of her women-centric movies. With clockwork regularity, she slipped easily into the skin of her characters, rendering her portrayals as authentic as possible.

The remake of *Koshish* would not have been possible but for her mettle. Both Kamal Haasan and Sujatha essayed the role of their lifetime as a dumb and deaf couple. Her angst was so real, it literally jumped out of the screen into the hearts of the spectators. The Kamal Haasan–Sujatha pair was a harmonic convergence of formidable talent and only a Balachander could do justice to their talent. *Uyarnthavargal* was a fine example of a film where she showcased her emotional density.

She did immense justice to most of her roles—whether it was as a helpless girl beleaguered by her former lover in *Oru Oothapu Kan Simitugirathu* or as the chirpy young girl in *Circus Ramadu*. Her finest acting seems to have come to the fore when she was paired with Kamal Haasan and Rajinikanth. It is not surprising that she never faced a lean period ever in her career. Despite being extremely selective, the star had 300 movies under her belt in just three decades.

Sujatha showed a distinct knack in spacing out her career. The gaps between her films helped her deliver great performances, especially switching between Tamil and Telugu films. There was a two-year interval between *Avargal* (1977) and *Gorintaku* (1979). This helped the actor to internalize the next character. She did several box-office grossers under Dasari Narayan Rao. Sujatha also had the honour of being paired with the director in quite a few movies, including *Soorigadu*. She received critical acclaim in movies like *Sujatha*, directed by Dasari Narayan Rao (this script was specifically written with her in mind). The actor did exceedingly well for herself opposite ANR, NTR, Shoban Babu, Krishna and Sharad Babu in Telugu. She was fortunate to be cast opposite Sivaji, Siva Kumar, Vijaya Kumar, Rajinikanth and Kamal Haasan. Though she had been sharing screen space with Rajinikanth, there was never any romantic on screen association with him (with the exception of *Avargal*).

Her subtle acting prowess attracted the attention of good Malayalam directors. She got the opportunity to act opposite the seasoned K.P. Ummar in the film *Drisakshi*. The elusive air comes alive in the song '*Orikkal matrum*'. She struck a hearty balance between sensitivity and sobriety in *Brasht* and *Or Vilipadakale*. The star was arguably great as a fine actor in *Chandrolsavam*, *Jalothsavam* and *Mayukkam*. Sujatha mesmerized Kannada moviegoers in *Devalaya* and *Nanna Devaru*.

Very early in her career, Sujatha drifted into mother roles. She wore white sarees, mouthing platitudes, playing the role of a mother to the hilt and displaying nuances that made the role unique. Her most cherished performance was in *Kiccha* (Kannada) as the hero's mother. She carried on with the mother role in *Neelakantha* (Telugu) playing Ravichandran's mother. Sujatha caught the critic's eye as Ramesh Aravind's mother in *Tutta Mutta* (Kannada). She did not hesitate to act even as the hero's mother—heroes with whom she had played the heroine in earlier films. Both Kamal Haasan and Rajinikanth had the unique opportunity of being both her hero and her son. She won a lot of praise for the ease with which she played senior roles. She was Rajinikanth's mother in *Uzhaippali*, *Kodi Parakkuthu* and *Baba*, Kamal Haasan's beloved in *Kadal Meengal*, and later, his mother in *Mangamma Sabatham*. Sujatha won the Nandi Award for her character role in *Pelli* (Telugu) but her absolute masterpiece was *Sri Ramadasu*, where she is Pokala Damaka. Audiences doffed their hats to this character. The actor reduced her workload in the latter half of her career, choosing to play character roles only sporadically. Yet her cameos in *Aval Varuvala* and *Arul Atagasam* sent her fans into nostalgic raptures.

The star's acting was a spillover from her real life—discreet, private and dignified. She kept entirely to herself, never revealing what the real Sujatha was like, be it her marriage, her children or the ailment she suffered from. The world came to know about it only after she was gone. Even then a true epitaph could not be written, as no one knew anything about her. The charming actor's only extravagance was her appearance as the face that endorsed Lux beauty soap. In doing so, she joined the ranks of the most beautiful divas of the film industry.

The truth is that sometimes actors are superior to the roles assigned to them. Sujatha was one such fine actor who remained underutilized by the South Indian film industry. And yet we will remember her as the actress who rode proudly, gracefully, into the sunset, leaving behind a legacy of timeless classics...

24

Lakshmi

Julie Morris, an Anglo-Indian girl, loses her heart to a Hindu boy from upper-middle-class family. The two are so carried away by their newfound love that they cross the societal boundary of morality. The girl pays the price. Cinematic history was made with the release of *Chattakari*, directed by K.S. Sethumadhavan, creating a storm in the minds of young cinema audiences. Lakshmi's chirpy disposition and naïveté made her a marvel in the industry. Every other character in the film was believable and looked easy to play, but the sensational star who immortalized the protagonist was a young actor with a proclivity to experiment. The film's bold theme of an unwed mother was right up her alley, which gave her a stamp on her persona. This well-known face of Indian cinema's real life is as heterodox as the roles she played.

Lakshmi was the second generation of actors in her family. Her mother, Kumari Rukhmini, was a popular artiste. Her father, Y.V. Rao, was a distinguished producer and director. This lineage gave her the legitimacy to enter the portals of cinema. She was spirited and bold, a right blend for an actor with a difference.

Her debut film, *Jeevanasam* (1968), announced her entry in South Indian filmdom when she was just thirteen. Though the film received only a lukewarm response, her performance was noticed. She was promptly cast in *Maattukkaara Velan*, a blockbuster where she vyed for attention alongside the likes of MGR and Jayalalithaa. *Kasethan Kadavulada* revealed her talent for comedy. She performed the secretary's role, giving a lighthearted tone to the character, pitting her talent against the versatile queen of comedy, Manorama, in this movie. Her timing and ease of acting won her much appreciation.

The film that established her as a consummate actor, though, was *Dikkatra Parvathi* (1974). Directed by the famous Singeetan Srinivasa Rao, the film highlights the story of a farmer trapped in the clutches of a moneylender. Lakshmi did justice to the role of the farmer's wife who protects her husband. The unusual ending of the film was on the lines of parallel cinema. The star had no qualms in accepting a deglamourized role early in her career. Her laudable performance won her the Filmfare Award for Best Actress.

This film was a turning point in her career as makers of parallel cinema approached her. Lakshmi earned the reputation of being an actor of substance. Her meaningful role in a film like *Sila Nerangalil Sila Manithargal* (1976) fetched her the National Award for Best Actress. This film was based on Jayakanthan's popular novel of the same name. Lakshmi gave a realistic representation of a girl's life after going through the trauma of rape. The actor dominated the entire film, verily living the character of Jaya. This was the beginning of her foray into women-centric films. In each of the films she took on, she experimented with different concepts. In *Avan Aval Adhu*, she plays a barren wife ready to legitimatize surrogacy to become a mother—a revolutionary concept back in the 1980s! Only an actor of Lakshmi's calibre could have essayed the role!

The actor was never averse to playing roles akin to real life. She was committed to good acting and was not worried about always playing the lead. Like every heroine of her time, she too, had her share of portraying run-of-the-mill characters. So she did some films that had the standard song-and-dance sequences with the hero that appealed to the masses. She made a conscious attempt to pick and choose meaningful roles, though. She was lucky to star in films like *Oru Nadigai Naadakam Paarkiral*, based on another Jaykanthan novel. This offbeat story showcased her real persona as a fiery independent woman fighting for her private space. There was enough bandwidth for her growth as an actor as the story also lent itself to comedy. Lakshmi was more of an actor than a star. She has given some racy performances with megastars like MGR, Sivaji, Rajinikanth and Kamal Haasan. She was also extremely comfortable with actors like Muthuraman, Jaishankar, Srikanth and Raghuvaran. She tested waters in the mythological genre too, with films like *Sri Raghavendra*. She is one of the few actresses to have accepted middle-aged roles in her late twenties, as she viewed them as challenging experiences. The star has acted with younger actors as well, in *Udaya Geetham* and *Kudumbam Oru Koyil*.

Once in her forties, the star gracefully accepted roles befitting her image and age. 'Why should I spend lakhs of rupees to tighten my skin, look like a teenager and compete with my grandchildren running behind parlours?' she exclaims. She was fortunate to bag some absolutely wonderful films that helped her to enhance her brand image. The film *Kanmani* has her playing a convincing lawyer. She shared celluloid space with the versatile star, Sujatha. Another effective cameo was

Julie, unsurpassed to this day

A rare combination of sense and sensibility

Meeting her match in Sujatha

Redefining a stereotype in Samsaram Oru Minsaram

with Sivaji in *Ananda Kanneer*, where she is a loving mother and a devoted wife. She portrayed the Brahminical tradition of wearing a saree and speaking the language effectively, which she repeated in *Sirai* (a film with a novel, bold theme where the rape victim seeks refuge with the rapist). Lakshmi's poignant perfomance won her the Urvashi Award. In the film *En Uyir Kannamma*, she has a significant role again. She portrayed a pivotal role in the box-office grosser *Padayappa* (earlier she had played the lead opposite Rajinikanth).

Lakshmi did not shy away from playing character roles while her erstwhile heroes were still playing the lead, nor did she mind playing a cameo with her former heroes' offspring. Her best character role to this day is in *Jeans*, where she plays a modern and progressive grandmother. It was a hilarious comedy with her in the role of the grandmother of Aishwarya Rai.

Her debut Telugu film, *Bandhavyalu*, came about when she was only fifteen and although it did not create any great splutter, it certainly opened the floodgates of Telugu cinema for her. She soared to great heights playing myriad roles as the beloved, wife, sister, sister-in-law. With every film she did, she paved a roadmap for success. The language was not difficult because of her lineage. This also eased her acceptance in Tollywood. She did a couple of movies with the thespians, ANR and NTR. Later, she acted with every male lead in the industry. She has also played second lead in *Jeevana Tarangalu*, where she almost stole the show from Vanisri, the main lead. The film was a box-office grosser. Directors and producers of the industry noticed her impressive acting skills. *Panthulamma*, which brought her much acclaim, won her the Best Actress Award. She joined the league of the most celebrated heroines of her era. She repeated her magic of *Chattakari* in its Telugu version, making Julie legendary. Her mentionworthy body of work included movies like *Pandanti Jeevitham* and *Chattaniki Kanlulevu*. The coveted Filmfare Best Actress Award was hers, once again, for her powerful screen presence in *Sravana Meghalu* (1986). Her progression to mother roles here, too, came about with consummate ease. She earned accolades for her portrayal as Nagarjuna's mother in *Ninne Peladuta*. This romantic comedy proved that even a mother could look glamorous. She hogged more limelight than the lead pair! The mother magic continued in the Mahesh Babu starrer *Murari*, for which she was given the Nandi Award for Best Character Actress. She reaped a rich harvest, playing a cameo in *Lahiri Lahiri Lahirilo* and *Chintakayalaravi*. *Mithunam* was her benchmark performance. Her daughter's comment sums it all: 'Splendid performance, Mom.' Lakshmi and S.P. Balasubrahmanyam as the middle-aged protagonist blaze the screen, creating some great chemistry which was enjoyed by the young and old alike.

The first blockbuster, *Chattakari* (1974), was to her the key to the kingdom, paving way for her illustrious journey in Malayalam cinema. The film *Mohiniattam* introduced her as a nimble-footed dancer. She has also played a Carnatic vocalist in the film *Gaanam*, living the part of a musician. As a tribal girl in *Ponni* and *Picnic*, she looked and played the part beautifully, earning critical acclaim. In *Ponni*, she was paired with another great actor, Kamal Haasan. She etched her name forever in the annals of Malayalam cinema, giving her best to the industry.

She re-entered Malayalam cinema after a gap, with the film *IG* in 2009, acting as the mother of the protagonist, commanding a screen presence, giving the lead players a good run for their money. In *Pramani* and *Zachariayude Garbhinikal*, she looks fresh-faced and wonderful, to the delight of her many fans.

The latter movie was a comedy where she displayed delicate vignettes of humour.

Lakshmi enjoyed the same exalted status in Kannada films as well. Ananth Nag and Lakshmi were a favourite pair, delivering several runaway hits. Their popularity reached giddying heights in movies like *Benkiya Bale*, *Chandanada Gombe*, *Makkele Devaru* and *Ibbani Karagithu*. After *Amma*, the hit pair went into oblivion for almost a decade and resurfaced in *Shivashakthi*. Even after such a long gap, they recaptured their earlier chemistry in this film. Their last film together was *Gulmohar*.

The actor more than deserved the Filmfare Best Actress Award for the film *Hoovu Hannu* (1993). The state government of Karnataka honoured her for this film. The Best Supporting Actress State Award for her excellent cameo performance in *Vamshi* (2008) was another feather in her cap. Very few stars have had such a sterling record of success in Kannada movies like Lakshmi's. Her tightrope walk between artistic and commercial roles was truly commendable. Acting, according to her, is a labour of love with no age bar. She has proved this time and again, even in her later days in cameo roles. After her exhilarating performance in the beautiful film *Julie*, she did not act any more as a heroine in Bollywood. She did some character roles (as a grandmother) in *Jeans* and *Hulchul*. She received as many eyeballs as Aishwarya Rai and Kareena Kapoor, the glamour dolls in these films.

Lakshmi was no stranger to the small screen either. She has competently anchored several reality shows, mostly in Tamil, a few in Kannada and Malayalam as well; all of these shows have enjoyed a good amount of popularity. She loves this medium as she feels the talk shows have made her more aware and responsive to societal needs. 'We are oblivious to problems on the sets or at home and the revelations by strangers on the talk show made me realize the dark side of life.'

Lakshmi acted in a prolific 400 films across all the South Indian languages and was the recipient of the topmost awards for her range of roles—right from Filmfare to State to National Awards. She has won Filmfare Awards for Best Actress simultaneously in two languages in the same year—*Dikkatra Parvathi* and *Chattakari*. She is probably one of the very few actors to have been decorated with the Nandi Award for her mother role (*Murari*). The adventurous lady was confident enough to accept roles on pure merit rather than sticking to playing the 'eye candy' female lead role.

She is undoubtedly one of a kind, a woman who led life on her own terms without ever being bogged down by societal norms. She never bothered about her image or about what people would say and chose instead to always follow her heart. That explains the multiple marital relationships she got into, without fearing public criticism. She never believed in hypocrisy; a holier than thou attitude had always been alien to her nature. And this has only endeared her to her fans even more and added to her charisma as a public figure.

Cinema critics have always rated her very highly for her fluency in dramaturgy. The actor has never had a starry air about her; be it in a big budget film or a small film or TV show, she has always given her work the same unconditional commitment. It would not be an exaggeration if we canonize her as a legendary emoting queen in the history of South Indian cinema.

'I have always exercised my right to pick and choose...' Lakshmi, the immortal star, retains a cult following and even today, she can be a tough competitor to any new star on the horizon...

25

Srividya

Hers was a poetic face with large lustrous eyes. A smile that revealed perfect pearly teeth. A demeanour that radiated absolute feminity…

Srividya was a much loved actor who notched up a record number of 800 appearances on the silver screen of South Indian cinema. Every journalist worth his/her salt has written about her expressive eyes. There has been no actor ever after who conveyed so much more than what the script demanded. Her face mirrored the most subtle emotions more than even her voice. Above all was her persona that had the grace to withstand the blows dealt by fate. The actor had traversed way beyond the normal experience of life, which helped her in her performances.

Srividya, a native of Chennai, had inherited an impeccable pedigree, which few could boast of—a musician of repute as a mother, an artist of eminence as a father. Her parents desired to name her Meenakshi but her grandfather named her Srividya instead. Little Srividya was attracted to dance due to her association with the Travancore Sisters (Lalita, Padmini and Ragini). The adept pupil mastered Bharatanatyam under the tutelage of Dandayuthapani Pillai. She began to give performances, including some with the renowned sisters.

The young girl was soon lured by the arclights, thanks to her frequent visits to the studios with Padmini. An offer from the great A.P. Nagarajan resulted in a film offer, pairing her with Sivaji Ganesan. In *Thiruvarutselvar*, Srividya had a dance cameo. Her next memorable performance was as the celestial dancer Menaka in *Kumara Sambhavam* (1969), under the baton of P. Subramaniam.

The eagle-eyed K. Balachander's insatiable quest for new talent found a jewel in Srividya. He experimented with her in *Nootrukku Nooru*, where she plays a young girl out to trap a professor (played by Jaishankar). The director repeated her in *Vellivizha*. This set the stage for bigger things, including a film titled *Sollathan Ninaikkaren*. She pulled off a praiseworthy act as one of the three sisters falling in love with the hero, approaching the role with great dignity and maturity. This Balachander staple became iconic as Bhairavi in his *Apoorva Raagangal* (1975). She enthusiastically accepted the challenge posed by the ace director to play a middle-aged musician at the age of twenty-two! She essayed with ease the role in which the protagonist falls in love with a much younger man (played by Kamal Haasan) despite being married (to Rajinikanth). She decoded this complex role, handling her love life and a recalcitrant daughter with panache.

Soon after, the actor received a flood of offers, but mostly they were not of any great consequence. Yet she added an indefinable touch to the characters she played, making people watch the films purely to see her act. Her fans warmed up to her in the movies where she was paired with actors like Muthuraman, Jaishankar, Sivakumar and Vijayakumar during the latter half of the 1970s.

The Srividya–Sivakumar pair first appeared in *Annai Velankanni* (1971). The pair was noted for their chemistry in *Karaikkal Ammaiyar* as Shiva and Shakti. They did seven films together as a lead pair, with the exception of *Kasturi Thilakam*, where they played siblings. The most mentionworthy was *Sollathan Ninaikkaren*. Their last film together was *Kadalukku Mariyadhai* (1993). Several viewers recollect her dramatic portrayal in the film (specially the last scene) till today.

She came up with heartwarming portrayals in movies like *Kalangalil Aval Vasantham* (1976). She played Raji, a woman who suffers from insanity. The actor wowed her audience with her act of wandering in the forest and hills, looking for her husband, singing the song *'Paadum vandey paarthadhunda'*.

The sheer range and bandwidth of her roles in cinematic history are amazing. She was a newlywed in *Nalla Pennmani* (1976), unaware of the marital storm that awaited her; the pitiable Maragatham succumbing to forbidden pleasures in *Unarchigal* (1976); a disciplinarian named Kavitha, dominating her husband and children in *Avar Enakke Sondham* (1977); a bold girl heading a transport company in *Aaru Pushpangal* (1977); an avenging angel in *Durga Devi* (1977). Then she played the title role in *Rowdy Rakamma* (1977), a woman redeemed by the local police inspector while essaying a naïve woman, helpless in preventing her husband's affair with his secretary, in *Ivargal Vidhyasamaanavargal* (1980). In 1977, she received the state government's Kalaimamani Award and the Best Actor Award for the movie *Madhura Geetam*.

During the golden years, she often shared screen space with the maestro Sivaji Ganesan. She matched the thespian's calibre in films such as *Imayam* (1979), *Naam Iruvar* and *Neethiyin Nizhalandnaangal*. Srividya was surprisingly paired with Kamal

Eloquent eyes that spoke volumes

An indelible scene from Apoorva Ragaangal *with Kamal Haasan*

Emotional subtlety was the hallmark of her superlative performances

Haasan in a few movies after *Apoorva Raagangal*, including *Indran Chandran*, *Punnagai Mannan* and *Kadhala Kadhala* and as his mother in *Apoorva Sagodharargal*. She was never paired romantically with Rajinikanth. But she played his sister-in-law in *Aaru Pushpangal*, his older sister in *Manithan* and *Uzhaippali*, and his mother in *Thalapati*.

Srividya also did a string of cameo roles, back to back, which were clichéd and stereotyped, but she gave them a different tenor and tone. Her increasing weight issues and the emergence of newer heroines unfortunately diminished her chances in Tamil films. She switched over to mother roles when she was merely twenty-nine. She commenced her second innings playing character roles in *Kelviyum Naane Badilum Naane*, as Aruna's mother. This phase lasted for nearly two decades with three generations of actors and countless films. Her heroes were still playing the lead while she became their mother (Rajinikanth and Kamal Haasan). Her last Tamil film was *London* (2005).

Srividya's association with Malayalam cinema began in 1969 with *Chattambikkavala*. She quickly caught the fancy of Malayalam moviegoers, as she was ever willing to experiment with her characterization. She had the right accent and body language. The actor nonpareil acted in 200 or more Malayalam films, acting alongside all the leading stars right from Satyan to Mammootty. The film that shot her to fame was *Chenda* (1973) by A. Vincent who taught her how to pose in the best angle before the camera, the art of projecting herself and everything technical that she needed to know. 'He was my best teacher,' the actor claimed. For the first time, she was cast opposite Madhu, the reigning superstar of Malayalam cinema. She did the most number of films with him and they became a winning combination. Srividya sometimes did fall prey to stereotypes but she always made it a refreshing experience.

The Bharathan–John Paul combination extracted the best from Srividya. She was the brilliant Sharada, wife of a professor, in *Kaattathe Killikkodu*, who fights tooth and nail to save her marriage. Bharat Gopi played the professor and the young Revathi was the student infatuated with the professor. She was so good that she was cast in the Tamil version as well, *Unjaladum Uravugal*.

Srividya was a riot in the movie *Panchavadi Palam* (1984), a political satire by K.G. George. The actor did ample justice to the role as the overbearing and interfering wife, Mandothari. She was spot on in movies where she played a Syrian Christian character, be it *Ayanam* or *Poomukhappadiyil* or *Ninneyum Kaathu*. *Irakal* exploited her emotive ability, especially in the scenes with her brother-in-law. She won the Kerala State Award for her iconic portrayals in several films—*Jeevitham Oru Gaanam* (1979), *Idavazhiyile Poocha Minda Poocha* (1979), *Rachana* (1983) and *Daivathinte Vikrithikal* (1992).

In *Daivathinte Vikrithikal*, she stood out as the Anglo-Indian matriarch, Maggie, effortlessly mirroring the frustration and pent up feelings of the character and winning the Best Actress Award for the same. Srividya as Devaki in *Pavithram* is a middle-aged woman who discovers she is pregnant. The accomplished actor registered a brilliant act, reflecting the sheer horror, shame and pride of a woman caught in such a situation!

The star left her footprints in Telugu, Kannada and Hindi cinema too. She had acted in more than two dozen films. She made her debut in Telugu films as a dancer in the Dasari Narayan Rao-directed *Tata Manavadu* (1975). This is the only film where she did a special dance sequence. Later, she did films like *Thoorpu Padamara* and *Kanyakumari* under the same director. Most of her later films were made during the 90s, when she took recourse to acting as a therapy. Some were good and some just passed muster at the box office. But the actor was in her full element in every one of them. The two odd Hindi movies hardly did anything for her image, though.

The star received maximum TRPs in both Tamil and Malayalam TV serials. She dazzled on the small screen, effectively breathing life into her roles. Shri Kumaran Thampi wrote a story exclusively for her—*Amma Thamburatty*. This famous serial was taken off air after the demise of the star, as she was irreplaceable! The multi-talented actor's singing talent came to the fore in Malayalam movies like *Amaran*, *Ayalathe Sundari*, *Oru Painkilikkadha* and *Nakshathra Tharattu*.

Srividya's troubled marriage left her emotionally scarred and financially shattered. But never once did she air her grievances in public. She bailed herself out, working round the clock, giving her all to acting. Just when things were going her way though, she fell prey to her physical ailment. Even that she bore bravely with her trademark grit and determination.

Srividya was as graceful in death as she was in life, leaving behind a vaccum not easy to fill. She was the only actor to be honoured with a state funeral. Then Chief Minister Achutanandan put it beautifully, 'She was a part of good cinema that brought laurels to Kerala though she was born a Tamil. Kerala adopted her as a daughter.'

26

Jayasudha

For one generation, she was the girl-next-door, for the next, she was the glamorous aunt, for today's generation, she is the popular mother whom everybody likes…

Jayasudha belongs to the last generation of 'acting' actors. She etched her name in filmdom with her prowess as a mischievous girl and as a suffering wife of a sadist husband and a doting mother in innumerable films. She has always been so natural that she earned the sobriquet 'Sahaja Nati' (spontaneous actor). Filmmakers earmarked her as their prime choice for character-driven roles. She held her own in the multi-starrer era of 1970s and 1980s.

Jayasudha aka Sujatha has had it all in her life—two wonderful children, an iconic film career, and now a new avatar, that of a politician. Although a native of Madras (Chennai), with a strong comfort level in Tamil, it is surprising that she did more films (225 films) in her native tongue, Telugu, without knowing how to read and write in the language. Her father never wanted her to become an actor but fate willed it otherwise. Her aunt, the famous actor/director Vijaya Nirmala, gave her a launching pad that transformed her entire life. She was offered a cameo in her aunt's home production, *Pandanti Kaapurami*, to play the daughter of the legendary star Jamuna. The young girl slipped into the role that became a passport for bigger things to come. Her role in the movie belied her age (she was only twelve) given the maturity she showed in her performance.

She made her entry at a time when stalwarts like Jamuna, Vanisri and Sujatha ruled South Indian cinema. Jayasudha climbed the ladder of success at a slow and steady pace, doing supporting roles as daughter and sister and friend, as in *Bharatha Vilas* where she played the daughter of Sivaji and *Deerga Sumangali* where she made a guest appearance. Balachander cast her as a sister in *Arangetram* and as an extroverted modern girl opposite Kamal Haasan in *Sollathan Ninaikiren* (1973). She gave a very good account of herself in this multi-starrer, vying for attention alongside Srividya and Jayachitra. She was cast again in *Apoorva Raagangal*. This noticeable role gave her visibility. She justified her director's trust as a defiant teenager falling in love with an older man; Rajinikanth was her father in the film! Balachander was a tough taskmaster and he exacted a hundred per cent from her in this role. Their efforts paid off and she earned a reputation for unconventional roles. She did a cameo in *Ninaithale Inikkum* and its Telugu version, *Andamaina Anubhavam*.

Jayasudha's debut film as a lead actor was *Lakshman Rekha* (Telugu), which was based on a Marathi novel. Her inborn talent came to the fore in this complex role. Then came her claim to fame in the title role of *Jyothi* (1976) under the direction of Raghavendra Rao. This was a remake of the Hindi film *Mili*. The star's magical acting catapulted her to the height of stardom in Telugu cinema. She handled the role of a blind girl deftly, showing maturity far beyond her years. She won the Filmfare Best Actress Award and the Nandi Award for this film. The same director facilitated another opportunity for the actor to earn one more Nandi Award, this time for his movie titled *Aame Katha* where her emotive brilliance received much appreciation, followed by the State Award. Raghavendra Rao then cast her in his next movie, *Mathura Swapnam* (based on A.J. Cronin's novel, *Citadel*) starring other bigwigs like Jaya Prada and Krishnam Raju. Jayasudha as the wife of the doctor (Krishnam Raju) essayed a praiseworthy role.

She had an innate instinct for choosing roles that enhanced her image as an actor. Her slender figure, emotive voice and expressive eyes were tailor-made for demanding performances. Despite being a lead heroine, she did a number of cameos as well, as she gave importance to the storyline and her character in the film. This was the main reason for her success in several multi-starrers, including *Bobbili Brahmanna* (Krishnam Raju, Sharada and Jayasudha) and *Palnati Simham* (Krishna, Radha and Jayasudha).

Jayasudha had no inhibitions about wearing a swimsuit if the story demanded it. She was one of the first stars to wear the costume without any objection in the Tamil film, *Sigappu Roja*, and its Telugu version, *Erra Gulabilu*. She wore miniskirts in *Nomu*, carrying off the image of a carefree teenager with absolute ease. In *Shokadu*, her uninhibited laughter as a rustic girl became the theme of a popular song, '*Siri malli puvenuvu*'.

Dasari Narayan Rao was another director who presented the actor in sixteen successful films. He unhesitantly cast her opposite the leading heroes of the time like ANR, Shoban Babu, Mohan Babu and Krishna. She began as his heroine and later progressed to character roles in his films. The most mentionworthy movies under his banner were *Shiva Ranjani*,

Premabhishekam and *Meghasandesam*, with the last two films getting her the Nandi Award. *Sivaranjani* where she plays a village girl, who becomes a filmstar, was a box-office grosser. She received universal accolades for her portrayal of a deglamourized prostitute deeply in love with the protagonist, in *Premabhishekam*. 'It was a gratifying moment for me when I won the coveted State Award yet another time,' she recalls. In *Meghasandesam*, where she plays ANR's wife, she showed absolutely no compunction in facing the camera with bare, minimum make-up.

'Romance was not easy for me,' Jayasudha claims. That being true, she did herself proud in movies like *Driver Ramudu*, *Amara Deepam*, *Adavi Ramadu* and *Naa Desam*. Her popularity rose to soaring heights with these films, enlivening the audience with her svelte steps and pearly smile. She was a self-taught dancer who danced her way to the cash register in several movies. Her glamour quotient was very evident in movies like *Yuvaraju* and *Ramudu Kadu Krishnudu*. The ease with which she switched between her simple persona and a glitzy glam role was really commendable. *Yugandhar* showed her in another light as a character with the right mix of winsomeness and valour (she learns self-defence tactics to avenge her brother's death) while in *Illalu*, she essayed a winning role with grey shades that demonstrated her genius. The few movies that she has acted with Krishna are praiseworthy, including *Lanke Bindelu* and *Palnati Simham*.

She challenged herself once again under Balachander's baton in *Idi Kada Kadu*, wearing the visage of feminist roles that were a rage in the 70s. She was paired opposite Chiranjeevi and she pulled off the role with astounding intensity as a victim of a sadist husband. The protagonist showed individuality and confidence, earning another Nandi Award. The years 1980–85

In Sollathan Ninaikiren

As a chirpy young girl in Apoorva Ragaangal

Sahaja Nati—*Consummate actor*

saw the star reaching the zenith of her fame. In one year, she had acted in twenty-four films, improving the nuances and contours of her acting skills all the time. By the 80s, she bid farewell to her Tamil connection, as she was very busy doing Telugu films back to back. She graduated from singing and dancing roles to serious ones, as seen in *Gruhapravesam* (1976). This was another women-centric film where she excelled as the protagonist who redeems her wayward husband. This role decorated her with the Filmfare Best Actress Award.

Ace director Ram Gopal Verma cast her in films like *Money Money* and *Dayyam*. She set new records in acting with *Kalyugstri*, a remake of the English movie, *Highway Queen*. She sculpted a stunning act as a Brahmin girl turning to prostitution, parading on the highways. Her performance in *O Barya Katha* is said to have narrowly missed the Nandi Award.

She became even busier after the exit of Jaya Prada and Sridevi from Telugu cinema. But she made time to tie the knot with Nitin Kapoor. With the birth of her children, she progressed to doing character roles. She acted as a strict matriarch managing the family finances in *Kalikalam*. She excelled herself as a senior artiste in films like *Ontari Poratam* with GenX actors like Venkatesh and Swetha, as also in *Vijay* with Nagarjuna.

Jayasudha carved a new niche for herself in mother roles. Her landmark movies include *Sakhi*, *Style*, *Bommarillu*, *Parugu*, and *Kotha Bangara Lokam*. In *Amma Nana Oka Tamil Ammai*, she gave a new dimension to the mother character and it became a benchmark for the projection of mother characters in South Indian filmmaking. A down-to-earth honesty and diverse repertoire became the signature of the star's new phase. This only further encouraged her to chisel a series of heartwarming performances in films like *Alaipayuthey* (Tamil) and *Sakhi*

(Telugu) under the aegis of genius moviemaker Mani Ratnam. She had the complete and fond acceptance of her audience in *Thavasi* (Tamil). She did not hesitate to act as Chiranjeevi's mother in *Rikshavodu*. She was praised for her role in this film as a long-suffering mother languishing in jail. She was appreciated as the wife, and later, as the mother of Sharath Kumar in the Tamil movie, *1977*. Her success run still continues with her outstanding mother roles, such as in *Seethamma Vakitlo Sirimalle Chettu*. She verily transformed these ordinary characters into historic montages. Time and again, she has shown filmmakers and the audience that she is an actor on a different octave.

Jayasudha was no stranger to Malayalam movies. She did well in movies like *Sarovaram*, along with Mammootty, doling out a portrayal with an understated appeal. She was also noticeable in *Ishtam*, a crowd-pleaser of a film, where she plays a college teacher.

With a career abounding in achievements, Jayasudha also forayed into the production arena. She has produced movies like *Kanchana Sita*, *Kalikalam*, *Mera Pati Sirf Mera Hai*, *Adrustam* and *Vinta Kodallu*. In *Hands Up*, she explores her talent in the comic genre, managing to get quite a few laughs.

Jayasudha has constantly dug deep to rediscover her mojo, opening up new vistas to cement her journey spanning four decades in the film industry. This perhaps helped her to build a strong fan base and make a mark in a hitherto uncharted territory like politics. She has not outgrown her passion for sports and cooking either. Cricket is and always was her first love. 'I would love to be reborn as Sachin Tendulkar,' quips the shining star.

27

Jaya Prada

Her journey from Rajahmundry to Rampur is as dramatic as her films. Jaya Prada, born as Lalita Rani, is a timeless beauty who walked the Indian cine terrain, earmarking an identity for herself, which was unbeatable. She zoomed in on celluloid inadvertently. A dance performance during the annual day of her school paved the way for an entry into filmdom. She was paid a princely amount of ten rupees for a three-minute cameo in the movie, *Bhoomikosam*. After this minuscule role, she went back to school, resuming her normal life after the shoot. Filmmaker Prabhakar Reddy then cast her in *Naku Swatantram Vachindi* (1975), rechristening her Jaya Prada after the banner Jaya Prada Combines. Her performance as the ferocious Chandramma seeking a vendetta for her husband's murder was well received. This cameo filmed against an earthy background announced her arrival as an actor to reckon with.

Jaya Prada was born on the banks of the Godavari river in the small hamlet of Rajahmundry. Her father, Krishna Rao, was a film financier and her mother, Neelaveni, introduced her to the fine arts of music and dance. The star says she has her mother to thank for, moulding her into what she is today. Her childhood days were spent mastering the cultural nuances; her day would begin very early with lessons in sitar, followed by dancing sessions. Even so, she was not inclined to be in the profession of acting but fate willed it otherwise.

The beauty queen's defining moment in her cinematic journey commenced under the legendary K. Balachander. He looked beyond her beauty and spotted her latent talent. The stark, realistic black-and-white movie *Anthuleni Katha* presented the actor to the world of cinema. Jaya Prada as Sarita was a director's actor, immortalizing the protagonist, just like Sujatha did in the Tamil version. The interplay of emotions and pathos was exhibited by the actor as if to the manner born. She garnered a huge fan following after her success in the lead role in her debut film. She was bestowed with the Nandi Special Jury Award for this film. Sarita brought out the actor in her, but the bewitching beauty dazzled the audience even more with her natural glamour quotient. K. Balachander would rein her back to good acting from time to time. The movie *47 Natkal* showcased her in a new light. The protagonist is cheated by her husband (Chiranjeevi) in an alien land (France). Jaya Prada excelled in emoting the part of the frightened wife trying to escape the torture. This gave her a new identity in the realm of histrionics. It also weaned her away from the glamour stereotype she was wont to play in her Telugu films. This was the first woman-centric film in a long time and the actor acquitted herself very well in both the Tamil and Telugu versions. The director polished her potential, casting her in films like *Manmatha Leelai* and *Ninaithale Inikkum*.

Filmmakers exploited her likeness to women in Ravi Verma paintings in film after film. Her excellence in dance was utilized to the optimum by the thespian K. Viswanath in *Siri Siri Muva*. This film was a trend changer, presenting the Venus replica in an entirely different light where she played the dumb dancer. Her dancing to the tunes of the director helped her steadily climb the ladder of success. She says, 'Viswanath was my acting school'.

The thespian gave her a big break in Bollywood through *Sargam*, a runaway hit, more so for her dancing skills. Jaya Prada justified his confidence in her by delivering a classic performance in *Sagara Sangamam*. The dancing star was pitted against another volcanic talent, Kamal Haasan. It was just not the dance but also the dramatics of the lead players that made this movie iconic. The emotionally charged romance displayed by both remains evergreen in the eyes of cinegoers to this day. The brilliant director discovered another facet of the star when he gave her an opportunity to sing '*Mounamelanoyi*'. And Jaya Prada became a singing star as well. Both director and actor scaled the peak of popularity and Jaya Prada won the coveted Filmfare Award for her performance. Viswanath cast her in yet another Hindi movie, *Kaamchor*, where she overcame the criticism of her Hindi accent. She pulled off her role with ease and confidence. The director recast her in *Sanjog*. Her double role in this film gave her a distinct identity and acceptance in Bollywood and the film became a milestone in her career. The star remains truly indebted to the great K. Viswanath who made it all possible in two languages.

Dasari Narayan Rao was another director who helped her to carve a permanent place for herself in the industry. He introduced her in *Devude Digi Vaste* and she fulfilled all expectations. He recreated her magic in front of the camera in twenty-five movies after that. The actor was so indebted to him that she did not hesitate to accept a cameo in his box-office

Vivacious diva—Jaya Prada

The bold and beautiful artiste

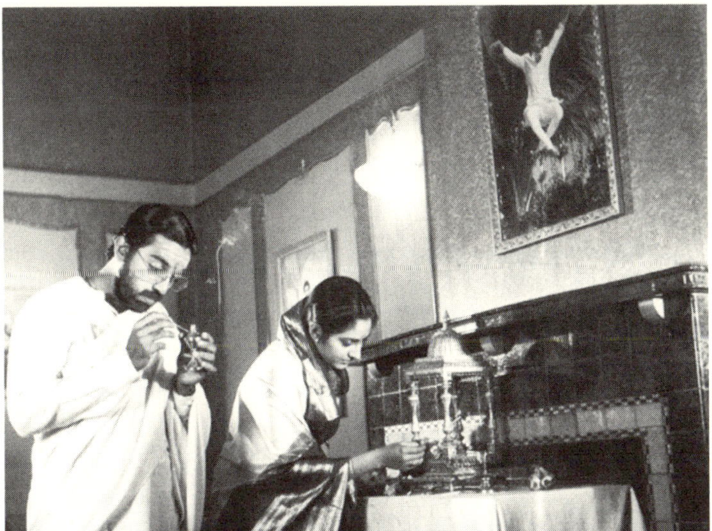

A sensitive portrayal in Sagara Sangamam

grosser *Edu Anthustula Meda*, which had superstars like ANR, Sujatha and Jayasudha. The veteran recalls her readiness to do the dance sequence in his movie despite her hectic schedule as a number one star. As a mark of gratitude, he mentioned her name in the song, *'Chakkani chukka...Jaya Prada'*! Her best performance, though, was in *Megasandesam*. As an ethereal dancer, she captivated the audience with her nimble feet and expressive eyes. The chemistry between the two protagonists, ANR and Jaya Prada, was exemplary. The film went on to win a National Award.

The successful star surrendered to the director's vision and fascinated her fans when she was paired opposite legends like ANR and NTR. She was barely in her teens when she was cast with NTR in *Adavi Ramudu*. She soon overcame her awe and displayed such brilliance that it stormed the box office. The song *'Aaresukoboyi paresukunname'* became a great hit. Dasari narrates an anecdote about her commitment—'Despite driving through the night, Jaya Prada was ready with make-up on the set, the next morning.' She shot twelve hours straight without a break for *Circus Ramudu*. This movie had NTR playing the lead with her. The next unforgettable movie to hit the marquee was *Yamagola*, a fantasy comedy with Jaya Prada opposite NTR. The star regaled the audience with her comic capers. The film was another super hit starring the pair. This star pair acted in ten box-office grossers becoming the most sought after pair in Telugu cinema at the time.

Bapu cast her in a mythological role in *Seeta Ramadu*, an epic film. Her consistent performance invited the attention of famous banners like Raghavender Rao and Ramoji Rao. Jaya Prada became one of the busiest actors in the late 70s and 80s. If six movies were released in a year, four of them had Jaya Prada in them. She starred with all the leading heroes like Shoban Babu, Chandramohan, Sharad Babu and Krishna. Her pairing opposite Krishna began with *Mana Voori Katha*, intermittently stretching over two decades and twenty-five films. Jaya Prada did a mature character role in *Chandravamsam*, with Krishna in the lead. She didn't mind competition, taking it in her stride, be it with her archrival Sridevi or her other co-stars like Jayasudha and Sujatha. She equalled Sridevi in terms of her glamour quotient and was on par with Jayasudha in terms of acting skills. What was most admirable was her professionalism on the sets. The on screen chemistry between Sridevi and Jaya Prada was remarkable. The cold vibes between the two women would disappear when they faced the camera. Their sister act could put blood sisters to shame. They repeated these in Bollywood too, as their Telugu films were made in Hindi with Jeetendra in the lead (*Tohfa*, *Mawali* and *Maqsad*).

Barring *Sharabi*, where she played a *tawaif* (earning accolades for the same), her portrayals in Hindi films were along traditional lines, depicting a sacrificing devout woman. This helped her acquire a huge female fan following and worked to her advantage when she later turned to the Hindi belt (Uttar Pradesh) for her political career. She became the highest paid female star in the mid-80s. The star had definitely come a long way from the nominal remuneration she had been paid for her debut Telugu movie. Till the 90s, the heroine did a great number of movies but they were all a montage of stereotyped glamour roles. Ironically, she stayed at the top despite the clichéd images.

Jaya Prada was a polyglot who left her footprints in Kannada, Marathi, Bengali and Malayalam films. She has done excellent films with Raj Kumar like *Sanadi Appanna*, *Kavirathna Kalidasa*, *Huli Haalina Mevu*. She had the unique opportunity of acting with father and son (Raj Kumar and Sandeep) in *Shabdavedhi*. The lady was certainly doing a tightrope walk, given her other new avatar of a busy parliamentarian. But she still delivered some unforgettable performances, including the particularly memorable *Krantiveera Sangolli Rayana*, a big budget historical biopic, where she was Kittur Rani Chinnamma. She certainly proved that a politician could also be a good actor and vice versa.

Jaya Prada has given some sterling performances in Bengali films as well, like *Swapne Dekha Raj Kanya* and *Sesh Sangat*. She is also a film producer, producing films for her brother, and lately, for her nephew and a theatre owner. She has written and directed the Telugu film *Class Medal*, with her nephew Siddharth in the lead. This multi-talented actor has even released a music album with celebrity composer, Bappi Lahiri. She has acted in a Bhojpuri film with Manoj Tiwari, a remake of the Telugu film *Matrudevobhava*. Filmfare has honoured the accomplished star by bestowing her the Lifetime Achievement Award. Her fans accorded her much respect when she forayed into the small screen. She tested waters by anchoring the show *Jayapradam*. 'I did this programme as I wanted to be in every house and prove that an artiste can be everywhere.' And of course, she became an overnight success in the electronic media.

In 2002, she walked into the Marathi film arena, doing a cameo in *Aadhar*. Around this time, the star had completed 300 movies and was still raring to go. Cinema audiences witnessed her stupendous acting skills in the Malayalam film *Pranayam*. This role challenged the actor in her and she became iconic as a middle-aged Christian woman, Grace, caught between two men in her life. Jaya Prada did an exceedingly good job in conveying the sensitivity of the character. She gave an excellent verdict of herself, pitted against two stalwarts Mohanlal and Anupam

Kher. She was no alien to Malayalam cinema, having previously acted in great movies like *Devadoothan* (a musical mystery-cum-romance). 'Malayalam films make me perform,' says the actor.

Jaya Prada fulfilled her dancing aspirations through *Amrapalli*, a dance ballet. She found enough time despite her political engagements to realize this dream. Her personal life has seen several ups and downs with her brother acting as her rock-solid anchor throughout. She has no regrets about her failed marriage or her political misadventures. She says politics has made her strong. She is convinced that she will serve the poor and stand up for the needy. A two-time member of parliament and one-time Rajya Sabha member, Jaya Prada has seen both the elixir of cinema and the nadir of politics. But she holds her head high, with pride in her heart, wanting to straddle both cinema and politics for as long as she can. As she herself aptly puts it, 'Anything is possible in life.'

28

Raadhika Sarathkumar

The year 1978 witnessed the metamorphosis of an ugly duckling into a beautiful swan as she stepped into filmdom. She was tracing her famous father, M.R. Radha's footsteps; a legendary actor in his time. Raadhika Sarathkumar is a versatile actor with unconventional looks who changed the image of a heroine in South Indian films. She made her debut in the Bharathiraja film, *Kizhake Pogum Rail*, quite by accident. The director happened to see her photograph in her friend's house and offered her the role. Teenaged Raadhika was taken by surprise. 'I was actually scared of him. But the director approached my mother and got her consent. I was absolutely naïve and raw.' The Bharathiraja discovery went on to blaze a trail that few in the industry can match even today. She is the most uninhibited star, widely known for her cheerful and bubbly nature. 'I was called a tomboy often. I never gave any importance to being beautiful. Raadhika has come a long way and is truly a fine example of a feisty woman who designed and shaped her own destiny.

Bharathiraja's assistant, Bhagyaraj, called her a *'poosanikai'* (pumpkin) when he saw her on the first day of the shooting. She candidly admits she was plump at the time. 'I still haven't forgiven him for that!' In her debut film, *Kizhake Pogum Rail*, she excelled in the role of Paanjali, a village belle. She brought out the effervescent nature of the character on the screen, justifying the director's choice displaying the interplay of feelings like joy, sorrow and excitement like a seasoned actor. It was difficult to believe that it was her first movie. 'I think after my first shot in that movie, my learning process started, and so far in my career, I am still learning,' she adds. The story revolved around an eastbound train, used as an effective medium for two lovers to exchange their messages. This unique feature aided Raadhika to make her character unforgettable and won the hearts of the public. The debutante had a huge canvas to reveal her talent; initially, as a happy-go-lucky teenager falling in love, and thereafter, portraying the anguish of separation from her lover. In the latter half, she beautifully encapsulates the suffering and shame of having to obey the command of the villagers (to walk naked around the village, early in the morning, to stop the torrential rain). This mind-blowing performance interwoven with wonderful songs made it a runaway hit and Raadhika, the star, was born! The wildest of guesses would not have been right about this girl. For who would have thought that the plump, gauche girl would transform into an actor of quality and élan!

Raadhika showed slow but steady progress thereon, acting in movies that suited her personality. One such movie was her debut Telugu film, *Nyayam Kavali*. The production house was looking for a new face and chose Raadhika and Chiranjeevi as their lead pair. She played the role of the brave Bharati, at once showing anger, hurt and vindictiveness. It was certainly a complex role but she essayed it with ease. Though she was not conversant in Telugu, she managed to mouth the lengthy and powerful dialogues like a true blue native. The movie became a launching pad, catapulting her to instant fame and winning her the Filmfare Award for Best Actress. She became a permanent fixture in Telugu films thereafter. Tamil directors and producers began to recognize her as a serious actor as well. 'I too began to concentrate on my career after *Nyayam Kavali*,' she admits.

Her acting prowess came to the fore in the movie *Dharma Devathai*, where with great aplomb and style, she plays the role of a young police officer fighting goons to save the modesty of a young girl, continuing where Vijayshanthi left off. It was a blessing that South Indian films readily accepted women police officers. She was equally at ease playing a widow valiantly protecting her daughter from being molested. Here was an actor with the optimum combination of valour and feminity. She bagged the Filmfare South Best Actress Award for this film.

In *Radha Kalyanam*, she plays the female lead. This film gave her an opportunity to showcase her talent as a young middle-class girl falling in love with her tenant, an aspiring musician. She left no stone unturned in playing the young lover who uses all her wiles to woo and chase the unsuspecting tenant, eventually forcing him to fall in line with her wishes. She walked straight into the hearts of thousands of cinema lovers as Radha. The emotions that she brings to play after her marriage to a widower, where she boldly confesses her old love, adds another feather to her cap. Effortlessly, she brings out the sense of tradition instilled in her by deciding to stay put in the marriage even when the husband gives her the freedom to walk away, displaying maturity far beyond her age. The movie was remade in Hindi as *Wo Saat Din* and in Tamil as *Andha Ezhu Natkal*.

Punthotta Kaval Karan was the first movie that presented

her as both a young and old character. She delved deep into the psyche of a young wife who could not bear children, showing frustration and despondency at once. The dialogues between Vijaykanth (husband) and Raadhika (wife) smacks of the onscreen chemistry between the two. She gave a very good account of herself as an older character bringing dignity and a quiet sobriety to the depiction. This showed her capacity to interpret the role, making it unforgettable. Her outstanding acting in this film got her the Tamil Nadu State Film Award (special recognition for Best Actress). She also earned the sobriquets, 'Iron lady' and 'Female Sivaji'.

Raadhika continued her honeymoon with Telugu cinema. She and Chiranjeevi became a hit pair in romantic as well as action-oriented films. Out of the twenty-eight films she did with him, many became box-office grossers. In the film *Abhilasha*, they even choreographed a dance themselves in the absence of the dance master! Raadhika came to be recognized for her powerful dialogue delivery and found that her own signature style was here to stay. The different roles she took on in Telugu moulded her and added new dimensions to her talent. Films like *Radha Kalyanam*, *Kirayi Rowdylu*, *Billa Ranga*, *Yamakinkarudu*, *Prema Pichollu* and *Palletoori Monagadu* helped her soar high into the galaxy of Telugu stardom. The Nandi Award was bestowed on her for Best Supporting Actress in the movie *Prema Katha*.

Raadhika became iconic as Lalitha in the film *Swathi Muthyam*, directed by the great K. Viswanath. 'A dream come true for me,' is how she puts it. She immortalized the character of a widow with a five-year-old son ekeing out a living in a small hamlet. Kamal Haasan, who plays the other lead as an autistic, unexpectedly marries Lalitha to save her from the barbs of society. It was a revolutionary idea, where a much younger man marries a widow in a spur-of-the-moment decision. Raadhika gave her career's best performance in this movie as the silent, dignified widow accepting her new husband. Her deft handling of the subject added to the success of the movie. Though she did not win any awards for her role, the movie was almost nominated for the Oscars, which in itself is an achievement of sorts! 'Looking back, now I realize the significance of the performance which never hit me then,' claims the star. After this film, Raadhika was acclaimed as one of the serious actors who could handle any heavy theme. It helped her to break out of the breezy heroine mould of Chiranjeevi starrers.

The early 1980s and 90s saw her switching between Tamil and Telugu movies, cementing her position in filmdom with *Ninaivu Chinnam*. She excels as the wife of Prabhu. She played the role of a rustic simpleton with absolute ease, winning the coveted State Best Actress Award. *Paasa Paravaigal*, with Lakshmi, Sivakumar and Mohan, penned by Karunanidhi, was a superhit and Raadhika, as the bereaved young woman, acquitted herself with the right deportment and poignancy that the role demanded, making her powerful presence felt once again.

She added to her kitty of awards with *Pasumpon*, an endorsement of her prowess, showcasing a mélange of emotions where she competes with stalwarts like Sivaji and Sivakumar and walked away with the Special Award for Best Actress. She was truly in her element, etching a lifelike character in *Kizhakku Cheemayile*, proving Bharathiraja's trust in her all over again, to exhibit the bonding between brother and sister. She was recast in the Telugu version, *Palnati Pourusham*, which was equally successful.

Raadhika is an indefatigable actor who went the extra mile to execute the role of middle-aged Radha in *Keladi Kanmani*,

'Rail Raadhika' shot to fame with her first film, Kizhake Pokum Rail

Sizzling Raadhika making her mark

Raadhika and Kamal Hassan, in an award-winning performance in Swathi Muthyam

Nuances of versatility in Keladi Kanmani

extending her friendship and support to the protaganist, S.P.B., a widower. She earned the Filmfare Best Actress Award in Tamil and went on to act in the Telugu version, *O Paapa Laali*, as well. This story of a platonic friendship between a man and woman went down very well with film audiences.

Meendum Oru Kadhal Kadhai, produced by the star herself, won the National Award for the Best Picture. She also plays the lead in the love story of a mentally unstable couple. Among her several other films in Tamil, she made a mark (as a vamp) in a cameo in *Jeans*. She did not hesitate to play a deglamourized role in *Gopurangal Saivadillai*, remade in Hindi as *Naseeb Apna Apna*, expertly registering her acting mettle in the film's climax.

She did a cameo as the wife of Mammootty, a music

maestro, in *Swathi Kiranam*. Raadhika breathed life into the character in a most subdued manner, making it extremely memorable. The dignity that she lent that character added another milestone to her career graph.

She left her indelible mark as a fine actor in every movie she did, be it Tamil, Telugu, Malayalam, Kannada or Hindi. 'I was most comfortable doing Telugu films where there is a lot more professionalism and camaraderie. The most difficult were Malayalam films,' confesses the versatile actor.

Raadhika had the privilege of acting with all the established heroes in five languages, including the great Amitabh Bacchan! Her competence and aggression always challenged the male leads. It is not for nothing that she is known as the 'Iron Lady' of South Indian cinema. The star has had resounding success in the small medium as well, acting in Tamil and Telugu serials produced under her own banner, Radaan TV. She has the unique distinction of being an accomplished film actor turned successful entrepreneur, founding Radaan Mediaworks India Limited. The busy actor, producer, director and entrepreneur is also a hands-on wife and a mother who has truly mastered the art of multi-tasking.

29

Sridevi

The unrelenting glare of the arclights, the lens of the camera never failed to heighten her statuesque figure, aquiline features the sum total of her touch-me-not beauty. Her majestic screen presence did not require any of the techno savvy razzmatazz. She has been compared to the Hollywood diva, Shirley Temple, as both began young. This prima donna of Indian cinema dominated the silver screen for three decades and enjoyed the prized distinction of reigning as the undisputed numero uno star for nearly a decade. She carried on the tradition of South Indian leading ladies making it big in Bollywood. The actor has around 300 movies in her kitty and she is the only star in Bollywood history to have made a highly triumphant come back...

Sridevi, christened at birth as Shree Amma Yanger, was born in Sivakasi, Tamil Nadu, to a Tamil father (Ayyapan) and Telugu mother (Rajeswari). She was introduced to the tinsel world when she was barely four, as Lord Murugan in *Thunaivan*, directed by Devar.

The legendary MGR spotted her first and made her a child

star. Attracted by her cherubic face, he cast her in his blockbuster, *Nam Naadu*. She became a well-known face by the time she was ten. She was soon acting in Telugu and Malayalam films and became a rage as a child-woman actor. After acting in nearly thirty-five films, she was introduced as a sister (in an adult role) of Lakshmi in the famous hit *Julie*, in both Malayalam and Hindi. The actor had been introduced as a lead in a Telugu film, *Annuragalu*, when she was barely ten years old. The director asked her mother to drape her in a saree, to see if she would fit the role. The tall girl played a visually impaired character in the film. Though the film failed, Sridevi's performance was noticed.

Sridevi is one of the several child stars to have made a success of her adult roles. K. Balachander, the famous director of South Indian cinema, introduced her as a heroine in the film *Moondru Mudichu*. This was a remake of the Telugu film *O Seeta Katha*. Kamal Haasan played the lead and Rajinikanth enacted the role of a villain. Sridevi recalls that Kamal Haasan would bully her constantly during the shooting. He himself has admitted in one of his interviews that he had behaved like a school leader during the making of this film. With this film, Sridevi transformed from a child wonder to a girl-woman. She delivered a sterling performance matching Kamal Haasan's talent.

Her meteoric rise as an actress was in *16 Vayathinile*, which was her launch pad to stardom. She played the role of a sixteen-year-old girl (Mayilu) dreaming of becoming a teacher. She was paired opposite Kamal Haasan and Rajinikanth (villain). She displayed her phenomenal talent as an innocent village belle. The songs '*Senthoora puvve*' (Tamil) and '*Sirimalle puvva*' (Telugu) became whopping chartbusters. Sridevi glided through the entire role, delivering a hypnotic performance. Mayilu became a household name.

After the runaway success of the Bharathiraja film, the director cast her in an exacting role in *Sigappu Rojakkal*, a suspense thriller. She was paired opposite Kamal Haasan who played a woman hater in the film. Sridevi delivered a superlative performance. This offbeat film was also made in Telugu as *Erra Gulabilu*. *Varumayin Niram Sivvapu*, another Balachander film, earned critical acclaim for both Kamal Haasan and Sridevi. The two competed with each other to display a tapestry of emotions as poverty-stricken characters. The film was made in Telugu as *Aakali Rajyam*, and later, in Hindi too (*Zara Si Zindagi*). The pair registered another convincing win in the film *Meendum Kokila*. Sridevi played the title role of a naïve wife of a briefless lawyer. Her comic timing brilliantly came to the fore in this film.

The Balu Mahindra-directed *Moondram Pirai* reinforced both Sridevi's talent and her wonderful vibes with Kamal Haasan. Her body language and expressions as a woman suffering from amnesia after an accident were laudable. She exuded glamour as a young woman prior to the accident, and later, as an amnesia patient with the IQ of a seven-year-old. She managed to bring an amazing authenticity to her character. This unmatched performance won her the Tamil Nadu State Film Award for Best Actress and the film was remade in Hindi, as *Sadma*, with the same pair.

The now famous duo made further waves in the movie *Vaazhvey Maayam*, where Sridevi is portrayed as a woman trying to redeem the debauched protagonist (Kamal Haasan). Though it was a clichéd love triangle, she managed to zoom ahead with style and confidence, winning accolades for the same. The Sridevi–Kamal Haasan pair is featured in the CNN-IBN 2012 list of the 'Greatest Romantic Couples on Celluloid' for having done forty films together in Tamil, Telugu and Malayalam.

An endearing role in Meendum Kokila

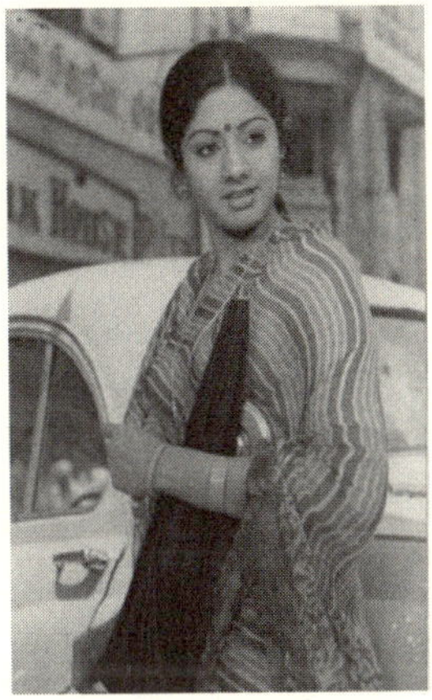

In the suspense thriller Sigappu Rojakkal

Her performance in Moondram Pirai *won her the Best Actress Award*

In Pathinaru Vayathinale

Rajinikanth was paired opposite Sridevi in movies like *Dharmayuddham*, *Priya* and *Pokkiri Raja*. But unlike Kamal Haasan starrers, Sridevi was cast only to increase the glamour quotient of Rajinikanth's films. Yet the actor reinvented herself and showed her best form on the screen. The actor within her could be seen even in such ornamental roles, as in the movie *Adutha Varisu*, where she plays the central character.

The audience loved the ANR–Sridevi and NTR–Sridevi pairing as well. Despite the age difference, both of them set the screen on fire. The child of *Badi Pantulu* and *Bhariya Biddalu* was a full-grown woman romancing the legendary stars. It was K. Raghvender Rao who gave her the glamour image in movies like *Kondaveeti Simham*. Her breathtaking beauty loomed large across the celluloid. This perhaps helped her in being cast opposite older heroes. With NTR, she did some blockbuster films like *Vetagadu*, *Kondaveeti Simham*, *Sardar Papa Rayudu*, *Bobili Puli*. She awed the audience with her spectacular appearances as a spoilt rich brat, a chirpy young girl or a carefree teenager falling in love with the macho protagonist. She was the choreographer's delight too, as she was an extraordinary dancer.

Sridevi struck gold when she was cast opposite ANR. She was barely sixteen when she became his heroine in *Mudullu Koduku*, *Premabhishekam* and *Bangaru Kanuka*. *Premabhishekam* entered the annals of cinema history with Sridevi and ANR immortalizing the on screen romance. This modern Devadas falls for a simple, straightforward girl in the film. Sridevi showed her acting mettle sans glamour and walked right into the box office.

The silver screen demi-goddess displayed a mosaic of shades in *Devatha*, *Mosagadu* and *Kartika Deepam* (she was noticed in this movie despite the presence of Sharada). These family dramas got her a large female fan following. She donned the role of a homemaker and the 'other woman' with equal aplomb. Most of these films were remade in Hindi with Jeetendra in the lead and Jaya Prada as her co-star. Krishnam Raju and Krishna were the other heroes who aided her ascent to the top; Sridevi has acted in around fifty films with Krishna. The actor was so busy that she once shot for eighteen songs for different films in the same locale with Krishna!

The star progressed to acting with heroes who matched her age like Chiranjeevi, Nagarjuna and Venkatesh. Her trademark charm and fetching looks made the films runaway hits. K. Raghavender Rao showed her in *Jagadeka Veerudu Atiloka Sundari*, as an ethereal angel from a fantasy world falling in love with a human being. This was her most iconic role in Telugu films. The director uncovered a new facet of her sculpted stunning features—untouched, elusive and at the same time human enough to fall in love. This archetypal movie reached dizzying heights of success. The song '*Abbani teeyani debba*' was an instant chartbuster.

Akhari Poratam showed her as a CBI officer exposing unlawful activities, with Nagarjuna as the hero in the film. This presented her in a new light in a robust performance. She had come full circle, acting with both the father (ANR) and the son (Nagarjuna). Ram Gopal Verma featured her in *Govinda Govinda* along with Nagarjuna. The song '*Andhuma andhama*' was a befitting ode to her beauty and Sridevi's role was a heady mix of comedy and character in the film. She is the wildlife photographer who is scared of animals. The expressions and timing shown by her in the film stand testimony to her immense talent. The interludes between the two protagonists provide light entertainment. The same director then cast her in a blockbuster,

Kshanam Kshanam, opposite Venkatesh. This became a cult classic and was one of the first road movies of Ram Gopal Verma. The film portrayed her as a chic modern girl, emoting fear and confusion, leading to a series of comic situations. Sridevi as a middle-class girl on a road trip with an unexpected companion (Venkatesh) gets into a fracas when chased by a bank robber and the police. The incidents that follow create a rib-tickling comedy while keeping alive the thread of suspense. She also sang the song '*Kingla kanipistunnadu*'. Her facile performance won her the Filmfare Best Actress Award. The star walked away with many honours, acting with the younger crop of actors like Arvind Swamy in the multi-lingual *Devaragam* (1996), which was her last South Indian film.

Sridevi has left an indelible mark on the Malayalam screen in memorable films like *Kumarasambhavam* and *Poombatta*. She shared screen space with greats like Sharada and Padmini and won the best child artiste award from the Kerala government for *Poombatta*. Malayalam filmmakers seized the opportunity to cast her in their films. The Kamal Haasan–Sridevi combination became a rage in *Satyavaan Savithri*. Her emotive prowess was witnessed in movies like *Vilkkanundu Swapnangal*, where she rubbed shoulders with Malayalam stalwarts like Mammootty and Sukumaram. *Aadhyapaadam*, *Aalinganam*, *Kuttavum Sikshaiyum* and *Aa Nimisham* directed by I.V. Sasi highlighted her comfort level in Malayalam cinema.

The actor's first brush with Hindi films came about with *Solva Sawaan*, which was nothing to write home about. But her favourite director, K. Raghevender Rao, roped her in for a master blaster, *Himmatwala*. Her re-debut announced her arrival in Bollywood with a bang (riding on the star power of the 'remake star' Jeetendra). But what really established her, as an actress was *Sadma*, a masterpiece nonpareil. There was no looking back for the star thereafter; she became the invincible queen of Bollywood. She inherited the crown from Rekha, another South Indian heart-throb. *Mr India* saw her scaling the summit (1987), followed by *Chandini* and *Chaalbaaz*. The superstar became a star luminary, trading tragedy, comedy and style with co-stars like Jeetendra, Rishi Kapoor, Anil Kapoor and Amitabh Bachchan. She had the opportunity of acting with the second-generation heroes like Sanjay Dutt, Salman Khan, Shah Rukh Khan and Akshay Kumar as well. The actor has been deservedly decorated with the nation's fourth highest civilian award, the Padma Shri.

Sridevi, had her share of ups and downs in the last decade of the twentieth century but there was a silver lining in the grey clouds in her personal life when she married Boney Kapoor. She bid adieu to stardust and settled down into family life. But once a star, always a star, and Sridevi set a record in the Hindi film industry as the only actress to make such a resounding come back with *English Vinglish*. She embraced success in her second innings, which no other come back star has ever done. The debonair diva (she is fifty years young, should we say) has been framed for posterity on the cover of the fashionista magazine *Vogue*. Some stars never fade...

30

Saritha

Her chubby face, dusky complexion and plump figure were hardly the right ingredients for the making of a star, yet this feisty girl went for a screen test and stood patiently, awaiting her turn. She was no. 162 in the queue for auditions under the lens of K. Balachander, the maven of Tamil cinema direction, when he was looking for a heroine for his film *Marocharithra* (1979). He saw the ember in her and decided that she would be the heroine, and sure she did—in twenty-three of his films! She was the blue-eyed girl of Tamil cinema, her colleagues' envy, and her pride in being a Balachander protégé. Perhaps this is the stuff dreams are made of...

Saritha's countenance did not have the glam measure that films required, but was a crucible for the gamut of human emotions that meaningful cinema is all about. She could inhabit the character she played and brought in a lived-in feel. Her performance had no trace of artifice. She cared not a bit for her screen presence of appearing beautiful; she had her head tonsured to play Sujatha, a cancer patient in one film and put on several kilos to look ungainly and become the hysterical

Julie Ganapati in another. Her fiery intensity on screen remains unmatched, Saritha made a tangible contribution in her brief sojourn in the film industry.

Reminiscing about her mentor, K. Balachander, she says, 'Every film of his that I have acted in has been a milestone in my career. KB is like a godfather. I grew up under his banner. I didn't know anything about acting, it was he who taught me the nuances.' Paradoxically, she attributes her success to her dark complexion and plump figure. 'Perhaps, if I looked glamorous, directors would have concentrated on my looks, more than on my performance.' She is glad that she was chosen only for performance-oriented roles with good scripts.

Marocharithra, her debut film with Kamal Haasan in 1978, was about a cross-cultural romance between the lead pair. The film became a blockbuster and another cult classic. Owing to its success in Andhra Pradesh, the film was released in the neighbouring states of Tamil Nadu and Karnataka. This film was listed among CNN-IBN's 100 greatest Indian films of all time in 2013.

In *Thappu Thalangal* (1978), which is again a Balachander movie, Saritha plays a prostitute in a whorehouse where she meets Rajinikanth who is a local thug, and the two of them bond over cough syrup. They decide to break free of their sinful ways and lead a sane life and the impediments they face make up the rest of the story. Saritha earned great appreciation for her superlative performance as Sarasu in this movie.

In Balachander's *Thaneer Thaneer* (1980), a gripping tale about a village's quest for water and their desperation to get it, she plays a pivotal role, subtly tempering love, anguish and despair. The film, at a superficial level, was about water, but metaphorically, it depicted the indifferent attitude of the authorities and the corruption that was rampantly prevalent. Saritha made an indelible impact. IBN Live included the film in its list of the 100 greatest Indian films of all time.

Vandichakkaram is a 1980 Tamil film starring Saritha and Sivakumar in the lead roles and it won both of them Filmfare Awards. *Agni Satchi* (1981) is the story of an oversensitive and neurotic character, Kannamma (Saritha), a poet who is in love with Arvindan (Sivakumar), a theatre director. Given their creative temperaments, love blossoms and they decide to get married. Kannama's parents hide the fact that she has a psychiatric problem. Her obsessions soon manifest, leading to a tumult in their relationships, particularly with his family members who goad him on to seek a divorce. But he does not abandon her because she is pregnant. He is very protective and seeks medical help. Saritha's performance in this film is ineffaceable and it won her the Tamil Nadu State Award for Best Actress.

In *Achamillai Achamillai* (1984), she plays the jilted wife of an honest man turned politician who gives into wiles and crime, and when he does not correct his ways, she kills him and surrenders. The story shows how politics can transform even the simple and virtuous to unholy ways. The actor's transition from a naïve, trusting girl to that of a virago who resorts to murder for a cause is brilliantly assayed and elicited appreciation from critics.

Her film *Mouna Geethangal* (1985) with Bhagyaraj went on to become a box-office hit. She plays his betrayed wife, and much as he tries to explain himself and seek forgiveness, she is unable to condone his infidelity. She chooses to live alone despite being pregnant and faces the trauma bravely.

Then followed Malayalam films like *P.C. 369*, *Kutettan*,

Deglamourized but meaty roles came her way

In Thaneer Thaneer, *a political satire*

Oru Kochukatha Aarum Parayatha Katha, Muhurtham Pathnonnu, Muppathinu Kathodu Kathoram. There were also Telugu and Kannada films, some of them remakes of her Tamil movies. She won four Filmfare Awards in Kannada movies for her unforgettable performances in films like *Kamana Billu, Chalisuva Modagalu, Hosa Belaku* (Filmfare Best Actress Award), *Keralidha Simha, Malaya Marutha, Eradu Rekhegalu, Mouna Geetha* (Filmfare Best Actress Award), *Mugila Mallige* (Filmfare Best Actress Award), *Thappa Thala* and *Bhakta Prahallada.* She received the Karnataka State Award for her performance with Sunder Raj in *Sankranthi.*

Julie Ganapathi (2003) is a remake of the American film *Misery.* Julie (Saritha) is a huge fan of a popular television show and begins to identify herself with the protagonist. The author of the series, Jayaram, is on his way back home after completing his work, when his vehicle meets with an accident and he is seriously injured. Julie rescues the author and takes him home. Slowly, he realizes that she is psychotic; she compels him to change the script to suit her judgment. Her hospitality turns into a trap where he is almost abducted and not allowed to leave the place. Saritha was sans make-up in this film and also gained weight to suit her image of an abnormal woman. Though the movie was not a big hit, the film was appreciated for her impressive and engaging performance.

The spirited star had yet another facet to her, she was a much sought after multi-lingual dubbing artiste. She would act during the day and dub for other heroines at night. She found it challenging and did it with a passion. Even at the peak of her career, she made time for dubbing. Saritha has lent her voice for heroines in Tamil, Telugu and Kannada. Jyothika, Soundarya, Nagma and Sushmita Sen sported her voice. Vijayashanthi was one star who would insist on Saritha's voice for her films.

Saritha says, 'I would watch bad films to find out why they didn't go well with the audience. Looking back, I'm very happy and thankful to the directors to have come up with powerful women-centric scripts for me.' After 140 films in which she walked away with substantial roles, she took a break between 1979 and 1989. The break was meant for her personal life, marriage and children. At fifty-four, the versatile actress is now set for a second innings in her career. Only this time, she has taken to the small screen. She has enjoyed playing the role of Thamarai in the serial *Selvi*, a family drama made by the veteran Raadhika, which was well received.

Six Filmfare Awards (four in Kannada and two in Tamil) between 1980 and 1989; one Nandi Award for the Telugu film *Kokilamma*; four awards as the best dubbing artist for the films, *Ammoru, Maavichiguru, Ayana Bangaram* and *Anthapuram*; the Kalaimamani Award from the Tamil Nadu government; three Best Actress Awards from the state for her films, *Oru Vellaadu Vengaiyagiradhu* and *Poo Pootha Nandavanam* and one award from Karnataka, is a testimony of her calibre as an actress.

31

Vijayashanti

Vijayashanti walked into the annals of South Indian cinema, illuminating the silver screen with her unconventional charm and beauty, rewriting the code of courage for women and inspiring millions of women to follow suit. She candidly admits that some of her bold roles transformed her from a shy introvert to a spunky woman.

Vijayashanti was christened Vijaya by her aunt Vijaya Lalitha. Her illustrious career spanning twenty-eight years began in 1979, at the tender age of thirteen, with a cameo role in the Tamil film *Kallukkul Eeram*, with Bharathiraja in the lead. Simultaneously, she made her debut in Telugu opposite Krishna in *Kilaadi Krishnudu*. The famous actor-director Vijay Nirmala handpicked the 'lovely-looking girl' to act opposite the leading hero, Krishna. Another cameo role of a sister came her way in the multi-starrer *Satyam-Shivam* (1981), with the legendary heroes of Telugu cinema, NTR and ANR. This role captured maximum attention and heralded the arrival of Vijayashanti as a budding star. She began to concentrate more on Telugu films as offers came pouring in, asking her to play the lead. She shifted from Tamil films to Telugu ones. Her most memorable performance in Tamil was her role in *Mannan* opposite the superstar Rajinikanth. Ace actor Sivaji Ganesan commended her role of an arrogant industrialist in this film.

Her pathbreaking roles commenced with *Neti Bharatam* (1983). The lead pair Suman and Vijayashanti brought their characters to life on the screen. It is a story of a gangraped girl fighting for her identity. The actress beautifully brought to the fore the character's anguish and her determination to overcome the situation. The film went on to win several awards. This bold theme projected Vijayashanti in a new light and it became a turning point in her acting career. There was no looking back for her after this film. She weaned herself away from the glamour doll image and began to accept meaningful performance-oriented portrayals.

Movies in 1985 like *Vande Mataram* and *Pratighatana* reinforced her acting flair. In the former, she enjoyed a broader canvas to showcase her acting skills. In the first half, she plays the very essence of feminity as Indira, and in the latter half, she metamorphoses into a tigress that tames lions, a woman who puts the thunder of fear in the villains. In this role, she proved to her critics that she had not forgotten the feminine side of her persona. She also serves up a heavy dose of patriotism, which gradually came to be her trademark.

Similarly, she played an extraordinary role in *Pratighatana*, as the protagonist teacher who creates a new roadmap to mould young minds. She also takes on the mantle of redeeming society by opposing certain anti-social elements. For the first time, a Telugu film gave more importance to the leading lady rather than the male lead. Vijayashanti excelled in this role, infusing vibrant life into it. Telugu cinema was turning towards more women-centric roles and message-oriented stories around this time. These films brought her not only name and fame but also served to inspire several women and youth audiences. She won the Filmfare Best Actress Award (Telugu) while the state government bestowed the Nandi Award for Best Actress on her for this film.

Karthavyam (1990) was her first movie from her own production house, Surya, aimed at showing women as the main protagonists. To quote her, 'In most films, women were used only to lend glamour. Six songs and a few sleazy scenes and that's all. We were never tested or allowed to show our talent. That's the reason I launched my own banner, Surya Movies, to make movies with woman as the protagonist.' She produced a film on the life of Kiran Bedi, the first woman police officer. Vijayashanti played the lead role of a cop. She looked and played the character without any training. She once mentioned in an interview, 'I never learnt any karate or gymnastics but I had to mentally prepare myself to do the odd fights and stunts.' The powerful dialogues and the action-packed story were a box-office grosser and a trendsetter in its time. *Vyjayanthi IPS* became a household name with every young girl wanting to become a police officer. The *muhurat* clap for this movie was given by none other than Kiran Bedi herself, who praised Vijayashanti for her lifelike portrayal. This movie was made in four languages and it was a success story across the regions. Her soaring fame gave jitters to several male leads of the time. She could carry the complete movie on her shoulders, a feat that had been a male prerogative until then in filmmaking. Every director wanted to cast her in similar roles with at least four fight sequences. Following *Karthavyam,* Vijayashanti became the highest paid superstar, demanding almost one crore for a film. Vijayashanti

Astute actor

In Karthavyam, *an inspiring performance*

won the National Film Award for Best Actress and the Nandi Award for Best Actress for her performance in this film.

This adventurous lady performed action sequences without duplicates, a feat unheard of those days when even heroes used body doubles! She could climb walls that were several feet high and could jump down dangerous waterfalls. She enjoyed quite a superwoman image in her heyday, capturing the imagination of every young girl. Her grit became synonymous with her persona. Her larger-than-life portrayals not only got her a huge fan following but also served to transform her personality. Such was the impact of her stardom that she was once featured along with Amitabh Bachchan on the cover page of a reputed magazine as the highest paid star. Even the popular male stars were not paid that kind of remuneration. Vijayashanti became the envy of most of the film fraternity of her time. It is not surprising that she could earn such a reputation due to her screen image. Going back in time, if one were to see these films, they have the same effect even now, more so in the twenty-first century when women live their lives in extreme danger. Bravery has seen many faces—one of them is Vijayashanti.

She was never stereotyped in action formula films. In every one of her movies, she has worn a different character's mask. Though all her roles were, in a way, a fight for justice, she has done it in varying styles. The film *Police Lockup* was made in Telugu and Tamil and it was another of Vijayashanti's actions films, sans uniform. Her dual role shows her playing a simple housewife of a cop and a CBI officer. She gives a very good account of herself in both the roles. The fight against the villains is à la Robin Hood and Tarzan style. This laudable performance earned her another Filmfare Best Actress Award.

The 1997 starrer *Osey Ramalumma* topped off her climb to

the summit. Vijayashanti was assigned the plum role of a lifetime and the name Ramalumma became like a second skin of her identity. With this film, she earned the love and admiration of the people of Telangana. The story was based on a woman rebel of the region and Vijayashanti and Dasari Narayana Rao were cast in the lead. A landlord rapes the protagonist and she rebels against the system and kills him, taking the help of Komranna (Dasari Narayana Rao). Shunning her police image, Vijayashanti breathed fiery life into the character of a tribal girl. She showcased all her talent and displayed all the emotions ranging from naivete to anger on the screen. With one stroke, the star had wiped out the public memory of her in the role of a police officer and etched the tribal girl's fury and her thirst for revenge on people's minds instead. Yet again, she managed to instill courage and the fighting spirit in women and the socially downtrodden. The blockbuster set a record as the most-viewed film ever, in the history of Telugu cinema. Vijayashanti went on to scale further dizzying heights of fame with this movie. She won the prestigious Nandi Award for the second time. She also won the Best Actress Award.

She was conferred the Filmfare Lifetime Achievement Award (2003) for her yeoman service to the film industry at a young age, when she was still in her early thirties! But she had completed nearly three decades as an accomplished actress, earning titles like 'Lady Amitabh' and 'Jackie Chan' for her prowess in martial arts and fight sequences. She was certainly a 'man' in a woman's world and she accepted the award with grace and dignity.

After taking an eight-year break, the great actress donned the pancake once more, to face the camera for the last time in *Nayudumma*. In this farewell film, she continued her signature theme opposing corruption, injustice and lawlessness. The mother and daughter role enacted by her was extremely memorable and it became her swan song. The curtains came down on her reel life and she embarked full-time on a political career, trying to realize the idealism she had essayed all along on the silver screen. 'I never aspired to become a politician. It just came my way. For, the other side of the coin is politics in our industry,' the star claims. Vijayashanti strives to champion the cause of the have-nots and is struggling to be accepted as a leader in a male-dominated field. But her charisma as a no-nonsense person has stayed with her throughout. Vijayashanti is one of the most feisty stars of South Indian cinema to have made it large both on and off screen...

32

Suhasini

Exuding effervescence and exuberance with a streak of distinctiveness that stems from her pedigree, oodles of buoyancy preceding her both in her reel and real life, Suhasini is a scion of the Hasan family synonymous with cinema. Her father is the illustrious Charuhasan, a lawyer turned actor, producer and director, and her paternal uncle is none other than Kamal Haasan, an icon who needs no introduction to film enthusiasts.

Suhasini was the first girl to have joined the film institute to do a course in filmatography. Ashok Kumar, a famous filmatographer, insisted that she join him as his assistant to practically learn the art and technique from behind the camera. Meanwhile, Dame Luck had chartered a different path for her, and she had a film offer coming her way. She made her film debut in 1980 with the Tamil film, *Nenjathai Killathe*, for which she won the Tamil Nadu State Award for Best Actress. She brought with her a new genre in acting, breathing in a fresh air of spontaneity and realism into the otherwise dramatic milieu, in her role as Viji. Before she could realize the whirl she found herself in, the success of the film swung her to stardom and then there was no looking back. She had found her calling. When Suhasini began to get film offers, she made an effort and learnt Telugu, Kannada and Malayalam. Ironically, despite her mother tongue being Tamil, and her background, she gained huge popularity in her Telugu and Kannada films.

In the Telugu film industry, she did about a hundred movies, many of them becoming box-office hits. She did a number of films with Chiranjeevi and Shobhan Babu. *Swati* with Bhanuchander got her the Best Actress Award. *Manchu Palliki* in Telugu (remade in Tamil as *Palaivana Cholai*) is the story of a girl who befriends four boys, wins their love and affection, but does not reveal to them that she has a heart ailment and dies an untimely death. A very poignant story, the film won rave reviews for her brilliant acting.

In *Mangamma Gari Manavadu*, Suhasini rocks as the ebullient Malli, along with the doyen Bhanumathi, and the movie created box-office history. In *Chantabbai*, a classic comedy, her role as Jwala was praiseworthy. *Bhavamaradalu* was another hit, with Shoban Babu and Raadhika, where Suhasini excelled as the possessive mother and wife, displaying perfect emotions. *Sravana Sandhya* presents her as a woman seeking a vendetta for the injustice done to her. It is remarkable that the actor could carve a niche for herself in the multi-star cast era with many leading ladies for competition, including the likes of Raadhika, Vijayashanti and Sridevi. The star was unforgettable as Jennifer, the school teacher reforming the protagonist (Chiranjeevi) in *Aaradhana*. She donned the black coat and played the lawyer to the hilt in *Maharaju*, opposite Shobhan Babu. The Best Supporting Actress Award was conferred on her for *Sirivennela*, directed by the veteran K. Viswanath, in which she plays the role of Subhashini, a mute painter.This was her defining moment in Telugu films. The movie revolves around her love for and devotion to Pandit Hari Prasad (Sarvadaman Banerjee) who plays a blind flautist.

Illalu Priyuralu is a Telugu adaptation of the famous Hindi film *Masoom*, and Suhasini plays the wife and mother of two children who is taken unawares when she hears of her husband's infidelity and his child born of the other woman in his life. She does full justice to the role, winning critical acclaim.

In *Akka Mogudu*, she is the lovable Ganga, whose antics are heartwarming. She progressed to taking on senior roles, playing mother roles in *Varudu*, *Leader* and *Pedda Babu*, a responsible collector in *Minugurulu* and an IPS officer in *Rakhi*.

Her Kannada films with Vishnuvardhan were big hits. *Bandhana*, a film based on the story of unrequited love and marital discord, was hugely successful because of the brilliant and sensitive performance of Suhasini. *Suprabhatha*, starring Suhasini and Vishnuvardhan, was another runaway hit consolidating her position in the Kannada film circuit. *Maathaadu Maathaadu Mallige* is an awakening film, giving a clarion call to villagers and farmers, since it deals with the subject of illegal exploitation of agricultural lands in the name of urbanization. Suhasini as the protagonist's wife and tough mother of three children, embodies the character of a busy rural housewife with a deep conviction of the value of her folk customs. The film won her much adulation.

Muttina Haara (String of Pearls) is a film set in the 1940s–60s, where she plays an army nurse. It is a heartrending story of the horrors of war. The movie won a National Award in the regional segment and Suhasini earned great appreciation for her performancc. *Bcnkiyalli Aralidha Hoovu* was a remake of Balachander's *Aval Oru Thodar Kathai* and the actor gave a scintillating performance, sweeping away a few awards. Her successful run continued with *Amruthavarshini*, an insightful movie that delves into the psyche of the male protagonist Ramesh who falls in love with a married lady. Suhasini's subtle performance as a woman caught in weird circumstances justifies the Best Actress Award she received. Her talent for comedy came through in *Eradaneya Maduve*, where she teams up with actor Ananth Nag, and made the film a box-office hit.

Her sojourn in Malayalam films has been evenly rewarding; she did full justice to some fabulous roles and thoroughly enjoyed the limelight. *Koodevide* (Where's the Nest) is a 1983 film, where Suhasini plays Alice, a teacher at a boarding school in Ooty. In a bizarre development, a student kills another student and an emotional drama unfolds. The film won several State Awards and was selected for the Indian Panorama. Suhasini won critical acclaim for her role in this film.

She plays the powerful role of Subhadra in *Vanaprastham*,as the female lead to Mohanlal who is a Kathakali dancer from a lower caste. Subhadra happens to see him enact Arjuna's character from the Mahabharata, and overruling the caste barrier, she begets his child, only to reject him later as she realizes she only loved the character he played and not him as a person. The consequences of this act and the trauma that the male lead undergoes leads to a startling denouement.

The film was nominated for the Grand Jury Prize. It was screened in the 1999 Cannes Film Festival. IBN Live ranked the film at number nine in its list of greatest Indian films.

Suhasini began her career with a significant Tamil movie, won instant recognition, then sashayed into Telugu, Kannada and Malayalam, until she had some good roles beckoning her back to Tamil. Her comeback Tamil film, *Sindhu Bhairavi*,

In Nejathai Killathey... *fresh and innocent*

In Sindhu Bhairavi, *a stellar performance*

In a courtroom scene

directed by the genius K. Balachander, remains a huge sensation even today among film buffs. In this movie, Suhasini plays Sindhu, an abandoned daughter who moves on with life confidently, until she meets a Carnatic musician and then comes the twists which change both their lives. She bears his child and gifts the baby to the childless couple, ultimately to withdraw from their life. Her virtuoso performance got her the National Film Award for Best Actress in 1986.

She attributes her stupendous success to the good fortune of having seasoned directors introducing her—Mahendran in Tamil, K. Balachander in Kannada, Bharathiraja in Telugu and Padmarajan in Malayalam.

In 2013, Suhasini played the iconic role of Komalathammal, Ramanujan's mother, in the biopic made on the mathematical genius Ramanujan who journeyed from Kumbakonam to Cambridge. The film was simultaneously shot in Tamil and English. The role was very challenging since it also has negative shades, and she is an unusual mother, being ambitious. She is so proud and excited that she has been chosen for this plum role and being an Iyengar herself, she loves to sport the role bringing in her identity and her native charm to the performance. 'It is amazing to enact and portray the tradition, values and knowledge of this community today. It feels like magic,' says Suhasini.

Suhasini is seen in a huge number of advertisements and TV shows, all very successful; there's no questioning her versatility! Her directorial venture *Indira* with her cousin Anu Haasan and Arvind Swamy was a noteworthy film based on caste-related issues set in a rural backdrop. Her slick direction and realistic approach merited great appreciation. She has also directed teleserials like *Penn* in Tamil. She has written the screenplay for a number of movies, which include her directorial debut *Indira* as also one of the most successful Bollywood films of 2008, *Guru*.

Suhasini married ace film director Mani Ratnam in 1988; he is her friend, philosopher and guide for life. Given the family gene pool of talent, she swam through the straits of cinema with relative ease. She is truly one of a kind in the cinematic medium, someone who can claim to have donned several caps, including those of a camerawoman, scriptwriter, director-producer-actor (both on the small and big screen), TV host and a sought-after motivational speaker at management institutes.

This articulate and savvy lady hopes to be a part of movements that involve society, conservation, women and arts. She has the zest to live long, armed with the wisdom she has gleaned over a period of thirty-three years spent in the film industry. She has enough reason to rejoice and savour her glorious hours on and off screen.

33

Revathi

Brimstone when the arclights are turned on, her unpretentious face lights upon her petite figure, bringing the character to life. Hailed as the Shabana Azmi of the South, Revathi is known for her intense and impeccable rendition of roles in discreet and nuanced performances. She is one of those rare actors, in a class of her own, not cast for the glamour factor alone, but an instant choice for an emotionally compelling role.

A quirk of destiny drew her into the world of films, when one of her group photographs taken at a school fashion parade caught the eye of famous director Bharathiraja. He had her traced and voila! Asha Kelunni was rechristened Revathi for her debut in Tamil cinema. *Manvasanai* (1983) is a love story where she played a small town girl. She made her presence felt and soon found herself acting in several Tamil, Telugu and Malayalam films.

The year 1986 saw her act in Mani Ratnam's *Mouna Ragam*, which was her tour de force. The apparently simple film that starts on a banal note of a middle-class family with a girl-meets-boy love story formula, and then moves on to an unpredictable turn with the boy's accidental death and the impact on the girl, which disturbs her emotionally. The family, unaware of the events, coerces her into an arranged marriage. Despite the husband's unconditional love for her, she remains estranged within the confines of her new home and seeks a divorce. The treatment of the theme is very sophisticated and Revathi delivers a sensitive performance as a bold girl who challenges the institution of marriage to break away from a binding relationship and live on her own terms.

Kattathe Kilikkoodu gave her a foothold in Malayalam cinema. She won the Best Actress Award for *Kakkothikkavile Appooppan Thaadikal* in 1987, a heroine-centric film. Revathi and Ambica are sisters and Revathi, who is kidnapped as a child, reunites with her sister much later, as a gypsy girl. The film went on to become a sleeper hit.

Revathi moved on to the league of heroine-oriented films; *Priyanka* was a fine example, a Tamil adaptation of Raj Kumar Santoshi's *Damini*. In this film, she takes on the title role of Priyanka, going through a bizarre sequence of events, where she witnesses her domestic help being molested by her brother-in-law and his friends and drags him to court, facing the ire of the family. The actress won great appreciation for her performance and also the Filmfare Best Actress Award.

In the Malayalam film *Gramophone*, she has played the role of Sarah, an old Jewish woman of Cochin. The role has great scope for emotional poignancy and she does it full justice. The film is shot in the backdrop of the small Jewish minority community living in Cochin.

Ankuram (The Seedling) is a Telugu film with Revathi in the lead role, playing a middle-class newly married young woman caught in the strange situation of trying to return an abandoned child to his father, and the story unfolds against the backdrop of issues like social stigma and Naxalism. The film conveys the message that educated citizens have a social responsibility towards their fellow citizens and Revathi played the role with amazing conviction.

Thevar Magan is the story of a sophisticated America-returned son of a village chieftain and the serious feud between the paternal brothers leading up to a tragic denouement. Revathi makes an impact as a rustic girl who is overwhelmed by the condescension of the hero (played by Kamal Haasan) who reluctantly marries her to stand by his word. Her song *'Inji idduppazha'* is one of the highlights of the movie. *Idu Saadhya* is a 1989 Kannada film in which Revathi created a world record—this is the first film to be shot within a span of forty-eight hours.

The range of roles and themes that have come her way is ample proof of her versatility and potential as an actor. In *Anjali*, Revathi plays the mother of a terminally ill, mentally disabled child, conveying the emotional trauma it means for the family. The film was dubbed into Hindi and Telugu and released under the same name. *Anjali* won three National Film Awards and was chosen as India's official entry to the Oscars in 1991. *Marupadiyum* is an adaptation of the highly acclaimed Hindi film *Arth*. The story is about a filmmaker who has an extramarital affair with an actress and decides to leave his wife. Revathi plays the wife who battles the trauma of infidelity and finds her identity to resume life as an individual. This film, too, won her the Best Actress Award.

After her glorious innings as a heroine, she gracefully moved on to roles befitting her age and later, ventured to direct. In her directorial debut in 2002, Revathi has brilliantly captured

Revathi in a dramatic scene

Prabhu and Revathi—easy rapport

With Mohan in Udaya Geetham

the lives of the innumerable women who live for their family and are emotionally impoverished in their twilight years, when the fledglings take flight and don't look back. *Mitr, My Friend* revolves around an Indian family settled in the US for eighteen years. The protagonists are Prithvi, born and raised in America and Lakshmi (played by Shobana), the girl he marries, who is from a small town in India. The initial euphoria lasts for a while, but when their daughter grows older, cultural differences emerge between mother and daughter. The mother realizes that she has almost lost her identity, having lived only for her husband and daughter all these years. She resolves to live for herself from then on. The film is an unusual, made as it was in the Indian English genre, and it got Revathi the Best Regional Film (English) at the National Awards. *Phir Milenge* (We'll Meet Again) is another Bollywood venture directed by her, a unique film that touched upon the subject of AIDS. It is about a girl working in an advertising agency who has a premarital affair. When her sister meets with an accident, the protagonist decides to donate blood, but is shocked to find that she is HIV-positive. Given the stigma of the disease in the Indian cultural context, she loses her job. Angered by her unfair dismissal, she searches for a lawyer to fight her case. The film won several awards. Revathi enthusiastically returned to acting in *Molly Aunty Rocks,* which narrates the story of a middle-aged woman who has lived in the US for twenty years and then comes back to India to save her bank job. The cultural differences Molly (Revathi) is confronted with and her relationship with her in-laws and her daughters form the crux of the story and the star actor executes her role with absolute grace. The year 2014 promises to be eventful for this actor of substance with some good cinema slated for release. One of the films she is working on is *Margarita with a Straw* directed by the well-known Shonali Bose. She plays mother to Kalki Koechlin who enacts the role of a girl suffering from cerebral palsy. To do justice to the role, Revathi has been visiting patients to understand the psychological implications of the ailment; such is her dedication to her work. No wonder Revathi is known to be an actor who lives the role and brings a rare kind of intensity to every depiction. Yet another much-hyped film that released in 2014 is an adaptation of the Chetan Bhagat novel, *Two States*. She plays the heroine's mother, a conservative South Indian woman. The film narrates a campus love story that blossoms between a North Indian boy and a South Indian girl and how they battle the family differences that invariably follow.

Unlike most other actresses, Revathi is a sports enthusiast, given the army background that she grew up in. She has participated in many car rallies in India. She dislikes being branded as a feminist. She is the latest woman director to join the bandwagon of those espousing the problems of family relationships and women's issues.

Revathi has come a long way professionally, as an actor, director, successful and sought after TV hostess. In her personal life too, she believes in being socially responsible and using her popularity to do something for the society through NGOs, the most notable ones being the Banyan, the Ability Foundation and the Tanker Foundation. She can afford to bask in the glory of all the fame and honour she has accrued over the years; instead, she is still raring to go! And why not, when here's a woman who steadfastly believes she should live with a purpose, a Ulyssean drive, 'to strive, to seek, to find and never to yield'.

34

Nadiya Moidu

A star walks away from the arclights into the relative anonymity of domesticity, marriage, had the guts to say no to plum offers, bid adieu to the tinsel world at the zenith of fame, after a brief but eventful four-year romance with the silver screen...

Nadiya Moidu brought in a breath of fresh air into South Indian cinema and transformed the concept of the heroine in the 80s. She introduced a middle-class flavour, doing away with the image of woman playing second fiddle to her male counterparts. South Indian cinema, too, underwent a veritable change, making the middle-class protagonist fun, cool and outgoing. 'I don't know if I redefined any images, but I enjoyed playing all my roles as I have had a middle-class upbringing and values,' she confesses.

Zareena Moidu, known to filmdom as Nadiya Moidu, is a true-blue Mumbaikar. She is a native of Kerala who initially had only a working knowledge of Malayalam. This bubbly, vivacious actor is a product of a mixed lineage—a Hindu mother and a Muslim father, which ensured an eclectic upbringing.

Nadiya had never dreamt that she would, one day, blaze across the silver screen. It all began at a wedding where she had danced along with her sister and friends. A.M. Fazil, the famous moviemaker, chanced to see the wedding video and noticed her. He was looking for a new face for his film and decided he had found what he was looking for. He cast her in the film *Nokketha Doorathu Kannum Nattu* (1984). Nadiya made history with her debut film and thus began her journey in the tinsel world. In the film, Fazil presented her as the young Girly Matthew, with Padmini playing her grandmother. Nadiya gave a high-octane performance as a happy-go-lucky youngster eager to enjoy life before succumbing to a terminal illness. The protagonist succeeds in winning over her grandmother's love and at the same time, falling in love with the handsome neighbour (played by Mohanlal). 'I just had to be myself and Padmini Aunty and the crew were most supportive. The whole shoot felt like a cakewalk,' recollects the star. She further adds, 'It is an immense blessing. Because it takes that one film to make an actor into a star and for me it was my first.'

Her debut film won her awards galore, including the Filmfare Best Actress Award and the Critics Award for Best Actress. Fazil cast her again in the Tamil version, *Poove Poochudava* (1985). Padmini and Nadiya recreated the magic and the film was a box-office grosser. She did have a tough time mouthing the Tamil dialogues but nobody noticed that. The tunic-clad high-spirited heroine became a trendsetter for teenagers. Her style and clothes were emulated all over Tamil Nadu. Suddenly, every teenager was wearing Nadiya bangles, Nadiya sarees and the Nadiya *kondai*. But the actor remained cautious. 'The roles I played had scope for me to be very glamorous. But I always chose a girl-next-door effect. I was aware that my dressing style was being imitated by young girls, so I was extra careful about it.' The actor also mentions that she had personally chosen the accessories and clothes for both films. 'They were so inexpensive; it is a surprise that it became popular.' With the offers pouring in, she was forced to quit college and concentrate on her film career.

Meanwhile in real life, she had given her heart to a boy whom she met at a Christmas party. Yet she continued with her career. 'It suited me fine as my fiancé had gone abroad for higher studies.' She was based in Mumbai and her father would accompany her for all the shoots. 'I would fly home as soon as the schedule got over.' Her sister, Haseena, was her most stringent critic and her mother, Lalitha, was her sheet anchor. The sprightly star's traits invariably rubbed off onto the characters she played on screen. She was cautious with her choice of roles, giving weightage to the story rather than the star cast.

In Malayalam, she was paired with Mammootty and Mohanlal. Her easygoing girl-next-door charm helped garner a huge fan base among Malayalam audiences. Being choosy, she did only ten films but they were each an example of a wonderful story accompanied by excellent characterization. *Panchagni* was a superhit film with Mohanlal, Geeta and Nadiya in the cast. Nadiya plays the protagonist, Savitri, with Naxalism as the central theme of the film. It was a praiseworthy act. In the Joy Thomas film, *Shyama*, she plays the title role. This romantic genre film opposite Mammootty helped her find her niche. The subtle chemistry between Mammootty and Nadiya enhanced the storyline. In *Vannu Kandu Keezhadakki* (a remake of *Khubsoorat*), she plays the free-spirited girl who changes the strict atmosphere in her sister's home by challenging the matriarch,

Nadiya's trademark charm

With Sivaji in Anbulla Appa*,*
fluency in dramaturgy

Nadiya's debut in Poove Poochudava
with the legend Padmini that won her
instant recognition

Laxmi. She shared screen space with two doyens, Mohanlal and Mammootty, in *Kandu Kandarinju*. Here, Nadiya handled the mature role of Aswathy with aplomb. Her versatility as an actor grew immensely in Malayalam films.

In all her Tamil films, she was paired with the younger crop of actors like Suresh, Mohan, Prabhu, Satyaraj, Vijaykant and Ramki, the only exceptions being Sivaji and Rajinikanth. In *Uyire Unakkaga*, Nadiya was pitted against the seasoned Sujatha. She looked as much at home in demure sarees as she did in her characteristic 'cool' clothes. Nadiya's compatibility with Mohan resulted in a couple of good movies like *Paadu Nilave* and *Unakkaagave Vaazhgiren*. In *Nilave Malare*, she essayed a mature role as the mother of a baby, showing her immense love for the child. This role brought all her maternal instinct to the fore, belying her age. In *Mangai Oru Gangai* (1987), she is cast as a young girl full of enthusiasm and vigour. The song '*Kaalai thendran ethanai*' has her singing in the beautiful locales of Ooty. The director showcases her gorgeous looks in her signature modern clothes, wide belts, dangling earrings and long hair tied with a bow. She looks and acts the part of Nancy in the film. All the filmmakers were quick to put to good use Nadiya's youthful looks, her dress sense, her dancing skills and her vibrant persona in films like *Unakkaagave Vaazhgiren, iniya Uravu Poothathu, Poo Mazhai Poliyudhu*. There is also a song titled after her, '*Nadiya nile Nadiya*' set to music by the maestro, Ilayaraja.

The Suresh–Nadiya pair ushered in an era of youth in Tamil films. *Poove Ilam Poove* was one such movie with Nadiya and Suresh playing a romantic couple. The biggest advantage for her was that most of her roles were fashioned after her real persona. *Poo Mazhai Poliyudhu* (Nadiya–Vijayakanth) was an

R.D. Burman musical. The foot-tapping numbers and rhythmic movements of Nadiya made the film very popular. She was cast opposite Prabhu in the blockbuster *Chinna Thambi Periya Thambi*. Both Prabhu and Satyaraj woo her, and eventually, she marries Prabhu. This was a romantic comedy, which highlighted Nadiya's comic timing. The film that brought her critical acclaim was *Anbulla Appa* (1987). She plays Radha, the daughter of the legendary Sivaji Ganesan. This film dealt with the father–daughter relationship. Nadiya's body language and good acting matched Sivaji's histrionics and the duo scorched the screen. She matched Sivaji's versatility by just being her own sweet self. Her character displayed the right measure of possessiveness, caring and adoration. This movie was an important milestone in her career. *Rajadhi Raja*, a Rajinikanth–Nadiya starrer, was the one of the defining hits of 1988.

Just as her career peaked, the affable actor decided to leave behind stardust and tied the knot with Shirish Godbole (her long-time boyfriend). Nadiya flew over the Atlantic and settled down in the US with her investment banker husband. In 2007, the couple, with their two daughters Sanam and Jana, returned to India. Right away, she started receiving offers for roles in movies. But Nadiya was not too keen as she now had two growing daughters. The right opportunity came by way of a Tamil film, *M. Kumaran S/O Mahalakshmi*. This became her comeback vehicle. Nadiya redefined the mother role with this film. She is the new age woman who dares to end a bad marriage and be a single mother. She does not hesitate to encourage her son to bond with his father. The audience lapped it all up and Nadiya's comeback film made history.

She found another strong story in *Thamirabharani*, where she plays the protagonist, Shakuntala Devi, a headstrong and arrogant woman. She did justice to the role as a psychologist mentoring young schoolboys in *Pattalam*. Her Malayalam films like *Doubles*, *Sevens* (in the role of a police commissioner) and *Aaru Sundarimaarude Katha* saw her giving splendid performances. In *ASK*, she plays the character of Rose and performs alongside consummate actors like Zarina Wahab, Prathap Pothen and Naren. In Shyamaprasad's *English*, she is a global Malayali in the UK. She plays a realistic multi-dimensional character, Saraswati, who goes beyond the template. She did another glamorous mother role in the Telugu film *Mirchi*, followed by the box-office grossers *Attarintiki Daredi* and *Drushyam*.

Nadiya also had her share of popularity on the small screen as an anchor for *Jackpot* on Jaya TV. She has proved to her detractors that a middle-aged woman can start life anew and make a success of it. Her unerring fashion sense and her fighting fit body make her a young girl at forty. The heartwarming star's life mantra, though, continues to be—'Cinema is my passion but family is my priority'.

Bibliography

T.P. RAJALAKSHMI

Randor Guy (2008). 'Women on Top'. *Galatta Cinema* 1 (12): 80.

Mohan V. Ram (22 June 2011). 'The Rani of cinema'. *The Hindu*.

T.P. RAJAKUMARI

Randor Guy (23 October 2009). 'Blast from the Past: Katch Devayani 1941'. *The Hindu*. Retrieved 14 March 2010.

Guy, Randor (11 July 2008). 'Blast From the Past : Haridas 1944'.*The Hindu*. Retrieved 14 March 2010.

K.B. SUNDARAMBAL

Biography on Sangeetam.com at the Wayback Machine(archived 17 February 2005; http://ragasinfilmmusic.blogspot.in/2009/12/vaazhkai-enum-odam-poompuhar.html

http://entertainment.oneindia.in/celebs/k-b-sundarambal/biography.html

M.S. SUBBULAKSHMI

'MS Subbulakshmi. 'Nightingale' of Carnatic music'. *Rediff* (India). 12 December 2004.

Srivastava, Gauri (2006). *Women role models: some eminent women of contemporary India*. Concept Publishing Company. pp. 55–57. ISBN 978-81-8069-336-6. OCLC 74991412.

www.msstribute.org/

PASUPULETI KANNAMBA

http://www.totaltollywood.com/profiles/profiles.php?category=2&id=kannamba

'Ashok Kumar 1941'. *The Hindu* (Chennai, India). 25 January 2008.
'Harishchandra 1944'. *The Hindu* (Chennai, India). 3 July 2009.

BHANUMATHI RAMAKRISHNA
'Telugu Cinema Etc - Idlebrain.com'.
http://www.aptalkies.com/artistdetails.php?id=5024&title=Bhanumathi%20 Ramakrishna
http://www.southindia.com/banu.htm

ANJALI DEVI
http://www.youtube.com/watch?v=LP-ztnm1qCQ
http://www.youtube.com/watch?v=RmYXBSjT4Ak

VYJAYANTHIMALA
Randor Guy (26 March 2011). 'Vanjikottai Vaaliban 1958'. *The Hindu*. Retrieved 20 January 2012.
Dinesh Raheja (7 February 2002). 'An eternal love story: Devdas'. *Rediff.* Retrieved 12 May 2011.
'Devdas'. Upperstall.com. Retrieved 20 March 2011.
Randor Guy (21 December 2009). 'Blast from the past: Kanavaney Kankanda Deivam'. *The Hindu* (Chennai, India). Retrieved 27 March 2011.
http://www.hindu.com/mp/2010/03/06/stories/2010030653051100.htm (vyjantimala)

SAVITRI
'Star and a versatile actor'. Chennai, India: *The Hindu*. 15 August 2003. Retrieved 11 July 2011.
https://www.google.co.in/webhp?sourceid=chrome-instant&ion=1&espv=2&ie=UTF-8 https://www.facebook.com/pages/Mahanati-Savitri/
Telugu Cinema Celebrity Bio Data - Savitri - Idlebrain.com

PADMINI
'Friday Review Chennai : Beauty, charm, charisma'. Chennai, India: The Hindu. 2006-09-29. Retrieved 2011-06-07.
'Beauty, charm, charisma'. Chennai, India: *The Hindu*. 29 September
http://dancingqueenpadmini.wordpress.com/category/articles-on-padmini/

B. SAROJA DEVI
http://articles.timesofindia.indiatimes.com/2013-05-05/news-

interviews/39042239_1_film-industry-saroja-devi-indian-cinema
http://spicyonion.com/actress/saroja-devi-biography/
http://www.hindustantimes.com/News-Feed/Entertainment/The-sweet-bird-of-Southern-cinema/Article1-335942.aspx
http://www.thesundayindian.com/en/story/starring-mgr-jayalalitha/7148/
http://www.kalyanamalaimagazine.com/Content/Thiraichuvai/Nov_1_15/Potpourri_of_titbits_about_Tamil_cinema_Sarojadevi.html
http://www.goldentamilcinema.net/index.php/sarojadevi/articles-2/21-saroja-devi-a-kannada-queen-who-ruled-in-4-languages
http://www.goldentamilcinema.net/index.php/sarojadevi/4-dr-sarojadevi
http://www.youtube.com/results?search_query=clips+of+saroja+devi%27s+life&oq=clips+of+saroja+devi%27s+life&gs_l=youtube.3...2113.18609.0.18704.31.27.2.2.2.0.104.1984.26j1.27.0...0.0...1ac.1.11.youtube.hugfyvQBXQI
http://www.hindu.com/fr/2007/07/13/stories/2007071350330100.htm

VIJAYA NIRMALA
http://www.telugumovietalkies.com/vijaya-nirmala-profile/
http://www.imdb.com/name/nm0632560/bio
http://www.thehindu.com/features/cinema/they-call-the-shots/article2969786.ece
http://www.hindu.com/mp/2007/08/04/stories/2007080452250300.htm
http://www.thehindu.com/todays-paper/tp-features/tp-cinemaplus/looking-back-with-contentment/article4373727.ece
http://www.gulte.com/movienews/14947/Aged-Heroines-Half-Century-dreams
http://www.mtv.com/artists/vijaya-nirmala/biography/
http://www.imdb.com/name/nm0632560/filmoyear
http://www.imdb.com/name/nm0632560/bio
http://www.hindu.com/thehindu/mp/2002/04/30/stories/2002043000330203.htm
http://www.indiaglitz.com/channels/telugu/article/45175.html
http://www.indiaglitz.com/channels/telugu/article/91161.html
http://www.etrailblazers.com/index.php?option=com_content&view=article&id=70:vijaya-nirmala&catid=11:faces&Itemid=2
http://www.telugucolours.com/id2-pid468-chV/profile/vijaya-nirmala
http://www.cinema2cinema.com/cinema/BirthdayShow.aspx?stars.Name=Vijaya%20Nirmala
http://www.movieslist.in/actor-actress/vijaya-nirmala/films#.UckOu9gsZ0h
http://womenscollections.com/women-celebrities/238-other-celebrities/film-directors/1551-vijaya-nirmala-director

http://www.idlebrain.com/research/anal/threerecordholders.html
http://www.youtube.com/watch?v=tFjuhJvgB30
http://www.youtube.com/watch?v=h4Z-hDHuYT8
http://www.youtube.com/watch?v=IX1Zvkuh1PU
http://www.youtube.com/watch?v=LB9eR6pL8zc
http://www.youtube.com/watch?v=RuNctRREq30

JAMUNA
http://www.telugumovietalkies.com/jamuna-profile/
http://www.altiusdirectory.com/Entertainment/tollywood-actress-jamuna-biography.php
http://www.telugucolours.com/id2-pid336-chJ/profile/jamuna
http://www.thehindu.com/todays-paper/tp-features/tp-cinemaplus/doyens-of-yesteryears-take-a-break/article3875660.ece
http://www.hindu.com/fr/2007/09/14/stories/2007091451130400.htm
http://telugu.way2movies.com/interviewssingle_telugu/Actress-Jamuna-In-Open-Heart-With-RK-10-334983.html
http://www.telugucinema.com/c/publish/stars/jamuna.php
http://www.youtube.com/watch?v=cvvKux_S1d4
http://www.youtube.com/watch?v=xCjuxajX_Dc
http://www.youtube.com/watch?v=KY9FMz3vOA4
http://www.hybiz.tv/Jamuna--Actress/173600
http://www.dailymotion.com/video/xjwvkd_aa-okkaru-veteran-telugu-actress-jamuna-01_fun#.UcJ_dNgsZ0g
http://www.youtube.com/watch?v=Gi19Xrw1WUE
http://www.youtube.com/watch?v=g7Xd3fTb3Ng
http://www.bharatmovies.com/stars/jamuna-movies.htm

MANORAMA
http://www.absoluteastronomy.com/topics/Manorama
http://chennaionline.com/movies/star-track/20124728114750/Rejuvenated-Aachi-Manorama-returns-to-big-screen.col
http://www.hindu.com/mp/2008/07/05/stories/2008070550460400.htm
http://spicyonion.com/actress/manorama-biography/
http://entertainment.oneindia.in/tamil/news/2011/manorama-life-support-hospitalized-311011.html
http://www.thamarai.com/news-details/450713450/manorama-gets-back-to-acting.html
http://www.thehindu.com/features/cinema/acting-and-reacting/article451893.ece

http://www.thehindu.com/todays-paper/tp-features/tp-fridayreview/aachi-an-achiever-all-through/article2270998.ece
http://www.hindu.com/fr/2004/04/09/stories/2004040901460700.htm
http://www.hindu.com/thehindu/mp/2003/07/07/stories/2003070701340300.htm
http://hindu.com/thehindu/lf/2002/02/27/stories/2002022700840200.htm
http://www.hindu.com/2008/06/28/stories/2008062857110300.htm
http://www.hindu.com/thehindu/mp/2002/09/30/stories/2002093001070300.htm
http://www.thehindu.com/todays-paper/tp-national/tp-tamilnadu/kollywood-raises-a-toast-to-aachi-on-completing-50-years-in-
http://www.hindu.com/mp/2008/06/30/stories/2008063050380100.htm
http://www.nilacharal.com/enter/celeb/manorama.html
http://www.rediff.com/entertai/2001/jul/28mano.htm
http://www.bollywood.com/actress-manorama-was-bitter-about-bollywood-shunning-her-deepa-mehta
http://www.tamilspider.com/resources/5197-Profile-Biography-Manorama.aspx
http://www.youtube.com/watch?v=b25oYlCns80
http://www.youtube.com/watch?feature=endscreen&NR=1&v=n01xK1D7Va4

SOWCAR JANAKI
http://www.thehindu.com/todays-paper/tp-features/tp-cinemaplus/shine-on-sowcar/article2097301.ece
http://www.hindu.com/2006/12/25/stories/2006122502790200.htm
http://udhayamgold.wordpress.com/2011/05/30/needhi/
http://usharaja60.blogsplug.in/2010/02/03/sowcar-janaki-is-fluent-in-english/
http://ibnlive.in.com/newstopics/sowcar-janaki.html
http://www.hindu.com/fr/2006/12/29/stories/2006122900820200.htm
http://entertainment.oneindia.in/kannada/news/2012/actresses-bangalore-international-film-festival-102178.html
http://www.thehindu.com/todays-paper/tp-national/tp-karnataka/a-teen-mother-who-went-on-to-become-a-star/article2437769.ece
http://spicyonion.com/actress/sowcar-janaki-biography/
http://www.telugucolours.com/id2-pid337-chJ/profile/janaki
http://www.ebharat.in/profile/sowcar-janaki/biography
http://newindianexpress.com/entertainment/tamil/article547010.ece
http://www.prokerala.com/news/photos/senior-actress-shavukaru-janaki-

being-felicitated-52386.html
http://www.hindu.com/2006/12/20/stories/2006122019310200.htm
http://cinema.pluz.in/news/kollywood/45772/shavukar-janaki-is-back-with-vanavarayan-vallavarayan.htm
http://www.kalyanamalaimagazine.com/Content/Thiraichuvai/April11_16_30/Potpourri_of_titbits_about_Tamil_cinema_Sowcar_Janaki.html
http://www.tamilstar.com/news-id-sowcar-janaki-recollects-kamal-haasans-kind-gesture-as-she-is-back-to-movies-tamil-movies-tamil-actor-19-06-122411.htm
http://www.kollyinsider.com/2012/06/sowcar-janaki-to-act-after-15-years.html
http://www.youtube.com/watch?v=vMrj-tt0bDc
http://www.youtube.com/watch?v=ra9Vyw2KZT8
http://www.youtube.com/watch?v=pDppycUpnSA&feature=c4-overview&playnext=1&list=TLKoUuJzZS5_w

URVASHI SHARADA
http://indianscreenstars.blogspot.in/2012/06/sharada.html
http://www.telugumovietalkies.com/sharada-profile/
http://www.youtube.com/watch?v=Xr0-3F47_Bw
http://www.youtube.com/watch?v=_1vfBkYgqSU
http://www.youtube.com/watch?v=g0uS89W4Nm4

SHEELA
http://en.wikipedia.org/wiki/Sheela
http://www.hindu.com/fr/2005/05/27/stories/2005052702800400.htm
http://www.hindu.com/fr/2005/07/22/stories/2005072201530100.htm
http://entertainment.oneindia.in/malayalam/news/2008/sheela-cultural-award-031008.html
http://www.metromatinee.com/artist/Sheela-950
http://articles.timesofindia.indiatimes.com/2012-09-02/news-and-interviews/33548039_1_film-industry-congress-party-sir-cp
http://keralamax.com/movies/interview-with-sheela/
http://indianscreenstars.blogspot.in/2011/11/sheela.html
http://www.youtube.com/watch?v=CAPznoZ_2Z8
http://en.wikipedia.org/wiki/Filmfare_Award_for_Best_Actress_%E2%80%93_Malayalam
http://entertainment.oneindia.in/celebs/sheela-malayalam-actress/biography.html
http://www.hindu.com/2004/06/12/stories/2004061215180300.htm

http://www.hindu.com/mp/2005/08/27/stories/2005082702970200.htm
http://en.wikipedia.org/wiki/Kerala_State_Film_Award_for_Best_Actress
http://www.indiaglitz.com/channels/malayalam/article/37576.html
http://www.youtube.com/watch?v=Y6QFJVsXh_0&list=PL61D20FB6CAA53825&index=17
http://www.hindu.com/mp/2009/07/20/stories/2009072051190400.htm

K.R. VIJAYA
http://www.hindu.com/2006/07/06/stories/2006070616070200.htm
http://www.thehindu.com/features/cinema/screen-goddess/article2642189.ece
http://entertainment.oneindia.in/celebs/k-r-vijaya/biography.html
http://www.tamilspider.com/resources/6136-Profile-Biography-Tamil-Actress-K-R-Vijaya.aspx
http://indianscreenstars.blogspot.in/2012/07/krvijaya.html
http://www.cinevedika.in/news/Actress+K.R.+Vijaya+Filmography+++-+Part+02_videoKmSFbgaLezc.html#.UdfTLawsZ0g
http://www.dailymotion.com/video/xjj6hr_madhuram-madhuram-ee-samayam-south-indian-actress-k-r-vijaya_fun#.UdfU9KwsZ0g
http://spicyonion.com/actress/k-r-vijaya-biography/
http://matineestars.com/malayalam/actress/k-r-vijaya/
http://www.telugumovietalkies.com/kr-vijaya-profile/
http://udaycinema.com/krvijaya
http://www.indiaglitz.com/channels/kannada/article/46903.html
http://dev.metrixindia.com/indopia/person/3483/k-r-vijaya/
http://cris-iyer.iyers.info/2011/12/06/tale-of-2-heroines.html
http://www.youtube.com/watch?v=Oc3OK_a1aKk
http://www.aplatestnews.com/usnewsvideo.php?vidtype=2&idx=actress-kr-vijaya-filmography-tv5-part-06-2012-11-20
http://www.youtube.com/watch?v=wZndY00q-yg
http://www.youtube.com/watch?v=ZArOwtm81HA
http://www.youtube.com/watch?v=MWad_ZDwIkY
http://goodtimes.ndtv.com/PhotoDetail.aspx?Page=5&ID=6852&AlbumType=PG#talk
http://www.youtube.com/watch?v=75uPJdKuHPU

DR J. JAYALALITHAA
http://www.rediff.com/movies/report/slide-show-1-everything-you-wanted-to-jayalalithaa-the-actor/20131109.htm#1
http://en.wikipedia.org/wiki/Oru_Thaai_Makkal

http://www.youtube.com/watch?v=wfv9WvFhkBY
http://www.gomolo.com/celeb/shivaji-ganeshan-and-jayalalitha-movies-list/1151/6032
http://www.outlookindia.com/article.aspx?270858
http://www.dnaindia.com/india/1028237/report-in-school-her-name-was-komalavalli
http://web.archive.org/web/20090303212850/http://tn.gov.in/tnassembly/assembly2001/archives/jjaya.htm
http://economictimes.indiatimes.com/jayalalitha-to-debut-in-hindi-for-campaigns/articleshow/1872517.cms
http://www.rediff.com/election/2004/may/06espec1.htm
http://news.bbc.co.uk/2/hi/south_asia/4762593.stm
http://www.tn.gov.in/spc/cmprofile.html
http://archive.tehelka.com/story_main4.asp?filename=op073104The_Enigma.asp
http://www.sunday-guardian.com/investigation/sasikalas-proximity-to-jaya-was-based-on-control-a-rule
http://www.outlookindia.com/article.aspx?205450
http://zeenews.india.com/news/states/i-m-the-political-heir-of-mgr-jayalalitha_418718.html
http://hindu.com/2002/02/15/stories/2002021508750400.htm
http://news.outlookindia.com/items.aspx?artid=728743
http://www.ndtv.com/article/people/who-is-j-jayalalithaa-211841
http://www.imdb.com/name/nm0412883/bio
http://www.hindu.com/fline/fl1810/18100100.htm
http://www.thehindu.com/news/national/tamil-nadu/article2019520.ece
http://news.bbc.co.uk/2/hi/south_asia/2976142.stm
http://www.thehindu.com/news/article2021167.ece
http://www.indianexpress.com/news/jaya-expels-close-aide-sasikala-husband-from-aiadmk/889588/
http://dbsjeyaraj.com/dbsj/archives/2127
http://www.tollywood.info/actor/j/jayalalitha.htm
http://www.youtube.com/watch?v=P1r-P-0qqb8
http://www.youtube.com/watch?v=_f_trrmWcHc
http://www.youtube.com/watch?v=1Y5lBiaXaVY
http://www.youtube.com/watch?v=6EYgxjlUs_k
http://www.youtube.com/watch?v=KtBiYJpRwVk
http://www.youtube.com/watch?v=8UzAt7ejLZ0
http://www.youtube.com/watch?v=6zRllmqyf8k
http://www.youtube.com/watch?v=WXJ-l0nENXU

http: / / www.youtube.com / watch?v=76K9MeRTlhE
http: / / www.youtube.com / watch?v=ftM4uNQN1QI
http: / / www.youtube.com / watch?v=nOH4XPIXuvc

BHARATI VISHNUVARDHAN
http: / / reelbox.tv / actress / bharathi-vishnuvardhan-vishnuvardhan
http: / / snehaloka.org / dr-vishnuvardhan / bharathi-vishnuvardhan /
http: / / reelbox.tv / actress / bharathi-vishnuvardhan-vishnuvardhan
http: / / www.chitraloka.com / news / 2079-bharathi-vishnuvardhan-honored-doctorate.html
http: / / www.deccanherald.com / content / 9384 / we-dont-try-own-each.html
http: / / www.karnatakaspider.com / resources / 4062-Profile-Biography-Kannada-Actress-Bharathi.aspx
http: / / www.ebharat.in / profile / bharathi-vishnuvardhan / biography
http: / / www.imdb.com / name / nm0080247 /
http: / / www.youtube.com / watch?v=KAqE5MqSUnA
http: / / www.youtube.com / watch?v=JwzYl0IuD5g
http: / / www.youtube.com / watch?v=dJIf-rayi68
http: / / www.youtube.com / watch?v=BI7BO2lkUzY
http: / / www.youtube.com / watch?v=3sW-rHyn1OQ
http: / / www.cinemawale.com / bharathi
http: / / entertainment.oneindia.in / kannada / news / 2012 / interview-vishnuvardhan-with-us-bharathi-099500.html
http: / / entertainment.oneindia.in / celebs / bharathi-vishnuvardhan / biography.html
http: / / www.karnatakaspider.com / resources / 4062-Profile-Biography-Kannada-Actress-Bharathi.aspx
http: / / www.thehindu.com / todays-paper / tp-national / tp-karnataka / bharathi-is-a-picture-of-poise / article675634.ece
http: / / www.thehindu.com / features / cinema / the-journey-of-a-kannada-film-icon / article72725.ece
http: / / articles.timesofindia.indiatimes.com / 2009-12-30 / mysore / 28062321_1_vishnuvardhan-kannada-film-industry-abhinava-bhargava
http: / / www.indiaglitz.com / channels / kannada / article / 60738.html
http: / / www.thehindu.com / news / cities / bangalore / kannada-and-telugu-are-two-faces-of-the-same-coin / article2084072.ece

KANCHANA
http: / / www.thehindu.com / features / cinema / nothing-is-permanent /

article3790964.ece
http://www.hindu.com/fr/2006/03/10/stories/2006031002950300.htm
http://www.hindu.com/2007/09/27/stories/2007092761160600.htm
http://www.idlebrain.com/research/untold/untold_kanchana.html
http://www.cinegoer.net/telugu-cinema/interviews/interview-with-kanchana-260812.html
http://www.behindwoods.com/tamil-movie-news-1/mar-10-03/kanchana-16-03-10.html
http://www.supergoodmovies.com/32631/sandalwood/rise-fall-rise-of-kanchana-great-gesture-news-details
http://www.indiaglitz.com/channels/tamil/article/65918.html
http://www.telugumovietalkies.com/kanchana-profile/
http://www.youtube.com/watch?v=YbKjsa0zXto
http://www.youtube.com/watch?v=WenfM3dMgfo
http://www.youtube.com/watch?v=p5MPfftvjBc (gur)
http://www.youtube.com/watch?v=43lbMKgAlaE

VANISRI
http://www.hindu.com/fr/2007/10/12/stories/2007101250490400.htm
http://www.imdb.com/name/nm0889148/bio
http://www.telugumovietalkies.com/vanisri-profile/
http://www.telugucolours.com/id2-pid466-chV/profile/vanisri
http://telugumovie.co/vanisri-telugu-actress-biodata/
http://www.justtollywood.com/profiles.php?n=Vanisri&pid=00001809&t=3
http://www.orkut.com/Main#CommMsgs?tid=5325468252751497804&cmm=33181599&hl=en
http://www.myfirstshow.com/news/view/12980/Vanisri-celebrates-her-birthday-today.html
http://www.absoluteastronomy.com/topics/Vanisri
http://forumhub.com/indfilms/28205.15.28.44.html
http://www.cinegoer.net/telugu-cinema/news-archives/december-2010/vanisri-urges-the-current-crop-of-heroines-to-be-wise-191210.html
http://www.idlebrain.com/news/2000march20/chitchat-vanisri.html
http://www.bharatwaves.co.in/news/ANR-was-elevated-because-of-our-presence:-Vanisri-22379.html
http://satyamshot.wordpress.com/2009/11/14/a-filmfare-special-on-telugu-cinema-aug-76/
http://evergreenstarsimages.blogspot.in/2011/06/vanisri-or-ratna-kumari-born-3-august.html
http://www.youtube.com/watch?v=qKkcZMC3v0M

http://www.youtube.com/watch?v=iwU-r2CDx_Y
http://www.youtube.com/watch?v=FZVCa1IMFJA
http://cinevedika.blogspot.in/2012/08/special-story-on-veteran-tollywood.html

SUJATHA
http://entertainment.oneindia.in/celebs/sujatha-tamil-actress/biography.html
http://muthusamyr.hubpages.com/hub/Sujatha-the-Veteran-South-Indian-Actress-Passed-Away
http://live.iencyclopedia.org/2011/04/telegu-actor-sujatha-passes-away.html
http://entertainment.oneindia.in/celebs/sujatha-tamil-actress/biography.html
http://malayalamscinema.blogspot.com/2011/04/actress-sujatha-left-us-with-tears.html
http://www.tamilspider.com/resources/6728-biography-south-indian-tamil-actress-sujatha.aspx
http://www.facenfacts.com/NewsDetails/7611/multi-faceted-actress-sujatha-dies.htm
http://www.movieslist.in/actor-actress/sujatha/films#.Uey5AqwsZ0g (movies list)
http://www.omnilexica.com/?q=Sujatha+%28actress%29
http://www.tollywoodblog.in/2011/04/actress-sujatha-passed-away.html
http://www.galatta.com/tamil/news/actress-sujatha-is-no-more/48457/
http://www.galatta.com/tamil/news/tributes-paid-to-sujatha/48513/ (tribute) (q)
http://www.thehindu.com/news/actor-sujatha-dead/article1605990.ece (q)
http://www.indiaglitz.com/channels/tamil/events/26394.html
http://www.indiaglitz.com/channels/tamil/article/66002.html
http://www.hindu.com/cp/2011/04/10/stories/2011041050170800.htm
http://variety.com/2011/film/news/tamil-actress-sujatha-dies-1118035074/
http://www.heartcareguide.net/2011/04/08/Kollywood-actress-Sujatha-dies-of-heart-failure-Total-Filmy/?r=1
http://www.rediff.com/movies/slide-show/slide-show-1-south-remembering-sujatha/20110407.htm
http://www.allvoices.com/contributed-news/8709987-actress-sujatha-passes-away
http://worldfilm.about.com/od/bollywood/a/sujatha1952-2011.htm
http://lite.epaper.timesofindia.com/mobile.aspx?article=yes&pageid=28&edlabel=BGMIR&mydateHid=09-04-2011&pubname=&edname=&articleid=P

c02806&format=&publabel=MM

http://www.southdreamz.com/34443/popular-south-indian-film-star-sujatha-58-no-more/

http://www.chennailivenews.com/Entertainment/News/20113907063901/Actress-Sujatha-dead.aspx

http://grouchydays.blogspot.in/2011/04/rip-sujatha-mother-for-all.html (mother roles)

http://prayagas.blogspot.in/2011/04/veteran-actress-sujatha-is-no-more.html

http://www.youtube.com/watch?v=B4voO_SAbDk

http://www.youtube.com/watch?v=y-7JyDsqp8I

http://www.youtube.com/watch?v=vCAsj8-T9ug

http://www.youtube.com/watch?v=XLVX0H9waCg

http://www.youtube.com/watch?v=QH-Uas1NTp4

http://www.youtube.com/watch?v=UbyKJttT2dE (;)

http://www.youtube.com/watch?v=khLLOPp2zvc

http://www.youtube.com/watch?v=46Yf95Gjcw8

http://www.youtube.com/watch?v=fGZ3RqWK_0A

http://www.youtube.com/watch?v=YT3WARxP6vE

http://www.youtube.com/watch?v=plVGqYat88Y

http://www.youtube.com/watch?v=6ipt4wi3v-c

http://www.youtube.com/watch?v=jpnwCSy7_jI

http://www.youtube.com/watch?v=TGYAoPXidYc

http://www.youtube.com/watch?v=j0gdWpNskkQ

http://www.youtube.com/watch?v=MGTm-Coeu2M

http://www.youtube.com/watch?v=Y8xjVi5ONqA

http://www.youtube.com/watch?v=1tHOiSMeHLk

http://www.youtube.com/watch?v=RoHclm604Fo

LAKSHMI

http://www.hindu.com/fr/2009/01/23/stories/2009012350710100.htm

http://www.indiaeveryday.in/karnataka/fullnews-anant-nag-and-lakshmi-pair-up-in-gulmohar-1167-5411209.htm (l & n pair up)

http://www.imdb.com/name/nm0482285/bio

http://udaycinema.com/lakshmi (short bio)

http://spicyonion.com/actress/lakshmi-biography/

http://www.galatta.com/malayalam/news/lakshmi-says-no-to-chattakkari-remake/61743/ (gelata)

http://indianscreenstars.blogspot.in/2011/12/lakshmi.html

http://www.idlebrain.com/movie/archive/mr-murari.html

http://www.tollywood.info/actor/l/lakshmi.htm

http://www.imdb.com/name/nm0482285/filmoyear
http://www.imdb.com/name/nm0482285/filmogenre
http://www.supergoodmovies.com/22450/sandalwood/towering-actress-lakshmi-back-in-neena-naana-news-details
http://www.cinebasti.com/celebrity/Lakshmi-Narayan/8580/biography
http://www.veethi.com/india-people/lakshmi_narayan-profile-1499-14.htm
http://www.findbestbiography.com/s_n_lakshmi
http://pages.rediff.com/lakshmi-actress-/650778
http://www.omnilexica.com/?q=Laxmi+%28actress%29
http://www.womenscollections.com/actress/151-telugu-actress/telugu-actress-1960-1970/1597-lakshmi
http://entertainment.oneindia.in/celebs/lakshmi/biography.html
http://www.cinegoer.net/telugu-cinema/interviews/interview-with-lakshmi-080212.html
http://www.youtube.com/watch?v=Y6QFJVsXh_0&list=PL61D20FB6CAA53825&index=17
http://www.telugucinema.com/c/publish/movieretrospect/tatamanavadu1973.php
http://www.imdb.com/name/nm0820286/
http://www.movieslist.in/actor-actress/srividya/films#.Ukkta39v50g
http://en.msidb.org/displayProfile.php?category=actors&artist=Sreevidya&limit=210
http://imprintsonindianfilmscreen.blogspot.in/2011/06/srividya.html
http://www.hindu.com/2006/10/20/stories/2006102005201200.htm
http://www.thehindu.com/news/national/kerala/society-to-hand-over-actor-srividyas-assets-to-govt/article1497947.ece
http://oldmalayalamcinema.wordpress.com/2012/08/12/srividya-actor-singer-danseuse-and-beauty-that-defined-a-generation/
http://oldmalayalamcinema.wordpress.com/2011/10/19/remembering-srividya/
http://oldmalayalamcinema.wordpress.com/2012/08/12/kaalangalil-aval-vasantham-a-tribute-to-srividya/
http://oldmalayalamcinema.wordpress.com/tag/tribute-to-srividya/
http://www.sify.com/movies/kamal-srividya-romance-is-now-a-film-news-tamil-kkfsUiiajaa.html
http://www.rediff.com/movies/2006/oct/20srividya.htm
http://oldmalayalamcinema.wordpress.com/2012/08/12/srividya-my-favourites-from-malayalam-films-1/
http://www.bchindwoods.com/tamil-movie news/oct 06 03/20-10-06-sri-vidhya.html

http://oosi.blogspot.in/2006/11/actress-srividya-in-her-last-interview.html
http://www.thehindu.com/news/national/karnataka/state-government-to-withdraw-film-awards-for-201011/article4953420.ece
http://www.mayyam.com/talk/viewlite.php?t=4704
http://www.hindu.com/fr/2006/10/27/stories/2006102700190400.htm
https://www.youtube.com/watch?v=tB8Ys7AMuG4
http://www.tubetamil.eu/raj-tv/thiraialayam-koppiyam-actress-srividya-tragedy-story-1368820859-879090.html

JAYASUDHA
http://www.nilacharal.com/enter/interview/js.html
http://www.telugucinema.com/c/publish/stars/jayasudha.php
http://www.hindu.com/2008/10/15/stories/2008101555530400.htm
http://indianscreenstars.blogspot.in/2012/04/jayasudha.html
http://articles.timesofindia.indiatimes.com/keyword/jayasudha/featured/4
http://www.youtube.com/watch?v=HWMCr53PQEM
http://www.youtube.com/watch?v=n4OPlreFTno
http://www.youtube.com/watch?v=K1FMj4dajC0
http://www.youtube.com/watch?v=4O6KZYBc0es
http://www.youtube.com/watch?v=hF2OKvbZF0I
http://www.youtube.com/watch?v=skowSuuD55Y
http://www.youtube.com/watch?v=qrHGsQr8xYk
http://www.youtube.com/watch?v=DSD2m6gMUj4
http://www.youtube.com/watch?v=VB-R6s8cZfU
http://www.youtube.com/watch?v=36nLxSwkei4 (fav 5)
http://telugu.way2movies.com/videossingle_telugu/Interview-with-Jayasudha-on-Her-Journey-in-Tollywood-9-229471.html
http://www.dailymotion.com/video/xjifju_matrudevobhava-famous-south-indian-actress-jayasudha-02_fun (mother)

JAYA PRADA
http://www.hindu.com/mp/2004/01/17/stories/2004011700010100.htm
http://web.archive.org/web/20051122103054/http://www.tollywoodinfo.com/modules/wfsection/article.php?articleid=61
http://www.telegraphindia.com/1071029/asp/entertainment/story_8480555.asp
http://specials.rediff.com/movies/2006/jun/20slide4.html
http://www.smashits.com/news/bollywood/movie-talk/4925/mahima-small-is-beautiful-too.html
http://web.archive.org/web/20071113004151/http://www.deccanherald.

com/Content/Nov112007/enter20071110350O4.asp
http://articles.timesofindia.indiatimes.com/2002-05-24/news-interviews/27112058_1_jaya-prada-marathi-cinema-south-indian
http://web.archive.org/web/20050227183117/http://filmchamber.com/tmpl.asp?it=wrjaya
http://www.rediff.com/election/1999/aug/20jaya.htm
http://www.sify.com/news/jayaprada-issued-notice-for-violating-poll-code-news-national-je1mueecigj.html
http://ibnlive.in.com/news/azam-circulating-nude-posters-of-mine-jaya/92312-37.html
http://news.oneindia.in/2009/05/16/jayaprada-steals-the-show-wins-rampur.html
http://www.hindu.com/2010/02/03/stories/2010020356440100.htm
http://web.archive.org/web/20060114222742/http://rajyasabha.nic.in/kiosk/rsfinal3/whoswho/alpha_n2.html
http://articles.timesofindia.indiatimes.com/2008-09-24/news-interviews/27893695_1_politics-jayaprada-nuclear-deal
http://articles.timesofindia.indiatimes.com/2011-04-18/news-interviews/29428056_1_jaya-prada-rampur-lok-sabha-award
http://www.imdb.com/name/nm0419685/bio
http://lifestyle.iloveindia.com/lounge/jaya-prada-3183.html
http://www.cinebasti.com/celebrity/Jayaprada/8734/biography
http://www.hindu.com/mag/2008/04/13/stories/2008041350120500.htm
http://www.hindu.com/fr/2008/06/06/stories/2008060650670100.htm
http://www.thehindu.com/todays-paper/tp-features/tp-cinemaplus/looking-back-with-contentment/article4373727.ece
http://164.100.47.132/LssNew/Members/Biography.aspx?mpsno=4165
http://articles.timesofindia.indiatimes.com/2010-02-05/news-interviews/28141607_1_amarji-amar-singhji-samajwadi-party
http://indianscreenstars.blogspot.in/2012/07/jaya-prada.html
http://www.masala.com/11681-jaya-prada-returns-to-bollywood
http://www.telugumovietalkies.com/jayaprada-profile/
http://lifestyle.iloveindia.com/lounge/jaya-prada-3183.html
http://www.rediff.com/movies/slide-show/slide-show-1-south-interview-with-jaya-prada/20110905.htm
http://movies.ndtv.com/regional/special-passion-to-work-in-malayalam-films-jaya-prada-131535
http://www.bollywood501.com/classic_f/jaya_prada/interview.html
http://www.chitramala.in/intervicws/jaya-prada-110946.html
http://www.jamactors.com/jamactors/jayaprada.php

http://en.wikipedia.org/wiki/Andamaina_Anubhavam
http://www.yentha.com/news/view/4/Interview-Of-The-Week-Jaya-Prada-Bold-and-Beautiful
http://headlinestoday.intoday.in/programme/an-affair-to-remember-jaya-prada/1/261052.html
http://www.redtagz.com/avaara.com/video_cinema_detail.php?cat=13000&catid=1&subcatid=1&vidname=Face%20To%20Face%20With%20Actress%20Jayaprada
http://www.youtube.com/watch?v=gXyVzR-4vsw
http://www.youtube.com/watch?v=e_AM2FRyfmY
http://www.youtube.com/watch?v=egi0f5ckSnA
http://www.youtube.com/watch?v=ULglYC5vDwU
http://www.youtube.com/watch?v=TIBgQHFw_PU
http://www.youtube.com/watch?v=S34waQYCs0s
http://www.youtube.com/watch?v=j1JhXssMk3k
http://www.youtube.com/watch?v=A5j3KrM6NFg
http://www.youtube.com/watch?v=4AChdLJezCY

RAADHIKA SARATHKUMAR
http://www.youtube.com/watch?v=ajyCU2ioePA
http://actressraadhika.blogspot.in/2010/01/raadhika-sarathkumar.html
http://entertainment.oneindia.in/celebs/radhika-sarathkumar/biography.html
http://www.veethi.com/india-people/raadhika_sarathkumar-profile-1065-14.htm
https://www.facebook.com/media/set/?set=a.407768465948162.90840.370162379708771&type=1
http://spicyonion.com/actress/radhika-biography/
http://www.tuticorinshops.org/2013/04/profile-and-biography-of-tamil-actress_7243.html
http://www.youtube.com/movie/kizhake-pogum-rail
http://www.youtube.com/watch?v=yDKVPvvs7fE
http://www.tollycircle.com/index.php/telugu-videos/radhika-biodata/
http://www.tollycircle.com/index.php/telugu-videos/radhika-biodata/

SRIDEVI
http://www.pinkvilla.com/entertainment/photos/sridevi-atat-people-magazine-cover-launch
http://asridevi.blogspot.in/2011/07/thunaivan-1967.html
https://www.facebook.com/sundeepsridevi/notes

http://www.iloveindia.com/indian-heroes/sridevi.html
http://www.koimoi.com/actress/sridevi/
http://entertainment.oneindia.in/celebs/sridevi-kapoor/biography.html
http://www.fridayrelease.com/celebrities/biography/sridevi/702
http://tamilnadu.com/personalities/sridevi.html
http://www.ndtv.com/photos/entertainment/indian-cinema-100-defining-moments-you-chose-15069/slide/1
http://boxofficeindia.com/cpages.php?pageName=top_actress
http://specials.rediff.com/women07/2007/mar/06wslid5.htm
http://www.dailymail.co.uk/indiahome/indianews/article-2216935/She-takes-Sridevis-comeback-English-Vinglish-broken-stereotype-proving-age-factor-heroines-comeback.html
http://www.mid-day.com/entertainment/2011/oct/201011-Sridevi-s-Bollywood-comeback-in-Tamil-Telugu.htm
http://zeenews.india.com/entertainment/celebrity/know-all-about-sridevi_7924.htm
http://www.boxofficeindia.co.in/himmatwala-14/
http://www.rediff.com/movies/slide-show/slide-show-1-your-favourite-sridevi-avatar-onscreen-vote/20120824.htm#11
http://www.bollywoodlife.com/news-gossip/sridevi-happy-birthday/
http://idiva.com/photogallery-entertainment/10-mustwatch-movies-that-werent-blockbusters/6659/7
http://www.indianexpress.com/news/the-forbidden-love/961045
http://www.bollywoodtrade.com/trade-news/adil-hussain-i-became-sridevis-fan-after-watching-sadma-/index.htm
http://movies.rediff.com/slide-show/2010/oct/18/slide-show-1-snake-movies-in-bollywood.htm#3
http://www.mid-day.com/photos/b-town-specials/the-best-of-sridevi/mr.-india/
http://idiva.com/photogallery-entertainment/sridevi-the-dancing-queen/8403/4
http://www.rediff.com/movies/slide-show/slide-show-1-pix-the-changing-faces-of-sridevi/20121009.htm#1
http://timesofindia.indiatimes.com/articlelist/entertainment/Top-10-Sridevi%27s-avatar/videols/16991142.cms
http://www.rediff.com/movies/2004/dec/02corner.htm
http://www.sridevi.biz/interviews_main.htm
http://asridevi.blogspot.in/2012/05/sridevis-interview-2012.html
http://www.hindustantimes.com/Entertainment/Bollywood/When-Sridevi-floored-Amitabh-Bachchan-again/Article1-940624.aspx

http://www.filmfare.com/interviews/spouse-special-boney-kapoor-speaks-about-sridevi-2548.html
http://www.indiaglitz.com/channels/hindi/article/86506.html
http://www.youtube.com/watch?v=y0A78W15yF4
http://www.youtube.com/watch?v=iZxZ7Zc5ujE
http://www.youtube.com/watch?v=SoqUvTzxW7I
http://www.youtube.com/watch?v=pbVClYoMXSg
http://www.youtube.com/watch?v=EG9F2chH1EA
http://www.youtube.com/watch?v=jTrVBJ3gfHY
http://www.youtube.com/watch?v=9TbCKSFGBsY
http://www.youtube.com/watch?v=h9_w8L1huFc
http://www.youtube.com/watch?v=2w7nnzFpCHo
http://www.youtube.com/watch?v=EM05orLPSdI
http://www.youtube.com/watch?v=w8Ao9KJJtSc
http://www.youtube.com/watch?v=I9FmiJoFRJQ
http://www.youtube.com/watch?v=bX-CWE28cb8
http://www.youtube.com/watch?v=7B_Z5VnVrLQ
http://www.youtube.com/watch?v=Vn_h3wAOJ-U
http://www.youtube.com/watch?v=VvKQTiwhnno
http://www.youtube.com/watch?v=jQoIUOVtytA
http://www.youtube.com/watch?v=FSNU4paNjTw
http://www.youtube.com/watch?v=osxoh9Di-yQ
http://www.youtube.com/watch?v=iux3Zu3qAQ0

SARITHA
en.wikipedia.org/wiki/Saritha

VIJAYASHANTI
http://spicyonion.com/actress/vijayashanthi-biography/
http://www.telugucolours.com/id2-pid469-chV/profile/vijayashanthi

SUHASINI
http://www.rediff.com/movies/2006/jul/14smr.htm
http://www.tribuneindia.com/2003/20030412/windows/main4.htm
http://spicyonion.com/actress/suhasini-biography/
http://www.indiangossips.com/2009/07/01/suhasini-mani-ratnam-back-in-tollywood/
http://newindianexpress.com/entertainment/interviews/Genius-of-Suhasini-Mani-Ratnam/2013/08/16/article1737047.ece
http://www.imdb.com/name/nm0007124/

http://entertainment.oneindia.in/malayalam/news/2013/mammootty-mohanlal-rejected-me-says-suhasini-mani-ratnam-117011.html
http://www.thehindu.com/todays-paper/tp-features/tp-fridayreview/humility-is-his-hallmark/article3217309.ece
http://www.hindu.com/fr/2007/03/09/stories/2007030901600500.htm
http://entertainment.oneindia.in/celebs/suhasini-mani-ratnam/biography.html
http://www.youtube.com/watch?v=t0ib1Jl4M-o (bday)
http://www.youtube.com/watch?v=E_RGpZ71MBs (pics)
http://www.youtube.com/watch?v=wapgbXxtIrI
http://www.youtube.com/watch?v=vVN5u8UCtHo
http://www.youtube.com/watch?v=j2QUjtzfFo4 (kbc)
http://www.youtube.com/watch?v=fjKwvVGjnBc (tv9)
http://www.youtube.com/watch?v=ZXdOQ-EvEwo (bck wid bng)

REVATHI
http://deepthiveera.hubpages.com/hub/ADMIRABLE-INDIAN-FILM-ACTRESS-REVATHI
http://spicyonion.com/actress/revathi-biography/

NADIYA MOIDU
http://www.indiaglitz.com/channels/tamil/article/38787.html (movies)
http://www.behindwoods.com/tamil-movie-news/apr-06-01/08-04-06-nadhiya.html
http://www.balconybeats.com/2011/5-reasons
http://www.thehindu.com/features/cinema/still-the-loved-girly/article4340325.ece
http://www.deccanchronicle.com/130522/entertainment-mollywood/
http://www.thehindu.com/features/cinema/english-autumn/article4742669.ece
http://www.hindu.com/fr/2008/08/01/stories/2008080150640100.htmhttp://indianscreenstars.blogspot.in/2012/04/nadia-moidu.html
http://www.sify.com/movies/mammootty-s-doubles-starts-rolling-imagegallery-malayalam-lbmpwTdgjgh.html
http://newindianexpress.com/entertainment/interviews/Nadiya-unplugged/2013/05/23/article1601655.ece
http://www.hindu.com/mp/2008/02/04/stories/2008020450670300.htm
http://newindianexpress.com/entertainment/television/article475297.ece
http://sindhutimes.wordpress.com/2009/04/22/nadia-moidu-actress-interview/ http://www.sify.com/movies/transcript-fans-chat-up-nadiya-

moidu-news-malayalam
http://www.sify.com/movies/malayalam/interview.php?id=13417668&cid=2408
http://www.sify.com/movies/tamil/profile.php?id=13917071&cid=2409
http://udaycinema.com/nadiya

Acknowledgements

'I can no other answer make, but, thanks, and thanks.'
—William Shakespeare

We gratefully acknowledge the people who have helped us in the making of this book.

Jayasree Tatineni, a reputed film producer's wife helped us meet several film stars. Her ready consent to help propelled us to continue our efforts. We are very grateful to her.

This book would not have been possible without the valuable insights and inputs from Randor Guy, an eminent film historian of South Indian cinema. Our sincere thanks to him.

We are very thankful to the stars for giving us their time and supporting us in this endeavour. They were very happy and forthcoming, because it was the first time they were approached for a book.

Then came organizing their photographs, and we met film News Anandan and Photo Gnanam who helped us with the right pictures, for the stories. We thank them.

Being avid readers of Bollywood columns, we got in touch with film critic and historian Bhavna Somayya for her feedback, and she was gracious enough to give us a blurb for the book. We are thankful to her.

We also thank Bala Theresa, Head, Department of Library and Information Sciences of St Ann's College, Hyderabad for giving us the impetus to write, and extending her support to our book.

Our special thanks to Rupa Publications India Pvt. Ltd for consenting to publish our book, and we sincerely acknowledge our sheet anchor, Dibakar Ghosh, for giving us valuable guidance, for patiently responding to all our queries always and for his qualitative suggestions all through the making of this book.

We wish to convey our gratitude to a lot of people, friends and well-wishers, who at some point or the other have contributed to this book in different ways.

Finally, an honorable mention goes to our spouses, J. Mahalingam and R. Shivkumar for just being there for us...